THE
GHOST OF
CHRISTMAS
SWEET

Connie Shelton

THE GHOST OF CHRISTMAS SWEET

Samantha Sweet Mysteries, Book 15

Connie Shelton

Secret Staircase Books

The Ghost of Christmas Sweet
Published by Secret Staircase Books, an imprint of
Columbine Publishing Group, LLC
PO Box 416, Angel Fire, NM 87710

Book layout and design by Secret Staircase Books
Cover images © Unholyvault, Andreas Meyer, Makeitdoubleplz,
Andrey Anishchenko

First trade paperback edition: October 2021
First e-book edition: October 2021
* * *
Publisher's Cataloging-in-Publication Data

Shelton, Connie
The Ghost of Christmas Sweet / by Connie Shelton.
p. cm.
ISBN 978-1945422980 (paperback)
ISBN 978-1945422997 (e-book)

1. Samantha Sweet (Fictitious character)--Fiction. 2. Taos,
New Mexico—Fiction. 3. Paranormal artifacts—Fiction. 4.
Bakery—Fiction. 5. Women sleuths—Fiction. 6. Chocolate
making—Fiction. I. Title

Samantha Sweet Mystery Series : Book 15.
Shelton, Connie, Samantha Sweet mysteries.

BISAC : FICTION / Mystery & Detective.
813/.54

For you, my readers—I cherish our connection through these stories.
Thank you!

Author's Note
A huge thanks to my editor, Stephanie Dewey, and to my beta readers who catch the many little things that my eyes miss: Marcia, Sandra, Susan, Isobel, Paula, and Judi—you are the best!

Chapter 1

Jingle Bells played merrily in the background as Samantha Sweet carried a two-tiered cake to the sales counter. The customer wanted snow—lots of snow—for her holiday party, and Sam had created an icing that flowed in soft ridges and peaks, then sprinkled the whole thing with transparent glitter that perfectly captured the sparkly appearance of a fresh snowfall in sunlight. Small edible pine trees clustered near the base of the lower tier and red garland made a festive swag around the top.

"Merri will love it," Jen said, looking up from the cash register. "She told me Christmas is her birthday—it's the reason she got her name—and she loves to play it up big with a combo birthday and holiday party."

"I ordered the red and green candles she wanted," Sam said, setting the cake into a protective box. She fished around in her baker's jacket pocket and came out with a small box, which she placed alongside the cake.

Jen glanced at the clock. "She's supposed to pick it up in an hour. Your timing was perfect."

Sam surveyed the sales room. One of the three bistro tables was occupied; the others were clean and waiting for anyone who came in. She walked over to the beverage bar to check supplies of sugar and cream and make sure the large carafes of her signature blend coffee were adequately full. As usual, Jen had made sure the area was spotless. Sam made eye contact and gave her a subtle thumbs-up just as the small bells over the front door tinkled.

Jingle Bells gave way to *Let it Snow*. Chilly air whooshed in, along with a tall young woman in a camel colored wool coat and fluffy black scarf. Her long, honey-blonde hair glistened with tiny specks of sleet, which quickly turned to water as she stepped into the warm bakery. She gave Sam a bright smile, showing perfect teeth.

"I hear that Sweet's Sweets is *the* place for the best cheesecake in the whole state," she said, a little breathlessly.

Sam laughed and pointed toward the glass display case in front of Jen. "I'm glad you heard that. Word gets around."

"Oh, this place is the talk of Albuquerque. You've got *fans*." The young woman pulled off her black mittens and extended a hand to Sam. "I'm Emily Plankhurst. I recently moved to Taos and your place has been tops on my to-do list, although it's taken longer than I expected to unpack and settle in."

Sam introduced herself and Jen, thinking the newcomer

was probably in her late twenties, a bit younger than Jen and Kelly.

Emily turned to the display of pastries, and Jen went into the descriptions of the current cheesecake offerings—plain, pumpkin with a ginger crust, and their signature amaretto—all seasonal favorites. Emily chose the amaretto and turned back to Sam while Jen scooped the slice onto a plate and added a fork and napkin.

"I'm supposed to tell you hello from one of your Albuquerque fans, Charlie Parker. She said she knows you and has ordered from your bakery for a few years now?"

Sam smiled, remembering the first time she'd met Charlie. It was at a spa resort in Santa Fe, where Charlie was attending an event and Sam was delivering the pastries. There had been an odd connection, something Sam later attributed to her having handled the wooden box that had only recently come into her possession at the time. It was her first experience with her own ability to provide a healing touch. She wondered how much Charlie had told Emily.

"Thanks, Jen," Emily said. "And I'd love a nice cup of tea to go with this." She set her plate on an empty bistro table and Sam showed her the box containing their selection of teas.

"Are you a longtime friend of Charlie?" Sam asked.

"No, not really. We met a few months ago at a funeral. Well, really, at the gathering after. A neighbor of mine passed away and it turned out Charlie had helped Linda and her daughter reunite after many years. Long story, and I was just a kid when the daughter went missing ... Anyway, we talked a bit. Charlie's office is in the neighborhood and I've run into her a few more times since. When she learned

I was moving to Taos was when she told me about your place."

"What brings you here?" Sam filled Emily's mug with hot water. "Taos typically isn't a hotbed of job opportunity for young people. But maybe you've found something. I didn't mean—"

Emily laughed, a pleasant sound. "Oh, no. No offense. I actually inherited a job. I'm the new librarian."

"At the public library? I'm in there all the time," Jen piped up.

"No, this is a private library. Well, I mean, we do have books to check out but mainly it's a research library. People come in who need to find obscure historical facts or photos. It started as my great-grandfather's collection of books and just grew as each generation added more. My grandpa was really crazy for history, and he added a lot. While he could." Emily had shed her coat and taken a seat.

The other customer left, and Sam busied herself clearing and wiping down the table while Emily took her first taste of the amaretto cheesecake. Her eyes rolled upward and she let out a slow moan. "Oh my gosh, Charlie was *so* right."

Sam smiled. "Glad you like it."

Jen spoke up. "So your grandfather is gone now? Is that how you inherited?"

Emily paused with a bite halfway to her mouth. "Kind of. He's in an Alzheimer care facility in Albuquerque. My grandmother Valerie passed earlier this year and left me the library. At first I thought I should stay home, you know, to be there for Grandpa. But he doesn't know me anymore, doesn't recognize anyone, so I wasn't doing any good there. And it meant a lot to Grandma to keep the library open.

So, here I am, and I love it. I was ready to get out of the city anyway."

Sam studied the newcomer for a minute, torn between getting back to the bustle of the kitchen and learning more from Emily. "I'd like you to meet my daughter, Kelly, sometime. She says the same thing about moving to this little town. She was in southern California for a few years and, well, I guess she began to feel the same way. She works part time next door at the dog grooming salon."

Emily brightened. "I'd like to meet her. Frankly, most of the patrons at the library are much older people, and I really don't know anyone close to my own age. I live in the adobe house right behind the library building. I guess it was originally a carriage house or something that went along with the home—way, *way* before my time. Even when I spent summers up here with my grandparents it was already a library. It's a cool and interesting place. Lots of little nooks and crannies to explore."

"Hey, we girls go out once a week or so, just dinner and a movie or something," Jen said. "You'll have to join us sometime."

"Cool," Emily said, taking a sip of her tea. "And great cheesecake. I will definitely be back for this. Oh—that reminds me ... before I go, I also need to order a cake. I'm hosting a little open house at the library on Saturday. I'd love for all of you to come."

Sam promised to check her calendar, and Jen sat down with Emily and an order form to get the details for the party cake.

"Emily seems nice," Jen told Sam twenty minutes later when she brought the order form to the kitchen.

"Very mature for her age, I thought. Okay, sorry, was

that an ageist remark in reverse?"

They both laughed.

"She's twenty-nine, so yeah, a little younger than Kelly, Riki and me. But I think she'll fit in to socialize." Jen handed Sam the cake order and they looked it over together.

"This will be a fairly easy one," Sam said. "Shaped like an open book. I've done them for Ivan's bookshop before. All we need to do is add a Christmas theme ..."

"And voila, you're done! You've got until tomorrow."

"And about twenty orders ahead of it," Sam reminded, lifting a sheaf of order sheets from the worktable. "Luckily, I have excellent help."

She said this last bit with a nod toward Julio, a guy who certainly knew how to get the most out of the large bake oven, and Becky, her head decorator. They'd hired three other decorators for the holiday season, experienced helpers who worked in shifts, and Sam set her own schedule which was, admittedly, more hours this time of year than she normally put in.

"We're all invited to the library open house," Jen said. "Emily included me and said I should pass the word to Kelly and Scott, Riki and Evan, and everyone from the bakery who wants to come."

Sam looked again at the cake order. "Maybe I'd better throw in a box of cupcakes or something. It sounds like she's getting generous with the invitations."

Jen shrugged and left to answer the tinkle of the front door chimes. At nearly the same moment, the back door to the alley opened, admitting Kelly and Anastasia.

"Hey," Sam said, opening her arms for a hug, "how's Grammy's girl?"

Four-year-old Ana ran to her, holding out a folded

piece of construction paper. "I made you a Christmas card for the bakery." The red paper was decorated with white cutout circles that formed a snowman and green triangles for pine trees.

"It's beautiful! I love it," Sam told her granddaughter.

"We just got back from arts and crafts class at Chris's Crafts," Kelly said

"Santa was there. I waited my turn patiently," Ana added.

"Did you tell him what you want for Christmas?" Sam asked. It had been a challenge to come up with gift ideas for a kid who didn't care for typical toys and already had more books and art supplies than she could possibly use.

"More markers! I need pink ones."

"Good. I'll bet he'll be sure you get some," Sam said.

"Santa told me what he's bringing me." Ana was practically dancing around the kitchen.

"And what's that?"

"A baby brother!"

What? Sam looked up at Kelly, who shook her head slowly and shrugged. Jen bustled in with another order form, Kelly gave Sam a peck on the cheek and said they needed to get home, and Sam was left wondering when guys in Santa costumes began promising things they couldn't possibly know about.

Verification of the bombshell news would have to wait. Kelly was driving right now, and Sam needed to get busy with frosting and cakes.

Chapter 2

The light was waning the next time Sam walked into the salesroom to check in with Jen. Their customer had come in to pick up the snow-scene cake—a super hit, according to Jen—and the glass display cases were nearly depleted, just as she liked to see them at the end of the day. She finished a quick inventory of supplies for the hot beverage bar; it was amazing how quickly cocoa, chai, and tea went, this time of year.

Leaving Jen to set things in order, Sam quickly placed a supply order online, then prioritized the custom orders for the two decorators who would arrive any time now and work until ten p.m. She always felt a little guilty for leaving while others stayed to work so late into the evening. She'd often worked late when getting Sweet's Sweets established, sometimes through the night, occasionally with a little magical help. But she put those thoughts aside and told herself that the two culinary students—Marcie and Christopher—wanted the work, had tuition bills to cover, and loved the practical experience. Without interruptions, the two could easily turn out the eight dozen cupcakes for the high school winter ball and the three sheet cakes for other customers, within reach of their quitting time.

Julio had cleaned the big Hobart mixer and all the baking pans, and had readied the dry ingredients for his customary morning routine of filling the displays with coffee cake in seasonal flavors, muffins for the breakfast crowd, cheesecake for the lunch group, and dozens of cookies for the after school kids and last-minute party trays. The day the tattooed biker had steered his Harley up to the bakery's back door had, indeed, been Sam's lucky day.

From the front room, Jen called out, "Good night!" Within minutes Sam heard vehicles out back, and she set her coat aside until she had greeted the decorators and got Marcie and Christopher started on their evening duties.

Five minutes later she was climbing into her hybrid all-wheel-drive SUV, noticing a bright half-moon above Taos Mountain. Mid December, and no snow on the ground here in town. Yet. They'd had a brief storm at the end of October, two more in November, but clear skies and bright sunshine had quickly done away with the four inches that fell at Thanksgiving. Up on the mountain there was undoubtedly more, but the operator at Taos Ski Valley was becoming antsy for a better base coat. Hotels and lodges were accepting reservations that would bring in guests, starting next week and filling every available room through New Year's Day. Sam thought briefly of her best friend,

Zoë, who operated a B&B and likely wouldn't have a spare moment for the next three weeks.

It was nearly dark when Sam pulled up the long driveway leading to their log ranch house beyond the north end of Taos. Beau's pickup was parked in front of the barn, headlights facing a ladder that leaned against the wall. She recognized his tall, lean shape and made out the figure of their hired hand, Danny. She stopped in her normal spot near the front porch, got out, and walked toward the men. Ranger the black Lab, and Nellie, their border collie, greeted her and then followed along.

"Hey you two. You're working late. Everything okay?"

Beau stepped over and gave her a kiss. "It will be by tomorrow. We're just tackling that leak in the barn roof."

She'd forgotten about that. After the last snow, Beau had mentioned a telltale wet spot inside, right over one of the horse stalls.

"We made good progress today," Danny said, pulling off his work gloves and slapping them against the leg of his jeans.

"We did. But we need to stick with it. They're saying another storm is on the way before tomorrow night." Beau shut off the pickup's lights and asked Danny to check that the two horses were in their stalls and the barn door was secure.

"Always something, on a ranch," Sam said with a warm smile toward her handsome husband. "I don't know how you managed it all before you retired."

Beau shook his head. "Me either. Very, very long days. That's all I can say."

"Well, I started a batch of green chile stew in the slow cooker this morning, so dinner's ready the minute I warm up the tortillas. Will Danny want to eat with us?"

"He told me earlier he has some other plans. I didn't ask what."

Sam kind of hoped Danny had a girlfriend, and she kind of hoped he didn't. When he'd come to work for them earlier this year, he'd been in the throes of a terrible breakup and the aftermath had nearly landed him in prison. Sam loved the soft-spoken young man as if he were her own kid, but he didn't have great luck with girlfriends. Anyway, lesson learned and she hoped he would be more cautious with his relationships.

The scent of green chile, meat and onions filled the house and Beau followed his nose, straight for the kitchen. Sam chuckled, taking a moment to hang her coat on the rack by the door and drape the strap of her backpack purse over a hook.

"Yum, that's good!" he said, nibbling on a morsel of the tender pork he'd evidently picked out of the pot.

While he shed his coat, Sam washed her hands and put the final touches on the simple meal, warming tortillas in the microwave and ladling generous portions of stew into bowls. They decided to carry their meal to the living room, where Beau quickly started a fire in the huge stone fireplace and tuned the TV to the basketball game he'd been wanting to catch. Any time a commercial came on, he switched to the weather forecast, where it looked like the storm was moving in more quickly than first predicted. Great for tourism, not good for two guys scrambling to get a roof repaired.

"Is that going to mess you up?" Sam asked, after the third time he'd checked the report.

"If we wake up in the morning with the roof covered

in snow, then yes. That won't be good. But I'm hoping it holds off until at least noon. We got a lot done today, just need to finish it up." But he didn't seem convinced.

Sam carried their empty bowls to the kitchen and lit the burner under the kettle for their evening ritual of chamomile tea. While it heated, she called Kelly.

"Can you talk?" Sam asked.

"Sure. Scott is herding Ana toward her bath, and I'm safely out of earshot downstairs in the kitchen. I know what you're calling about, and the answer is, I don't know. I was totally dumbfounded when Ana told me what *Santa* said."

"Who was the guy? Anyone you know?"

"I think it was Chris's husband—she's the craft shop owner. I've only met him once, and not in costume. There were two dozen kids there today, all running around in full sugar-hype mode after making their card projects and being fed cupcakes. Which, I have to say, came from the supermarket and weren't nearly as fantastic as yours. I need to have a talk with Chris."

"And maybe with her husband. Why would he say such a thing, giving Ana the idea that she might have a baby brother for Christmas?"

"Yeah, well, by Christmas would obviously be impossible. I don't know what to tell her. Even if it's true, it would be next fall. And I haven't had a moment to warn Scott about this, so she could be dropping this news on him any—"

Even over the phone, Sam could hear a loud thud in the background.

"Oh, yikes. Mom, I'd better go check on that."

The phone went dead and Sam had no choice but to wait.

Chapter 3

Kelly got out of her car in front of Puppy Chic and held up both hands, laughing as she did so. "Sorry, Mom, I should have called you back last night. It just got a little weird at our house."

Sam had assumed as much, after the strange crash interrupted their phone call.

"The big noise was Scott. Ana somehow dumped a toy teapot of water all over the bathroom floor and he made a dive to stop her. Didn't work. Obviously. He was fine but completely soaked from head to toe since he skidded across the spill. So, then we cleaned that up and I decided it would be best to squash the rumor Ana managed to start. We finished her bath and got her to bed and then my dear husband and I sat up until late—talking about all this."

"What does Scott say?"

"He says Ana's mentioned a little brother several times during their home schooling lessons. He has a feeling *Santa* didn't tell her any such thing, that she blurted out the baby news as wishful thinking. She'd love it if Santa really did bring a baby … but really, we're not even trying for one. Our lives are completely crazy right now and managing one precocious toddler is plenty. Can you imagine if a second child had Ana's … abilities?"

Being able to read the strange rune-like writing in the magical book, before she turned four years old, making offhand statements and having them come true, communicating almost telepathically with Eliza, the calico cat. Sam couldn't imagine the challenge of managing a household with more than one of these little prodigies running around. She said as much to Kelly.

"And, not to mention, Scott's books have taken off gangbusters this year. His publisher is talking about sending him on a book tour with the next one—twenty-five cities in thirty days! And that would leave me at home alone to handle the schooling and everything else he does for us all the time. A newborn might just send me over the edge."

Sam placed an arm around her daughter's shoulders. "Okay, first off, you know you wouldn't be doing it alone. I'll help, however I can. Beau would pitch in." She glanced in the front windows of Sweet's Sweets, where Jen was smiling as she served a customer. "Even Auntie Jen would help where she could."

"She's my best friend, Mom, not a miracle worker. She has a crazy schedule already."

"For the holidays. But things will work out."

"I know. They always do, and now I have the help of a book of spells and a magical box. I'm thinking invincibly and willing it all to turn out just right."

"Speaking of the holidays, here's a customer who's come to pick up a cake. Let me introduce you. She's new in town, runs a small private library, and has invited us all to a party—I'll fill you in on the rest later."

Emily Plankhurst pulled her Jeep Wrangler to a stop in front of the bakery and was halfway to the door before she realized the shouted greeting was coming from Sam.

"Emily, hi. I have your cake ready but wanted to take a second to introduce my daughter. I think I mentioned Kelly already?"

Emily smiled warmly and walked toward them. "You and Jen both have talked about Kelly. It's great to meet you, finally."

Kelly greeted Emily but seemed a little antsy to get inside. "Sorry, I'm already ten minutes late for work, but I'd love to catch up and hear more about your library. I'm sure my husband would too—he's always researching something."

She gave Emily's hand a squeeze and turned toward the grooming shop.

"Sam, before we go inside, can I ask you something?" Emily said. "I've been looking back through the old newspaper archives we have at the library. It's a great way to learn who's who in a town this size. Anyway, I've come across your name."

"Uh-oh," Sam said with a laugh.

"Your husband is the sheriff, right?"

"Well, he used to be. You probably haven't gotten to that point in the news, but there was a serious incident a few years back. Beau was injured and has since retired from law enforcement."

"Oh, I'm so sorry to hear that. Is he all right?"

"Perfectly fine. Just discovered he loves being a rancher and was tired of chasing down bad guys."

Emily nodded, understanding. "So, anyway ... I'm not quite sure how to explain this ... I ..." She cleared her throat and started over. "Charlie Parker, in Albuquerque, told me you had some type of special *ability*, and I don't know ... The way she said it, I get the impression it's not music or math. She mentioned a healing touch."

Sam felt her brows wrinkle together. "Yes, that's true, among other things. I'm not sure I see the connection."

"From the news articles—and I'll admit to reading between the lines—I get the feeling you're able to see things that lead to solving crimes."

Sam nodded. *Where was this going?*

Emily drew a deep breath and blurted out, "Do you believe in ghosts? Because ever since I've been living in my grandparents' house I believe I've seen the ghost of my grandmother. She talks to me sometimes, and a couple days ago she told me how to find a hidden space behind a wall in the library. I went there the next morning. The space is exactly where she said it would be, and inside the space I found a painting. It's not where someone would hang a picture—it was hidden there."

"Wow."

"I know, I'm sorry to just drop that on you. I don't know—"

"No, I think it sounds fascinating. I can't say whether I believe in ghosts or not. I've never seen one or communicated with one, that I know of, but ..." how to say this without giving out any secrets? "But I don't rule out anything. Strange things do happen. And since the hidden space *was* there and the painting was inside ... well, I'd say there's something to it."

"I haven't done any research on the painting itself, and I probably won't have time for a few days. But if you're coming to the library open house tomorrow afternoon, would you mind taking a look at it? I just—I guess I just feel like it's a mystery that needs to be solved. The painting could have been hidden there for a few months or a hundred years. I really have no idea."

A breeze came up the sidewalk, reminding Sam that even though the sun was shining it was a December day. "I'd love to see it. Right now, let's get inside and warm up. Stay for a coffee or cup of tea, if you'd like."

"Thanks, Sam. Don't say anything about my find to anyone else yet. I'd like for you to see it first. And maybe Beau, if you think he'd know anything about it."

Sam doubted that. Beau was much more rancher than art enthusiast. That particular talent fell to her friend Rupert Penrick, but Rupert had a new love in his life and was wintering in some tropical climate, the last she'd heard.

Emily walked to the bakery's front door and held it open for Sam. "Sorry I don't have time for a coffee right now. I should just pick up the cake and get home to prepare for the party."

When she saw the cake, she let out a squeal. Sam had done the book's binding in burgundy fondant, the pages in buttercream the color of aged paper, and had written the line "'Twas the night before Christmas ..." in a good rendition of Olde English script. On the left hand page, she and Becky had some fun with decorative touches— sprigs of holly, a brick fireplace and chimney, and a bag that appeared to be overflowing with toys.

"Oh, Sam. The detail is amazing! The rug in front of the fireplace actually looks like an old hooked rug my great-grandmother made. It's still in my house." Emily looked as though she might cry. "How will I ever be able to cut into it?"

"Maybe knowing that the cake is pumpkin spice with a ginger crème fraiche filling will be incentive enough."

"You put so much into this—how can I thank you?"

"Just tell people where you got it," Sam said, giving her a quick hug. "Word of mouth is how Sweet's Sweets stays in business."

"Absolutely—you know I will. And I will make a big deal of it if you'll come to the party."

"Planning on it." Sam lowered her voice, although Jen was occupied with another customer's purchase. "I can't wait to see that thing you were telling me about."

Chapter 4

Saturday at the bakery was a little crazy, but Sam managed to break away an hour before closing. The Morton Library was only three blocks from Sweet's Sweets, and Sam was surprised she'd never gone in to explore the place. It definitely had a loyal group of patrons, judging by the way cars had double parked to fill the small parking area and now filled both sides of the road. Sam found a spot more than two blocks away, locked her car, and walked toward the adobe building with its pitched metal roof, dormers, and blue painted trim around the windows.

She spotted her son-in-law's car in the crowded space, happy to see Scott and Kelly had come. She'd brought cookies as a hostess gift, regretting that she hadn't made time to create the special handmade chocolates her shop had featured in past years. Selling her chocolate factory had taken her somewhat out of that world, but maybe it was time to begin experimenting with them again, just for the holidays.

Right, and when am I going to find the extra time right now?

She put that thought aside and walked through the tiny outer vestibule and into a large room filled with people and bookcases, music and chatter. Almost automatically, her eyes sought out Kelly and Scott. They were at the far end of the room, so Sam took in the rest of it first.

The librarian's desk sat squarely in front of the entrance, the first stopping point for anyone coming in. Although the desk now sported a tablecloth and small Christmas tree, she could imagine Emily seated there, fielding questions, directing patrons to one of the stacks. Neatly labeled shelves covered various time periods and locations—Taos County, Colfax County, Pueblo Culture, Spanish Colonization, and more. It seemed there were sections for all aspects of northern New Mexico's history.

"Sam, so glad you could make it," Emily said, startling her.

"Oh! This place is amazing. I hope I wasn't staring with my mouth open. You said all this began with your grandfather's personal collection?"

"Great-great-grandfather. Morton Plankhurst."

"Ah. I wondered where the library's name came from."

"Yes, apparently Morton was a huge collector of books and papers—you won't believe the archive room. But then each of his sons added to it, to make the collection what it is today. My grandfather—the one who's now in Albuquerque—is the one who really went to work organizing it all. Before that, there were literally piles of books and boxes of papers. The original generations knew where everything was, but it was basically unusable to a patron who might walk in the door looking for information. When I was a kid, I came up here in the summer and Grandpa would put me to work. He taught me the Dewey Decimal System and insisted we catalogue everything."

"So you know the place inside and out."

"I thought I did." A wry smile crossed Emily's face. "Until, well the night Grandma Valerie ... well, you know."

Sam spotted a small plaque near the door.

This library is made possible by the generous contributions of our donors, including the Eliza Nalespar Foundation Trust.

"Eliza Nalespar had something to do with this?" Sam asked.

"Apparently she and my great-grandfather, William, were very good friends. Maybe more than that—I don't know. Eliza lived out toward the north end—"

"On Tyler Road. You won't believe this, but her house is where Kelly and Scott live now."

Emily's face went still. "Okay, *now* things make more sense. Scott Porter is the author who wrote ..."

"The history of Eliza's house and her work here in Taos. She was quite a famous author in her day, too."

"I've heard that. Oh my gosh, it's amazing how it all fits together. Scott came in, right after I moved here, said how sorry he was about my grandpa's condition, how he would miss him. I didn't realize—wow."

Sam sensed movement at her shoulder.

"Didn't realize how much help your grandfather gave me in researching Eliza's history, for my book," said Scott's voice.

Sam turned and gave Scott and Kelly quick hugs. Kelly

wore a bronze tunic and skirt, which perfectly accented her cinnamon curls that were pinned up in a messy bun. Scott looked almost professorial in a tweed jacket and black turtleneck shirt.

"I love this library," he said. "I've spent many, many hours here, ever since I taught at the UNM local campus."

Emily laughed. "I'm sure you could show me things I don't know about my own library. You do know that you have free rein here, any time."

"Your grandpa told me the same thing. I appreciate that."

Sam spotted Zoë across the room, near a refreshment table, and excused herself to say hello and to see how the cake was doing.

"Hey, girl," Sam said, giving her slender friend a hug.

"You know what—I'm glad you're not one of those who gets picky about calling any female over fourteen a *woman*. I'm happy to be a girl for the rest of my days, especially now that we both have more gray than brown in our hair. Something about 'old girl' just rings a lot better than 'old woman' doesn't it?"

Sam laughed out loud. Zoë had never been one to mince words.

"I love the cake," Zoë said, nodding toward the half-eaten slice on her plate. "You outdid yourself with this one."

"Seems it's a popular one. Emily will be lucky to get a couple slices to take home with her."

"Somebody said Kelly thinks she's pregnant?"

"Oh, don't let *her* hear you say that. I'm not sure she's used to the idea well enough to exactly welcome the news. At this point, it's not a sure thing."

Zoë made a zipping motion across her lips. "Hey, I've gotta get home. Guests checked in earlier this afternoon, but they'll be settled in their rooms by now and looking for dinner or entertainment suggestions. I really just popped over for a few minutes to wish Emily well."

Gazing around the large room, Sam noticed the crowd had thinned. Zoë was right—it was approaching the dinner hour for many. Sam had left the remaining green chile stew for Beau, so she didn't need to get home immediately. She nibbled a couple of crackers spread with a soft cheese that was delicious. Along with four or five carrot sticks, the snacks could easily suffice for her own evening meal. She was just wiping her fingers on a napkin and looking for the spot to discard her used paper plate when Emily walked up to her.

"One of the ladies volunteered to see the rest of the guests out and to lock up, so I'm free now if you want to take a look at the item we talked about."

Sam nodded eagerly. She followed Emily to the back of the library and through a doorway marked Private. The small storeroom held two tables stacked with boxes. "You can see that I still have plenty to keep me busy."

"This really is a lifetime endeavor, isn't it?" Sam said.

"Several lifetimes." Emily led the way out a back door, which she locked behind them, and they crossed a small courtyard to the house. "I know, it's Taos where nobody locks their doors. My city influence is still showing, I guess. Plus, there's just such a wealth of irreplaceable information in the library. I'd have to answer to three generations of Plankhursts if I let anything happen to all their work."

"I get it—I really do." Sam was busy taking in the details of the house. Built of adobe, same as the library, the home had sort of a cozy-huge vibe. The structure itself wasn't massive, but the rooms inside were larger than one would guess. White walls with bright touches of color in furnishings, pillows, and art. Sam caught the signature of Valerie Plankhurst on at least two pieces they passed in the hall. There were hand-carved wooden doors throughout, kiva fireplaces in the living room and in a smaller study, which was where Emily led Sam now.

Emily pulled the drapes across the one window in the room and switched on two lamps before she touched a spot on the wall and a large bookcase swung outward.

"This was where the painting was hidden?" Sam asked.

"No, actually, there's a similar panel in the library. I discovered this one the day after Grandma Valerie told me about the other. I have a feeling there are secret little cubbies all over this place."

"Amazing that you didn't discover some of them when you were here as a kid. Curiosity, and all that."

"I know—right? I wonder how often they grabbed my little hands or distracted me just as I was about to poke into some place I shouldn't." She reached into the space behind the bookcase with her left hand and pulled out a framed painting, about 36 by 24 inches. "This is what I found."

She cleared the top of the carved Mexican desk and carried the picture there, switching on another, brighter lamp.

The image was of a winter forest scene with snow-laden pine trees, a gray sky with shafts of sunlight beaming onto mounds of snow on the ground.

"I like it," Sam said, "mainly because I love winter scenery."

"But overall, it's just a lot of gray and white, right?"

"Well, kind of."

"Watch this, which I discovered totally by mistake." Emily picked up the painting and stood it upright, leaning the frame against the floor lamp beside an overstuffed armchair.

When the light shone on the image from above, the change in depth of the picture was immediate. Suddenly, the trees in the forest seemed to part and reveal small details in the distant background. The shafts of sunlight brightened and revealed small animal footprints in the foreground.

"Amazing, huh?" Emily said. "And you can't believe how much changes when natural daylight hits it. There's a cabin back in the forest, with lighted windows and what look like Christmas decorations."

"Let me check something," Sam said, moving closer and kneeling beside the painting. "JCF. That's the signature, and I'm pretty sure I know who it is."

She got back to her feet and pulled her phone from the pocket of her slacks. "JC Freeman was a famous Taos artist, some years ago. I'm guessing he died maybe twenty years ago, or so … Yes—here."

She began reading from the phone screen. "JC Freeman, artist, born 1943, died 2001. Best known for his unusual perceptions and ways of working hidden objects into his works. While well known during his lifetime, Freeman's work achieved its highest values after his untimely death at the age of fifty-eight. His works were often titled based on some obscure item in the painting, which drew admirers to his shows by the hundreds, people who wanted to be the first to find the hidden object."

Sam turned back to look at the painting. "There's more to his biography, of course. You may want to look him up and see if you can identify this one."

"Oh, I already know the name of this picture," Emily said with an impish grin. She took the frame by its upper edges and turned it around. "Right here on the back."

She pointed to a small white card taped to the brown paper backing which hid the back of the canvas and the stretcher bars. Sam stooped to read it.

"*The Ghost of Christmas*. Hmm, why does that sound familiar?"

"Ask Siri."

But before Emily even suggested as much, Sam was into a search for the title and the artist's name. In less than a second she had an article on her screen.

"They almost make this too easy nowadays," Sam said. "Your grandpa would be upset to know he wasn't needed to help people research things."

"You would think. But there's a lot in that library that can't be found on the internet, or so I was told."

"According to this, *The Ghost of Christmas* was one of Freeman's most mysterious paintings and no one could definitively spot the image the artist had hidden. Some claimed that was mere myth, that many people had seen the image, but popular consensus was that it was one of his trickier works of art." She read silently for a moment. "Uh-oh."

"What uh-oh? I'm not sure that's good."

"*The Ghost of Christmas* was tragically lost in a fire at the home of its owner, billionaire Phillip Crawford, who had purchased the painting directly from Freeman. The wealthy hedge fund manager was quoted as saying what a great loss it was to the art world, especially since it was JC Freeman's last known painting. The artist was diagnosed with a brain tumor, followed by a decline in his mental faculties, and he never painted again. He died a few years later."

"So ... if the painting got burned up, what's this? It seems like it would be really tricky for another artist to imitate Freeman's style."

"I was thinking the same thing," Sam said. "Plus, in my younger days I worked for the insurance agency here in town that insured Crawford's house and the contents. If I remember correctly, there was some question about the authenticity of the painting that burned."

"Did they call in experts to verify it?"

Sam stretched her memory back to those days, so long ago now. She shook her head. "As I recall, Crawford's house was one of those showplace homes just off the plaza, a multi-million dollar house, and that was only one of four or five houses he and his wife owned, all over the world. He demanded payment for the limits of the policy, but didn't make a stink about the painting itself. The main thing I remember my boss grumbling about was that the homeowner had only lived in the place a couple of years and hadn't paid enough in premiums to come close to what they were about to pay out for the claim. I don't even remember the artwork being much of an issue, even with my boss." She stared at the painting once again.

"But the insurance company did pay for it?" Emily asked. "So that means, if this one should turn out to be real, someone committed a fraud."

Sam knew immediately what Emily was thinking. If this painting was the original, how did it get into a hidden niche in her grandfather's library?

Chapter 5

They stared at the painting for a few more minutes. Emily swore she couldn't see any ghost in the design, and Sam was too tired this late in the day to worry about it. Finally, with the painting stashed safely back in its hiding place, Emily turned to Sam.

"How about a cup of tea? And I'm fairly sure there's enough of your wonderful cake left for us each to have a slice."

"Sure. That sounds nice."

Sam followed her hostess to the kitchen, where she put the kettle on while Emily walked back to the library to pick up the remaining cake.

"Whew, it's getting cold out there!" she said when she returned.

"It's your first winter up north, so yeah, I imagine the

difference from Albuquerque is noticeable. You'll get used to it. Be sure you have a decent coat and warm gloves. They'll save you."

They settled on a comfortable sofa in the living room.

"I'm in a pickle here, aren't I?" Emily said, once her slice of cake was gone. "I can't ask for authentication that this is the real Freeman without showing it to someone in the art business."

"Any reputable art dealer will know the story behind it."

"They would be legally bound to reveal that it survived the fire, right? And then the questions will start, mainly, how did my grandfather get hold of it? Why didn't he speak up when the media reported the painting destroyed?"

"Yeah, that is a sticky problem."

"It's not as if I can ask my grandfather how he got it. Poor Grandpa doesn't even know his own family anymore." Her voice cracked a little.

"I'm so sorry. I wish I knew what to say."

"If this is the real Freeman—and I feel sure it is—it was stolen and switched at the time of the fire. But my grandpa didn't do it—I just *know* he didn't! All I can think of is to do my own research and figure it out before I reveal the painting to anyone else." She was looking at Sam with a bright, inquisitive glint in her eyes.

"Oh, Emily, I don't know … I don't have the kind of law enforcement contacts I used to. We'd need to get hold of the police and fire department reports …"

"You said *we*! Sam, you're right, we *can* do this. You can help me prove Grandpa's innocence because you have experience at this. I'll dig through the archives here in the library. Maybe you could just ask your husband? He might remember things about the case."

"I can ask. But Beau doesn't have access to his department's records anymore either."

Emily acted as if she hadn't heard that part. "And the insurance company—you used to work there. Maybe someone you knew back then would go back through their old claims."

"Again, I'll ask. But don't get your hopes up. Normally, once claims are settled, the records might stay on file for a few years, but they don't keep that stuff indefinitely unless there's a question of a bogus claim or—"

"But if my painting is the real one, there *was* a bogus claim. Maybe someone questioned it back then and kept the file."

"Maybe so," Sam said, privately doubting whether any of this could be proven. But it was worth a try.

As she drove home a while later, she thought about Emily's situation and the urgency she felt about proving the painting was real. And the deeper question involving her grandfather's innocence. Could the authorities file charges against a man in his diminished state? Probably nothing that would stick. But they could ruin the family name in the process, maybe to such an extent that the Nalespar Foundation would pull the library's funding.

The historical work Emily and her family were doing was an important asset to the town. It had been the life's work of three generations, and was already important to this young woman who'd taken over the legacy.

Asking some questions and reporting her findings to Emily seemed the least she could do. It was exactly the sort of mystery Sam would love to help solve. If only it hadn't come up during her busiest season of the year.

Beau was in bed when Sam got home, no doubt

exhausted after working outdoors and climbing the ladder to the barn roof all day. Ranger and Nellie were tucked into their crates downstairs. She kept her own bedtime preparations as quiet as possible and slipped under the covers beside him. He groaned softly in his sleep and rolled over to drape one arm across her middle. She snuggled in close and tried to put aside thoughts of paintings and ghosts and fire.

* * *

Sometime in the dark, early morning hours Beau murmured in her ear. His gentle hand began stroking her thigh and a parade of small kisses started at her neck and trailed to her shoulder. Despite crazy schedules and long days, they still had the romantic touch in these quiet hours together. She rolled toward him in response and let the magic begin.

Later, in the shower together, they made jokes about being old, married grandparents. "Let the kids have their fun," Beau said. "We could show them a thing or two."

"Ew! I need to get that image right out of my head." She slapped his shoulder with a soggy washcloth and backed up under the hot water spray.

Beau left her to finish with shampoo and conditioner, while he toweled off and dressed. Fifteen minutes later, Sam found him in the kitchen making a bowl of oatmeal for himself and toasting an English muffin for her.

"There's still some peach jam left from that batch Zoë gave you last fall," he said. "Want that with your muffin?"

"Did I ever tell you, you're the best husband ever?"

"You might have mentioned it." He paused at the

refrigerator door and gave her a kiss.

Sam pulled a small plate from the cupboard for her muffin. "So, now that I've buttered you up with sex and loving words, can I ask you a law enforcement question?"

He chuckled and set down the jar of jam. "Sure."

"Do you remember a case about twenty-five years ago, where a big house burned down? I don't recall whether it was ruled to be arson or some other cause. As I remember, the house was a few blocks from the plaza—"

"Well, right there I can tell you it wasn't my case. Twenty-five years ago was before my time here in Taos, and if it was within town boundaries that would have been under police jurisdiction, not sheriff's department. Sorry."

"Ah, I should have thought of all that. I guess I was tired last night, and this morning I was, um, somewhat distracted."

She filled him in on the parts she remembered about the case, what she had told Emily Plankhurst last night, but nothing about it sparked a memory for him. He'd moved to Taos as a deputy about twenty years ago, and by the time he'd settled into his job the fire was old news and the rich guy had moved on, not rebuilding or staying in the area. She made a mental note to stop by the police department and see if she could talk someone into giving her a look at the old case file.

They finished breakfast and she could tell Beau was anxious to get outside. She ought to be heading for the bakery herself, but decided to see what background information she could find online first. She took her laptop to the dining table near the wide French doors, which gave her a view of the sprawling ranch property—gray-brown and winter dead at the moment. She could see Beau and

Danny tending the horses, a peaceful scene.

"Okay, to work," she told herself.

She began with a search for 'Taos arson Crawford' figuring those were the high points of any news stories that might exist. She found one small blurb in the *Albuquerque Journal North*, the edition for the northern part of the state, which stated what she already knew.

A fire in the Taos home of billionaire hedge fund manager Phillip Crawford destroyed one wing of the large house, including fine furnishings and art. The homeowners were not home at the time. An unnamed person died from smoke inhalation. The fire is being investigated as arson.

Sam searched but never found a follow-up in that particular publication.

The *Taos News* covered the story much more in depth, quoting police and fire department officials. It was big news for about a week, ending once the investigation team ruled that the fire seemed to be the work of an arsonist. Mainly, much was made about the home's owner. Phillip Crawford was variously described as a generous man and philanthropist, or a rich jerk. Taos neighbors, east coast heads of charitable foundations, business colleagues, and socially prominent people from New York to Los Angeles had weighed in with stories about him, none of which meant anything more than a way for Crawford to stay in the limelight.

Aside from the fact that a young man died in the fire (revealed in a later article to have been the boyfriend of the young woman who was housesitting for the absent Crawfords), the Freeman painting was, of course, one of the highlights since the artist was local. The artist had just suffered that brain tumor and was quickly becoming known as a recluse, so he didn't personally speak up. But that didn't mean there wasn't plenty of news, both about him and about the art. *The Ghost of Christmas* had been purchased by the Crawfords for $25,000 and was reputed to have tripled in value, depending on which 'art expert' was asked. Sam could only imagine what it would be worth now.

All in all, the news coverage leaned toward sensationalizing the mystery of the painting and whether its destruction might have been a motive for the whole disaster—the loss of a large house and subsequent insurance claim, the death of the young man, the shadow over the reputation of the billionaire who, himself, might have been the intended murder victim. It seemed like a convoluted mess, in light of Emily Plankhurst's discovery of the painting.

Sam jotted down the names of everyone local, figuring the socialites in New York weren't going to be of much use to Emily but the locals might actually know something. Her computer clock told her it was a little after eight, so she placed a call to the insurance office where she had worked, all those years ago. The agency owner had moved on, selling out to a larger corporation, but one person Sam knew from her time was still there. She and Patsy Garcia had started as young 20-somethings who took the first office job they could get, but Patsy had stayed on and risen to office manager or administrative something-or-other, basically the highest position in the place next to the owner.

"Samantha Sweet! Oh. My. Gosh. It's been ages. How are you?" Patsy's bubbly personality never changed.

They exchanged chit-chatty pleasantries for a minute or two before Sam got to the purpose of the call.

"Can you look up an old case for me? Or at least check and see if it still exists? There's a dozen chocolate lava cupcakes in it for you." Another thing that never changed about Patsy, her love of chocolate.

Sam gave the homeowner's name and the date of the fire, which she'd learned from the news articles, holding out slight hope that the agency had kept its records that far back.

"Whoo, that was a big one. I'm sure we didn't destroy the record, you know, based on the size of the claim, the accusation of arson, and that poor young guy who died in there."

"The newspapers didn't make nearly as big a deal about the death as they did about the rich guy's art collection. I'm ashamed to say that I'd forgotten all about that tragedy."

"As I remember it, the investigators eventually ruled it an accidental fire, most likely caused when the house sitter and her boyfriend left candles burning near some curtains in the living room. The girl tried to swear they hadn't gone upstairs to the master bedroom. Don't quote me on any of this—it's just what's coming back to me now. I'll pull the file and let you take a look."

"I'll bring the cupcakes."

Chapter 6

Sam spent the rest of the morning at the bakery, pleased to see how much progress the evening crew had made with the orders. Becky was here now, putting the finishing touches on an elaborate wedding cake while Sam made quick work of two large trays of holiday cookies—snowmen, Santas, and green Christmas trees. For good measure, she set a dozen cupcakes in a bakery box, in case Patsy called soon.

However, the next call Sam received was from Emily.

"I've got something *really* interesting to show you, and if you can break away for lunch, I'll make us a sandwich at my house."

"Lunch? I, uh …" Sam looked over the chaos in the bakery kitchen, debating whether she could put Emily off for a while, but Becky gave her a nod and mouthed *we're good here.*

"It's something you really need to see in full daylight," Emily added.

"Okay, sure. I'll be there in fifteen minutes."

This time there were plenty of spaces to park in front of the library and Sam took advantage of the one nearest the door. Emily's grin was immediate.

"Oh, yay! You've got to come see this," she said, jumping up from her desk chair and motioning Sam inside. "I'll just lock the front door …"

"Am I keeping you from library business?"

"Oh, no. Sometimes I get browsers, but most of the serious researchers make appointments. I have nothing on the calendar until three o'clock this afternoon. What I need to show you is in the house." She flipped over a little Closed sign on the front door before leading the way out the back.

"I just need to retrieve the painting again. Sorry I'm so paranoid, but I'm locking it up every minute it's not actually with me. We'll go in the kitchen," she told Sam.

Sam entered the bright room with its large north-facing windows and white walls and cabinetry. Two plastic-wrapped plates with deli meat sandwiches sat on the small table. Emily was back in under two minutes.

"Gotta set this up facing the windows," she explained, carrying the painting to a straight-backed chair that sat at an angle in the middle of the room. "I discovered this when I took a research break and came in for a cup of tea this morning. Remember the little card on the back of the frame, the one that gave the title of the painting? Well, there's another notation in very tiny writing that I hadn't noticed last night. The study is kind of a dark room and we were working by lamplight."

"What's the tiny writing say?" Sam had to admit, her curiosity was piqued.

"Right below the words *Ghost of Christmas* it says 'Upper right quadrant.' See it?"

Sam looked. The small writing looked the same as the larger, the title. Either the artist or someone along the way—maybe in a gallery, maybe the purchaser—had written both notations.

"So … I placed the painting in bright light and started studying the upper right quadrant. Do you see the ghost?"

Once she was told what to look for and where, yes, Sam could definitely see a face and an ethereal shape woven within the obvious picture of the forest scene. It was so skillfully done that it really did take some study to figure it out.

"My gosh, that's amazing."

"Right? And look carefully at all the other little details. I thought there were only Christmas decorations on the little cottage in the background, but they're everywhere! The whole forest has tiny lights and glowing orbs. And the snow—he's managed to make it sparkle. I mean, the whole design is absolutely a …"

"… work of art. It's truly incredible." Sam could see what all the fuss was about, why JC Freeman had completely rocked the art world with his technique. She felt tears welling up, thinking of the loss of this talented man.

Emily evidently felt the same way. She stood with both hands clutched in front of her heart.

"There's no way this is a forgery," Sam said.

"My thought exactly. I can't imagine anyone on earth able to copy this technique. I mean, I've read a lot about Freeman since last night, and people describe his work, the effects he was able to achieve ... but you can't really appreciate it until you've seen one of these in person."

Sam thought of her buddy, Rupert, and wondered if he'd seen Freeman's work. Most likely so. He really did get around in the art world. He would absolutely swoon over this one. It had to be one of the best Freeman pieces ever done, and she was tempted to email him about it. But no one else could be let in on the secret yet. Well, maybe she and Emily could solve the mystery of this one, establish who owned it now, and have it available for Rupert to see after he and Mark came back from their Caribbean winter stay.

"May I take a picture?" Sam asked.

"Absolutely. But don't count on the details showing up. I have the latest-greatest cell phone and the photo of the painting doesn't at all do it justice."

"I won't show it to anyone, but it would be helpful as a comparison if I come across other photos of it in the insurance or police reports."

"How are those coming along, by the way?" Emily asked as she poured glasses of iced tea to go with their sandwiches.

Sam snapped two pics of the painting and agreed with Emily's opinion that they paled in comparison to the real thing. Over lunch she filled her young friend in on what she had learned from Beau—basically nothing—and from the insurance company—there should be more to come.

"Oh well, at least we're working on it," Emily said.

Sam's phone rang as she was taking the last bite of her sandwich. It was Patsy, and there was good news. Sam could take a look at the file, although she couldn't remove it from their office. The boss would be out all afternoon.

"Great timing," Sam said. "I need to run by the bakery

and then I'll be there." She ended the call and carried her plate to the sink, then picked up her coat from the back of her chair and turned to Emily. "Looks like we're still on track. Wish me luck."

Thank goodness the impending storm Beau was worried about had not materialized, Sam thought as she left Sweet's Sweets on her way to the insurance office. It had taken a bright, clear day like this one for the painting to reveal its depths. Once again, she thought of how some things simply could not be explained. How would the work of art look to her, if she handled the carved box first? Now *that* was something to think about.

The insurance offices had been remodeled and upgraded since Sam's day, partly, she suspected, through Patsy's influence as office manager. The desks and computers were new, and each agent had a glassed-in cubicle for privacy. The walls held generic art, but at least it was a big upgrade from the posters that used to hang there. She walked in, greeted her old friend, and handed over the bakery box.

"Ooh, my favorites!" Patsy said, drawing Sam into a hug. "You promise this won't go to my hips?" It was an old joke between them, both of whom had always battled their weight.

"You can always share them around the office," Sam reminded, noticing that most of the desks were occupied by staff talking on telephones.

"Only after I grab two for myself," Patsy said with a grin. "I've got the file you wanted, and you can use Rob's desk in there. Want some coffee?"

Sam shook her head and reached for the file. The phones were ringing almost constantly, and she appreciated the use of an office with a door she could close. She draped her coat over the back of the chair and pushed aside a stapler and a pen set, giving herself a little space to open the thick manila folder. Possibly, all the information existed in the computer system somewhere, but it was amazing how many forms were still completed on paper back then. She began at the back, hoping to take everything in chronological order.

The first contact came when an administrative manager at Crawford Capital had called the insurance company to report the fire. Apparently, wealthy people aren't bothered with such details. However, the insurance company loves details. The adjuster met with Phillip and Camilla Crawford at the site of the devastated house.

Mr. Crawford provided fairly precise details about the cost of constructing the home and about its furnishings. Sam supposed a guy whose business is following the stock market and knowing the price of dozens of stocks at once wouldn't have too much trouble recalling such details about his own home, especially since the house had been built less than three years earlier. Mrs. Crawford seemed conspicuously silent, as there were no direct quotes from her. Maybe it's just the way wives of important men are— smile and keep your mouth shut.

When asked for their version of events on the night of the fire, the homeowners claimed to have been traveling in Mexico. A handwritten notation by the adjuster indicated that fact had checked out. Normally, they would have a cleaner come to the Taos residence a few days before their arrival and a few days after they left. But since this trip was just a quick jaunt to Puerto Vallarta with friends, and they planned to return within a week, they'd engaged a house sitter to stay and care for their cat and use up the extra food in the fridge. Susan O'Malley was the eighteen-year-old daughter of their regular house cleaner, and they trusted her completely.

Susan was told not to have friends over, certainly no young men, the main concern being that the kids would get preoccupied and someone would accidentally let the cat out. Crawford claimed it never entered his mind that Susan would do anything dishonest.

But, as the news stories had reported, Susan did have a boyfriend over to the Crawford house. Speculation—both by the homeowners and the media—was that the couple had probably lit a bunch of candles and left them burning, too near the expensive drapery fabric. The good news was that Susan went downstairs around midnight for a snack, panicked when the living room (Crawford called it the lounge) was full of smoke, and ran from the house. Luckily, kitty cat raced out the open door right behind her.

Sadly, the boyfriend, Mike Miera, was trapped upstairs, and no amount of screaming by Susan roused any help in time to save him. By the time the fire department arrived, the entire west end of the house was in flames. Structurally, the east end was fine—still standing, anyway—although many of the furnishings had been so damaged by smoke and water that they were included in the insurance claim for reimbursement.

Sam skimmed the list of possessions the Crawfords were claiming. It seemed heavy on details such as who designed this handmade rug or that custom sofa. The fabric of the draperies, which investigators pinpointed as the starting point of the blaze, came from a New York designer and Sam supposed she should recognize the name. She didn't know the names, didn't care.

She paused only when she came to the Freeman

painting: Lounge – one painting titled *The Ghost of Christmas* by JC Freeman. Purchase price in 1990: $25,000; Current appreciated value: $72,000.

Nearly triple the value in the four years they'd owned it? Sam couldn't rule it out; she would need to research that further. It would also be interesting to know how much more the artwork had appreciated in value in the years since the artist's death.

Sam flipped through the pages in the folder, finding a lot of duplicate information. The fire investigator's report backed up what the police report said. The police report verified the alibi of the homeowners, and the story of the traumatized house sitter seemed to check out. All of this was reported in summary; Sam knew from experience that the law enforcement file would contain a lot more than just the conclusions.

The insurance company had asked for authentication of all items over a certain value, and the Freeman painting was among these. That particular report merely stated that the painting had been completely destroyed, with only a few fragments of canvas and frame remaining. Those fragments checked out as matching the photos and description of the piece of property, at the time it was insured. With sworn statements by the homeowners that they had seen the original art in its customary place only a few days before the fire, it was accepted that *The Ghost of Christmas* truly had perished in the flames.

With her phone, she clicked photos of several documents and made herself a list of all the names associated with the case, trying to err on the side of taking too much information rather than too little. One never knew what direction a lead might take her.

There was a lot of back and forth correspondence about how much the insurance would pay. The home and furnishings had been valued at six million dollars. Sam's eyes widened a little when she read that number. Yes, Taos real estate could be pricey, but she'd had no idea there were homes in that bracket so many years ago.

As was customary, the company denied full payment right from the start, making the argument that much of the structure could be rebuilt for a fraction of its insured value. Crawford and his attorneys fought them. The result was a two million dollar payout, which Sam supposed was next to nothing in the eyes of someone worth over a billion dollars. And a fifty thousand dollar painting was probably something that people like the Crawfords would pick up on a whim, without blinking an eye at the price.

The final page was stamped CLAIM PAID in big red letters.

Sam stood up and stretched her aching shoulders. She carried the file folder back to Patsy and handed it over.

"So, it looks like it took more than a year to settle this one, but the case was closed. Why is the folder still here?"

Patsy led the way down a short hall that went to an employee break room and bathrooms. Keeping her voice low, she said, "Our job was to decide how much to pay for the lost home and furnishings. You'll want to read the police and arson investigator's reports. Even though the homeowner was found blameless, the fire was ruled arson, and that means the death of the young man inside was considered a murder."

"No statute of limitations on murder." Sam felt the weight of a whole new aspect to this situation.

Chapter 7

Sam hadn't realized how many hours she'd spent poring over the insurance file. The sun was low in the western sky when she pulled onto Paseo Pueblo del Sur and headed north. The police station was on her way; she might as well stop and ask if she could get a copy of the police report. It would be good to look it over while all the names and numbers were fresh in her mind.

Just her luck, she got hold of an administrative person whose only desire at this moment was to shut down her computer and go home for the day. The woman did at least do Sam the courtesy of tapping the name Crawford on her keyboard.

"Sorry, nothing under that name—open or closed."

Sam's mind went blank for a second, then she thought of the unresolved crime, the one the police would be interested in. "Try Mike, or maybe Michael, Miera."

"Okay, got it. It's listed as an accidental death. Hmm. It's an old one."

"Yes. I'm working on an aspect related to it, and I'd like to take a look at the case file."

The woman looked at her as if she'd come from another planet. "We don't open our case files to the public."

"Who would I talk to?"

"Look, it's quitting time for the admin section. The chief went home half an hour ago."

Sam could tell she was quickly getting nowhere, and there was no point in pushing it. She might need this lady on her side someday. She thanked the woman for her trouble and left. Just as well. Her eyes were aching and her lower back wasn't going to withstand much more time in a hard chair. Plus, there was more than one way to work around an obstinate bureaucrat.

The sky was pitch black by the time Sam reached the ranch, where the absence of manmade light, other than the soft glow of lamps from inside the house, made a zillion stars pop into view. She got out of her car and stood staring at them for a full two minutes, breathing deeply to take in the frosty air and release some of the tiredness in her bones. It was amazing how quickly dusk became full darkness, this time of year.

Walking inside, she could hear Beau in the kitchen. He stepped out with a plate of raw hamburger patties. Both dogs were trailing him, completely interested. He ordered them to lie down by the fireplace.

"Hey, long day? Danny and I finished the barn roof early enough in the day that I got a head start on dinner. I've already lit the grill and you shall be treated to one of my world-famous burgers tonight."

"That sounds wonderful," Sam said, leaning toward him for a kiss before taking off her coat.

"Ten minutes." He headed toward the French doors and the deck beyond. "Oh, Kelly called. Said she had tried to reach you but didn't get through."

Sam pulled her phone from her bag and stared at the screen as she headed upstairs. She must have switched it off when she was at the insurance office and forgot to turn it back on. She tapped Kelly's number and set the phone on speaker while she reached toward her dresser top for the carved wooden box that held the answer for her aching shoulder muscles.

"Hey Mom, what's up?"

"You called?"

"I guess I did. The afternoon has gotten away from me and we're just now sitting down to dinner. I've got something I want to run by you. Later?"

"Perfect." Sam slid her phone into her pocket and picked up the wooden box. As it always did, the wood began to change from a dull brown and take on a golden-honey sheen. It warmed to the touch, spreading heat through her hands, arms, and shoulders. The energy boost was better than taking a pill or indulging in cocktail hour.

"I could get used to doing this *every* evening. Don't let me get hooked on you," Sam whispered to the box.

"Burgers!" came Beau's call from the living room.

Sam traded her bakery jacket for the cozy fleece one she loved to wear at home and hurried downstairs. Bless him, he'd thought of everything, right down to the fries he'd kept warm in the oven. They assembled their burgers with favorite toppings and carried their plates to the dining room.

"Long day at the bakery?" he asked, after he'd swallowed

his first huge bite of the juicy burger.

"Bakery and many other things. Remember that house fire I asked you about, the old investigation from before you arrived here? Well, an item that had been claimed as destroyed has turned up, and I've agreed to see what I can learn. Most of my afternoon was spent at the insurance office, going through the old claim paperwork."

"Sounds really exciting," he said with a wry grin.

"Yeah, well, not exactly a heart-pounding read. I'm in the fact-gathering stage right now. I was hoping to read the police file, too, but couldn't get past the front desk. Think there's any way a word from the county's most beloved former sheriff would carry any weight there?"

He gave her a sideways look. "You sure you want to get involved? You've been having more fun with the bakery and with Ana and Kelly than you ever did solving crimes …" But he could immediately see it was important to her. "I'll give Ben Martinez a call in the morning."

Sam suppressed a grin and thanked him. He still knew who was who in this town, despite his protests about sticking to the ranching life and ignoring law enforcement's current cases.

They finished eating and Sam cleared the dishes while Beau carried a cup of decaf to his favorite armchair and settled in front of a TV western. Once the dishwasher was filled and running its cycle, Sam called Kelly.

"I had an interesting visit with Emily Plankhurst this afternoon," Kelly began.

"Really? I saw her around noon and she didn't say anything about plans."

"It was very last-minute. I called to see if she'd like to get together for lunch tomorrow, and the plan kind of morphed into tea this afternoon, here at my house. The moment I mentioned that, she jumped on the chance to see where Eliza Nalespar used to live. And of course Scott became the ever-gracious host, showing off his writing room in the turret, which we believe was also Eliza's writing room, back in the day."

"Oh, that does sound like fun. I'll bet Emily was suitably impressed."

"She asked if we ever had visits from Eliza's ghost."

"Really? And what did you tell her?"

"We haven't actually seen any visible ghosts. Too bad. I almost wish we could experience more of this house's history."

"If anyone could, I'll bet it would be Scott—history buff, Eliza expert."

"Yeah, you would think. So, anyway, that's not the interesting part. While Em and I were in the living room with our tea, she told me she sees ghosts. Well, *a* ghost, I guess. She says she has been visited several times by the ghost of her grandmother."

Interesting that Emily had confided in Kelly. "Did she say anything about what this grandmother has told her?"

"Like hidden niches in the house and library? Yeah. A painting was hidden in one of them."

So it was okay to discuss those things with Kelly now.

"She's mentioned that to me, as well, but swore me to secrecy. I'm thinking I'd better touch base with Emily again to be sure how much of this story she's sharing."

"Well, that's all I know at this moment. Anyway, the other purpose of my calling you was to let you know that Scott and I are taking Ana to Albuquerque. We got tickets to see *The Nutcracker* this weekend. He's great at teaching her science, history, biology, math ... all those school subjects. But I'd like to see her get some culture too. And this is such a fun one. Plus, we'll see if we're brave enough to hit the big malls and get some Christmas shopping done."

"Sounds like fun for all of you."

"We'll only be gone a night or two, but I was thinking you and I should try to get together this week, if you can find the time."

"I'm hoping to get an appointment with the police chief—I'll explain later. Depending on when that happens, I'll pop by."

Before she forgot, Sam called Emily Plankhurst and asked how much Kelly knew about the painting and the possible insurance scam.

"As soon as I entered her home, and once Kelly and I spent some time together, I knew I could trust her. She gives me the same vibe as you do, Sam. I didn't tell her all of the story yet, but you are welcome to. I sense there's something magical in that house, especially when I went upstairs to see the turret room. Somewhere in that part of the house, maybe the attic, there's ... well, I don't know quite how to explain it."

"I'm seeing Kelly tomorrow and I'll tell her more about what we're working on. Speaking of which ..." Sam went on to share what she had learned from the insurance claim file. "I've got a list of the people whose names came up, at the time. I'd like to track them down and speak with each one, see what they remember from all those years ago."

"Should I help with that?"

"At this point, I think not. My questions will seem to come from curiosity—I'll think of a cover story. If you come into it, someone who knows of your grandfather's connection might put it all together before we do. I don't want you, or the painting, to be in danger."

Chapter 8

As good as his word, Beau called Ben Martinez first thing the next morning.

"He seemed a little put out at having to dig up an old file, but I think curiosity won out. We have an appointment to meet with him this afternoon at four."

"We?"

"Yeah, he can't share the file with a civilian, but he's bending the rule slightly to show it to me as the former sheriff. And that's only because it's a closed case."

"Is he certain he still has the file somewhere? Aren't old ones eventually destroyed?"

"Minor crimes, yes. But there was a death in this one, and the property damage was considered 'major' so they've held it."

"This is good news. Okay, four o'clock. Shall I come

home first or just meet you there?"

With a plan in place, Sam called Kelly.

"Ana and I are trying to make a batch of fudge, and we could probably use your help. Want to come over now?" Kelly sounded a tiny bit desperate, so Sam agreed.

Fifteen minutes later she was pulling up to the portico near the back door at the Victorian. Already, she noticed Christmas decorations at the front bay windows, a huge fresh evergreen wreath on the front door, and swags of greenery along the covered porch and pillars. Electric candles sat on every windowsill, but the Christmas tree in its traditional spot in the front window had not been set up yet. Eliza, the family's calico cat, sat in one of the front windows, as if she knew Sam would soon arrive.

"We're making Christmas candy!" Ana announced as Sam walked in the back door. Eliza had already sauntered into the kitchen. "I think we just dump all the stuff in the pan and we stir it and eat it, but Mommy seems a little scared about that."

Sam swept the four year old into a hug. "I think Mommy just wants us to read the recipe first and make sure that's how it's done."

From the counter near the windows at the back of the house, Kelly mouthed *thank you* to Sam. "Let's hang up Grammy's coat first and then we'll get started."

A half hour later, as Sam set the pan of fudge to cool on the countertop, Scott walked in.

"Writing is done for the day!" he announced in a jovial mood. "Is my student ready for today's lessons?"

"Candy!" Ana jumped down from her stool and bounded toward her dad.

"Um, only the one small piece," Kelly cautioned, "or

you won't even be able to keep her tied to her chair."

Sam gave a curious look as Scott and his daughter left the room.

"They're doing an advent calendar, and each little door opens to reveal a foil-wrapped chocolate. I try to suggest they wait until after lunch for it, but that never seems to work."

"Well, as you said, he's the one who has to keep her attention on the lessons."

"This month is pretty easy—for history they're studying how various cultures in other countries celebrate the holidays." Kelly ran hot water and a squirt of detergent into the fudgy saucepan. "So, now we have the rest of the morning—or however long you can stay. And I'm dying to know more about this secret artwork Em said she found in her house."

Sam filled her in, including how the ghost of Grandma Valerie had shown Emily where to look, right down to the painting's supposed destruction in the fire and what she'd learned from the insurance file, including the fact that she now had a list of suspects to interview.

"This afternoon Beau is taking me to meet with the police chief, and hopefully I'll learn more about the result of the case from a law enforcement standpoint. At this point, Emily just wants to be sure her grandfather wouldn't be in trouble over this thing."

"Sounds like you need a truthfulness spell, for when you talk to all these suspects." Kelly wiped her hands on a towel and tilted her head toward the back stairs that led to the attic. "Shall we?"

Sam smiled. "A truthfulness spell—do you really have one?"

"Who knows?" Kelly said, looking back over her shoulder as she mounted the first step. "I'm discovering new things in that book all the time."

The book. Its history was so long and complicated Sam couldn't even begin to put it all together, starting with the quirky Romanian who had put the leather-bound volume into Kelly's hands five years ago in England, with the story that it had belonged to a witch. The writing inside wasn't even readable, except to certain people at certain times, and the two women had more recently discovered that the contents of the crazy book seemed to change as new pages appeared.

"It's worth a shot," Sam said, following along as Kelly reached for a key above the door frame and unlocked the attic door.

The room with its steeply-pitched ceiling looked as it must have a hundred years ago, with a heavy wooden table, a couple of stools, a sturdy oak bookcase along one wall, and a window seat in the sunny dormer. The cat had followed them up the stairs; she now leapt onto the cushion and curled herself into a ball in the sunshine.

Kelly retrieved the book from the locked upper cupboard where she stashed it away from any prying eyes that might want to catch a glimpse. Experience had taught them that the book and the carved wooden boxes each woman possessed had, at times, been hunted and desired by others. They weren't willing to take chances with them now.

"Okay, so I'll be interviewing people who may know something about a painting that was thought to have been destroyed in a fire twenty-five years ago, but which has recently shown up. I need some way to improve their memories so they'll actually give me accurate information."

"And a way to know if what they're telling you is the truth."

"Well, *that* should be simple." They exchanged a look and broke into giggles.

"Okay, let's start with what we know works," Kelly said, pulling her own carved wooden box—the one anciently called Manichee—from the upper cupboard and holding it firmly in her hands.

As with Virtu, the box Sam owned, the wood began to warm and glow. Kelly handed it over to Sam. Almost right away, the rune-like figures on the pages of the book became readable in English.

"I wonder, if we had been Romanian witches, or French occultists or something … would these words appear in those languages?" Kelly mused.

"Most likely." Sam set the box down and peered over her daughter's shoulder at the yellowed pages of the book.

They had figured out, early on, that there were no chapters, per se, nor an index. Finding any particular subject was completely hit-or-miss. Well, maybe not *completely*. Kelly inserted her thumb at a random spot in the book and opened it.

Memory Improvement. The words were centered at the top of the selected page.

"Ha! Sometimes this really works," Kelly said with a triumphant smile.

She read aloud: "To improve one's own memory, spend two minutes in quiet contemplation while repeating silently the name of the item one wants to remember. The details will appear."

"Um, that sounds pretty basic and not at all super-natural," Sam said.

"Sometimes so-called magic really is just common sense."

"Okay, agreed. *But,* what I need is to improve someone else's memory for a particular event. Anything on that?"

Kelly paged forward. "'To improve the memory of another person or collective group of people …' Oh, gosh, you're going to laugh. 'Lead those persons in the same exercise as that for improving one's own memory.' Sheesh, no kidding!"

"Hm, not bad if it's you and me, just trying to find where we left our keys or something. Somehow I don't see it working in a situation where I'm basically interrogating someone we suspect of a crime."

"Nah. Better scrap that plan."

"What about my being able to tell whether someone is telling me the truth?"

"Let's see." Kelly continued turning pages, but the closest thing she found was a recipe for a truth serum. Since the prime ingredients were ancient root of a yewberry tree and two hairs from a Moravian bat, they quickly gave that up.

"I'm afraid I can't work with this eye-of-newt type stuff. If it's not an ingredient I have in my kitchen or can get at the herb store, I'm not taking any chances."

"Plus, trips to Moravia are running pretty expensive this time of year," Kelly said with a wink.

"Well, shoot. I guess I'll just have to channel my inner deputy and put my old skills to use when I talk to them."

"I wish you luck. For now, how about a cup of tea, and we'll see if the fudge is firm enough to cut a couple tiny pieces." Kelly stashed the book and the box where they'd come from, and called to the cat.

With their secrets safely locked back in the attic, they

descended to the kitchen once again.

"So, what do you make of Emily's sighting of her ghostly grandmother?" Kelly asked.

"At this point, I'm going with the idea of lucid dreaming. Emily has only mentioned her grandmother appearing to her at night, after she's gone to bed. Isn't it most likely that she falls asleep and starts dreaming, and then the vision seems very real because she has dreamed it that way?"

"Could be." Kelly was reaching for the tea canister and didn't quite meet Sam's eye.

"But …?"

"But the longer we live in this house the more I'm wondering … Scott has heard strange noises a couple of times, up in the turret room, times when he swears the spirit of Eliza Nalespar is nearby."

"Does she talk to him?"

"I'm not sure. I have to admit, when he's told me those things, I get a really strong case of the goosebumps running up and down my arms. It's as if my hair is standing on end, too. I've been a little afraid to ask many direct questions."

"Seriously?"

"Seriously. But, I'll put on my brave-girl pants next time and try to get details. I can say a friend talks to a ghost and ask if he's had that happen to him."

The kettle whistled and Kelly busied herself pouring the boiling water over their teabags.

"I'd suggest you do it when Ana's not around," Sam said.

"Oh, definitely. There are times when that child knows *way* too much."

"Too much of what?" Ana skidded to a stop in the kitchen doorway.

Chapter 9

As she drove toward the police station later, Sam thought of Kelly's quick response to Ana and how she'd switched the subject around to lunch. Parenting required a lot of different skills, and it had been many years since Sam had needed to flex those mental muscles.

Beau's truck was already in the lot at the administration complex when Sam pulled in. She spotted him on the front steps, about to enter the Police Department wing of the sprawling adobe brown building with the Territorial style white trim. She caught up with him in the vestibule.

It was a bit annoying the way the same surly female administrator from yesterday practically fell over herself to usher them to the chief's office when it was Beau making the request. Of course, today they had an appointment, and maybe the chief himself had told her who they were.

Or it could be the fact that, despite retirement from law enforcement, Beau was still a strikingly good-looking man, tall and slim, with those ocean blue eyes and winning smile. It wasn't the first time Sam had seen women react.

"Sheriff Cardwell, good to see you again," Ben Martinez greeted.

Beau held up a hand. "*Former* sheriff—but thanks. Yes, good to see you too."

They shook hands, and Beau reminded the chief he'd also met Sam in the past.

"I understand you're revisiting an old case," Martinez said, showing them to a conference table where a single file sat in front of the chair at the head. The folder's cover was heavy brown cardstock, filled with about four inches of pages held together at the top with a pronged silver fastener.

Beau gave a noncommittal nod. "I'd like for Sam to look over the reports, and of course we'd appreciate your thoughts, anything you remember about it."

Martinez indicated they should sit, and he pushed the folder toward Beau. "Certainly. Of course, I was a rookie officer at the time so I'm not sure how complete my memories will be. But the old chief, Fred Holfelder, he shared information, wanted all of our input."

Sam sat next to her husband and listened, fairly certain Martinez was posturing, and she wondered how involved he'd actually been. But the file would reveal that. The names of all investigating officers would be there.

Beau opened the cover of the folder and immediately pointed to the page on top. Conclusion: fire began accidentally. Death of subject was therefore accidental. Case Closed. There was a longer, more detailed version of the same verdict, but that was the bottom line.

Sam raised the top page and gazed over the next one in the stack. As she'd done at the insurance office, she then lifted the entire stack of pages and started with the initial report that had been filed when the call about the fire had come in.

Originally, this was a fire department case, but the police had been brought in quickly when the body of the young man was discovered. Part of the reason the police file was fairly thick, Sam discovered, was because it included a copy of the arson investigator's report. Handy for her. She wouldn't need to talk her way into yet another department, begging for access to information.

While Beau chatted with Martinez, she jotted the names of witnesses who hadn't appeared within the insurance claim parameters. The interviews with neighbors seemed fairly consistent. Around one o'clock in the morning, someone in the home next door had heard a woman screaming—the house sitter. They looked out their windows and saw the mansion in flames, called the fire department, then rushed out to assist the young woman who was wearing only a flimsy nightgown and crying 'Mike, Mike … Mike's still inside.' The neighbor relayed this information to the first firemen on the scene, then bundled the girl into a warm robe and a pair of slippers. In the word-for-word transcript of the interview, much was made about how the poor girl should be decently covered.

When authorities interviewed the house sitter, both at the scene and the following day, she denied hearing any smoke alarms until she'd gone downstairs where the smoke and flames were out of control. She'd run for the front door and called out for help, but the fire immediately intensified and she couldn't push past the flames inside to reach the boyfriend upstairs.

Sam scanned the interviews, mainly looking for names she didn't already have or new information, but the insurance file had been very thorough and she already knew much of this. The fire chief's name, Arnold Brown, appeared in the conclusion section. She jotted it down, in case she hadn't already made a note.

The arson investigator's report concluded that the cause of the blaze had been from multiple candles left unattended in a room with flammable draperies (the source of this information came from the house sitter herself). Sam knew that already, too, but something about the report bothered her. She wrote on her note, *Candles?* and left it at that.

"Are you about ready?" Beau asked, tearing her attention away from the final page in the file.

"Um, yeah, I suppose so. Chief Martinez, do you remember anything about the case that I might have missed here?"

Martinez preened a little. "It was the most horrific scene I'd witnessed up to that point in my career. Fire is a scary, scary thing."

Profound. Sam riffled the pages of the file one more time, then stood and followed Beau to the door.

"Chief, I saw one word in the file that bothers me. Accelerant. I didn't get to the details of the full report …" *because you guys are so impatient to go* "but it seems the fire department was considering that the case might be arson?"

"They always look at all possible causes," Martinez said with a smile. "It's just part of investigating every fire. They probably just noted that they'd tested for an accelerant on the scene and didn't find anything."

"Do you personally remember any discussion about that?"

He shrugged. "Not really. But, as I've said, my memory is a little fuzzy on the details. It was an early case for me, and I wasn't privy to all the interviews or conversations."

"Of course."

Out in the parking lot, Sam brought it up to Beau. "What did you think of the chief's last answer back there? Don't you think he would have been briefed or at least been in on the gossip?"

"Not necessarily. It makes sense to me that not every rookie cop was included in all aspects of an investigation. That would have been up to detectives and, more than likely, the investigators within the fire department."

Sam nodded, still a little unconvinced. She'd seen the squad room in Beau's office. The deputies hung around and talked about cases all the time. Even the rookies had ears. They knew things.

She was about to climb into her car when she heard Beau's name called out.

"Hang on, Sam. This is someone you'll want to meet," Beau said.

She closed her door and looked toward the man who was approaching. He was in his mid-sixties, muscular, with an outdoorsy vibe, wearing jeans and a fleece jacket. As he came closer she noted a good smile, straight teeth, and graying hair that hadn't thinned. Beau stepped forward and the two men shook hands.

"Beau! How've you been? Haven't seen much of you since you retired."

"Ranching's pretty much full time these days. Arnie, I'd like for you to meet my wife, Samantha." He turned to her. "Arnie Brown is the fire chief. You probably came across his name in that report you were reading, hon."

"Uh-oh. Reading reports about me?" the man said with humor in his voice.

"An old case," she said, shaking his hand. "One the police and fire department worked together."

"Ah. Well, there are probably many. Say, Beau, we gotta catch up sometime soon. I'd suggest a coffee or something now, but I'm running late. I'm retiring at the first of the year, so let's get together after that." Arnie gave them both a smile and turned toward the entrance to the county clerk's office.

Sam wished she'd had the presence of mind to formulate a question or two about the Crawford house, but the moment was gone. She blew it off and climbed into her car. At least she had other people to talk to, and maybe someone could shed some light on the JC Freeman painting and how a fake could have been substituted for the missing real one.

She pondered all this during the drive home, while she warmed leftover stew for their dinner, and while she and Beau ate and cleaned up the kitchen afterward. Was it as simple as the police and fire departments believed, an accidental fire that turned tragic? But then, wasn't it somewhat beyond coincidence that the valuable painting had been replaced by another at some point right before the fire? And if a crime had been committed, who had the most to gain by setting the fire and switching the painting?

Right before bedtime, Sam handled the carved box again, in hopes that her dreams would reveal something. But all that filled her head during the night were more questions, and she woke at five in the morning in desperate need of coffee.

Quietly pulling on her robe, she slipped out of the bedroom and went downstairs. Her list of names from all the reports was in her pack and she took it to the kitchen table while the coffee brewed.

How would an investigator approach this? By asking who had the strongest motive for the crime. Normally, when a building burned, the owner would be questioned first, then anyone with a grudge against the person. Okay. So Phillip Crawford was a good place to start.

Sam looked him up online. As a high-profile investor and major player, it wasn't hard to find profiles and social media links for him. She read through them, noticing that his biggest achievements were all more than two decades old, and there hadn't been many updates at all in the past ten years. He had apparently divorced Camilla within a few years after the Taos home was burned, and there had been two other wives since. Maybe those who described him as a thoughtless jerk were right. Maybe those were among the gaggle of ex-wives.

Crawford Capital was still listed among the financial funds, but no longer in the top five, or even the top ten. The mighty Phillip Crawford, it seemed, was a bit past his heyday. Sam wondered if she could possibly get him on the phone.

Among those with grudges, there were probably many, especially during Crawford's prime years as a carnivore on Wall Street. But putting together those types of connections, so many years later ... thinking about it gave Sam a headache. She poured the coffee.

She couldn't begin to understand Crawford's New York connections until she had a better picture of how that could tie to little bitty Taos, New Mexico. Logic said that if he'd pissed off some mobster or union boss on the east coast, it would be his New York or Greenwich homes that would have been targeted. That this had happened in Taos just didn't feel right.

What about the house sitter? Maybe she'd been pilfering jewelry or other things from the house and let the fire get started to hide those crimes. But in that case, she would have done it on a night the boyfriend didn't stay over, or she would have at least gotten them both out of the house.

And, Sam had to admit, David Plankhurst, Emily's grandfather, had to be considered a suspect. After all, he had ended up with a very valuable painting. How was Sam going to voice that possibility to Emily?

Chapter 10

Sam waited until it was a little after nine on the east coast before she placed the call to Crawford Capital. Meanwhile, Beau had come through the kitchen and grabbed a whole grain muffin on his way out to meet up with Danny, planting a kiss on top of her head and mumbling something about a broken gate.

"Crawford Capital, how may I direct your call?" Stated by what was apparently an actual human being.

"I need to speak with Phillip Crawford, please."

"Mr. Crawford is currently in a meeting. Who's calling please?" In a meeting. Office-speak for 'How can I get rid of you without disturbing the boss?'

Sam was ready. "It's Samantha Sweet with the Taos County Sheriff's Office." Yes, it was technically once true, now a lie.

"I can take your number and give the message to Mr. Crawford's administrative assistant."

It was the best Sam would get. She left her cell number and made a little bet with herself that she would never hear anything back.

Next on the list was Susan O'Malley, the house sitter, who would now be forty-three years old. Sam looked up the name. There were three O'Malleys in the directory, which meant they were probably older folks. No one actually had landlines these days. She got lucky on the second call, when the woman told her Susie was her daughter. Sam gave the shortest, least threatening recap of why she was calling and the trusting lady gave her Susan's number and let it drop that Susie lived right next door. Sam probably should have given her a little lesson in using caution about protecting a person's privacy, but at this moment that wouldn't be in her best interests.

She showered and dressed, checked in quickly with Jen to be sure all was going okay at the bakery, and was slipping her coat on when her phone rang. A New York area code.

"Samantha Sweet, Phil Crawford here."

"Really? I mean, thank you so much for returning my call."

"Paulina says you're with the Taos County Sheriff's Office? If this is a fundraiser, I won't be happy about the interruption."

"No, no fundraiser. We're actually looking into an old case here in town, and it goes back to the time when your house burned. A new lead in the case has turned up."

"What new lead? I thought that case was closed years ago."

"It has to do with the JC Freeman painting that was

destroyed in the fire. I believe the insurance company included that item in the settlement they paid for the loss of the property."

"Right, right. I guess so. This is all ancient history, and my lawyers handled the details."

"Yes, sir. The claim was paid. But the authenticity of that particular piece of art has been called into question. Can you tell me where you purchased the painting, *The Ghost of Christmas*?"

"Some gallery there in town. My wife and I attended an opening and the artist was there. Nice guy, not your typical artsy-fartsy type with greasy hair and lives in a cave or something. He was sociable, a mover. Turned out we had friends in common in Malibu. Camilla liked the painting and it seemed like an investment. Buy low, sell high, that kind of thing. We assumed it would appreciate in value. If nothing else, back then it was the thing—saying you owned a JC Freeman."

"Do you remember what you paid for it?"

"Not a clue. I don't pay much attention if it's under a couple million. This was definitely less than that."

"But the gallery would have a record of the sale?"

"I suppose. Don't they track provenance or something like that? Hey, art isn't really my thing. Ask me the price of anything on the Dow Jones. Ask me which hedge funds are most profitable this year. Don't ask me about a book or a picture, especially from a previous lifetime."

"I believe you and Mrs. Crawford have since divorced?"

"That Mrs. C and two others. Camilla, apparently, thought she had found greener pastures. Or a handsomer guy." He gave an unpleasant chuckle then cleared his throat. "No offense to your little town, but Taos isn't even in my rearview mirror anymore. I've moved on in my life. Now, if that's all?" Without waiting for an answer he hung up.

Whether or not Camilla had been caught cheating seemed irrelevant. Sam could see why Crawford hadn't been a serious suspect in the original case. Aside from having their alibi confirmed by the friends they'd traveled to Mexico with, obviously the house, the location, and the prestige of owning a JC Freeman painting meant little or nothing to him. He simply didn't care.

The insurance check had probably gone right into the down payment for someplace twice the size and four times the price in either California or New York. She'd seen it before—people enchanted with New Mexico until they actually lived here. Then things became too dusty, too backward, and too provincial for their big-city tastes. And most of the locals were none too sad to see them go.

She had the name of the gallery where ninety percent of JC Freeman's art had been sold, and it was on her list of visits to make. She would be sure to drop in the fact that she'd already spoken to Phil Crawford on the subject of his purchase of *The Ghost of Christmas*.

Sam was in her car, halfway to town when her phone rang.

"Sam, it's Emily." Her voice seemed agitated. "Do you have a few minutes to talk?"

"I'm in the car right now. Want me to come over?"

A sigh. "Yes, that would be wonderful."

One vehicle, a white Subaru, sat in the library's parking area when Sam pulled up. She could see lights through the front windows, so she left her car and walked inside. Emily was at the desk, handing a library card over to the patron, a middle-aged woman Sam vaguely recognized from the bakery. They exchanged quick smiles as the woman left.

Emily raked her fingers through her long hair and let out a long breath. "I hope she didn't notice my hands shaking."

"What's the matter? Has something happened?"

"Yeah, you could say so. I saw my grandmother again."

"Um ... I'm getting the idea this was different than the other times?"

Emily walked around the desk and turned toward the back corner of the room, where the lighting was not as bright. She pointed. "Yes—broad daylight, right over there. This time I *know* it wasn't a dream."

Sam found herself drawn and wary at the same time. Emily didn't seem to want to walk back into that corner, but Sam took her arm and they edged toward the bookshelves there.

"Describe it to me, this sighting. Did she speak to you?"

"She was dressed sort of ... young. Do you think ghosts change their clothes? Last time she wore all black. Anyway, today it was a really short tie-dyed dress, bright glass beads hanging around her neck, sandals, a colorful headband. She looked like a teenager from the '60s with her hair all wavy around her shoulders, but her face was as I remember her when I was a kid." Emily turned toward Sam with a nervous chuckle. "I guess both my grandparents were sort of hippies in their younger days. I just never actually saw her dressed that way in real life."

She stopped and pointed toward a corner where shelving on both walls met. All the shelves were packed with books.

"I had just walked in the back door and switched on the lights, and Grandma Valerie was standing right there, in front of those shelves, as if she was looking for a particular book. She turned toward me and smiled, and that's when I realized who it was. I just blurted out the first thing that came to me. I said 'I found the painting' and she just nodded her head, like she somehow already knew that."

"Sounds like she's looking out for you."

"Maybe so." Emily seemed to genuinely consider that possibility. "Then I told her I was worried about Grandpa, if people know the painting has been here in the house all this time."

Emily was still gripping Sam's arm as they remained a dozen feet or more from the corner where the ghost had stood.

"Did she respond to that?" Sam asked.

"She got this dreamy smile when I mentioned Grandpa, but then she said yes, she was concerned about him too. And then she said something kind of strange."

Sam looked at her when Emily didn't continue.

"She said, 'It's not what I thought. It's not what everyone thinks.' I have no idea what that means, Sam. What could she be saying?"

"Maybe there was more of a connection between your grandparents and the wealthy guy who owned the painting?"

"I can't imagine what that would be. I mean, I was just a kid at the time and I wasn't around Taos a whole lot. They must have had friends and a social life I knew nothing about."

"True."

"But, think about it. There's this earth-child couple with their beads and gauzy linen clothing—that's how I remember her dressing when I was little—and there's this

New Yorker with his high-power business and wheeler-dealer image. At least that's how I imagine him. What would they have in common?"

"Maybe Crawford had an interest in history and came in the library, and they became friends that way."

"I can check that," Emily said, walking back to the desk. She pulled out a simple box that contained 3x5 cards. "Don't laugh. This was my grandfather's library card system. The man never met a computer he liked, so he kept everything very old-school. There's a basic information card on each patron—name, address, phone number. And the patrons get a little wallet card, which he typed on this." She pointed out an IBM Selectric, which sat on its own stand nearby. "When they check out a book, they hand over their card. They get the card back when they bring the book back. Their information card lists what they checked out and when they brought it back. At a glance, I can tell who has books out because their library card is paperclipped to their client card."

"Looks like a system that could have been set up by your great-grandfather."

"It very well might have been." She held up the open box for Sam to take a peek. "As you can see, we have fewer than a hundred regular patrons, the ones who actually check out books. Many of our visitors just sit over at the study tables, look things up and take notes, without actually checking out the books. And of course, the archived papers and newspapers can't leave the library. The system seems to work, although I have to admit that I'm itching to computerize it all one of these days."

"So, Phillip Crawford?"

Emily's eyebrows pulled together as she flipped

through the card box. "Nope. No Crawford in here."

"Well, I suppose they still might have known each other," Sam said. "Crawford may have stopped by to study the research papers or—" Her phone interrupted and she glanced at the screen. "It's the bakery. I'd better—"

Emily nodded, and Sam tapped to take the call.

"Sam, it's Becky, are you in town or at the ranch?"

"I'm close by. What's up?"

"I just called Mrs. Mackley to let her know the sheet cake is ready for her party. She informed me it's supposed to be delivered, but I'm scrambling to get the Ortiz wedding cake finished on time. And Mrs. Mackley wants hers *now*."

"I'll swing by. Have Julio put the cake in the van. I can be there in five minutes."

"Bless you, Sam. Thanks so much."

Emily looked up. "Go, go. I didn't mean to interrupt your day. If you come up with any idea of what Grandma Valerie's message might be about, just let me know."

Sam assured her she'd give it some thought, then hurried out to her car.

It's not what everyone thinks. What in the world could that mean?

Chapter 11

Sam parked her car in the alley behind Sweet's Sweets, flipped through her key ring and brought up the one for the delivery van, and was on her way to Alva Mackley's house. This was a longtime, loyal customer. It wouldn't be smart to be obstinate about delivering the cake, even though nothing on the order form indicated delivery was expected. Hostesses like Alva entertained regularly, and many future orders depended upon pleasing her.

Sam knew the house; it was only two blocks from her first home in town. She walked up to the door empty-handed and rang the bell to be sure Alva had a place cleared to set the large cake.

"Oh, Sam, thank you so much!" exclaimed the elderly woman, who looked as though she had just returned from the hair salon. "The party starts in two hours and I have *so* much to do!"

"Show me where you want the cake and I'll be out of your way in two minutes."

"I'd love for you to stay for the party," Alva said. "Everyone always raves about your pastries. They'd love to include you. We're just a fun bunch of old gabbers."

She'd seen Alva's group of friends, all seventy-five and older, solid church ladies whose conversations tended to focus on the cute antics of their great-grandchildren. Sam couldn't see any way to clear her afternoon to sit in complete boredom. She made convincing apologies to Alva, pulling a few business cards from the pocket of her coat.

"If anyone needs something from the bakery, here's my number. We're fairly booked up for special orders through Christmas, but there are always cookies and scones in the display cases. Maybe those will be helpful to someone with last-minute plans."

She drove a block away before pulling over and taking out her phone. Susan O'Malley, the Crawfords' former house sitter, answered on the first ring.

"Mother said you would be calling." Illogically, Sam had a picture of an eighteen year old in her mind, but this was a mature voice roughened by cigarettes.

"Susan, I'd like to pick your brain for a few minutes about the Crawford case."

"Mother mentioned that. I have no idea what I could tell you. The police interviewed me a lot at the time. Did you talk to them?"

"A quick glance at their case file. I know the basics of what happened, but was hoping maybe you've thought of something else since then."

"Gosh, I don't know. Nothing comes to mind right this minute."

"Could I come by? Are you at home?"

"I'm at work, and this isn't the place to get into it. I'm a cashier at Happy Foods, and the only reason you caught me now is because I'm on break. Which ends, like, right now. I need to get back inside."

"Maybe later?"

"Yeah, sure. I get off at three. And I'm off tomorrow, but I really gotta get out and do some Christmas shopping, so it's hit or miss if you'll catch me at home."

"Thanks so much. I'll call first. Have a good d—"

The connection was already lost. "Well, that could turn out to be a bust," Sam said to the empty van. The one person who was actually there when the fire started, the one who might know if the painting on the wall that night was the real one, and Susan O'Malley wasn't exactly a willing witness.

Sam let out a sigh. She had the name of the gallery where Crawford had bought the painting, but fatigue was setting in and she realized she was probably hungry. She debated: go home and see if Beau had already eaten; grab fast food somewhere (she planned to go completely off fast food, but she still had more than two weeks until she had to form it as a new year's resolution); get to the bakery and hope work would distract her mind.

The search for answers on the case seemed to be going nowhere, whereas her business could always use her attention. She was only a few blocks from Sweet's Sweets so she headed in that direction.

Kelly's little car was parked behind Puppy Chic next door, and she spotted Sam at the wheel of the bakery van.

"Hey, Mom. Boy, did I get the third degree from Ana after you left yesterday. I told you, that kid knows too much, and she's not easily distracted once she gets a question in her mind." But she was grinning when she said it.

"Ah, right. We were talking about whether ghosts exist. Did you get the chance to talk to Scott about his experiences?"

Kelly shook her head. "No real chance without little ears present. Not that we don't believe open discussion is good for kids, just that she's at the age where everything is taken literally. I really don't want to plant fears in her head so she's screaming in the night about scary things under the bed or something."

"No, I completely get that. Ana's got some kind of special abilities anyway. Who knows how much she already has figured out about stuff like that." Sam had locked the van and hiked her pack up over her shoulder, and at that moment her stomach growled.

"A little hungry?" Kelly asked.

"Probably. I meant to grab something but the van just seemed to drive me right back to work."

"Hang on. I met Lisa Coppell for lunch—we hadn't seen each other in ages—and I couldn't finish all my sandwich." Kelly reached into the car and came out with a Styrofoam box. "Philly cheesesteak. Stick it in the micro for a minute and you're set to go."

"Great, thanks!"

"We need to get together socially. The guys haven't seen each other in a while. How about dinner at our place tonight? Nothing fancy—I put my famous Bolognese sauce in the slow cooker this morning."

Before she could respond, Sam heard the bakery door

open. Julio appeared on the step with a bag of trash bound for the dumpster in the alley.

"Good," he said, spotting Sam. "Becky's slammed."

"Uh-oh. Let me check this out," she said to Kelly, "and I'll get back to you on the dinner plan."

Becky *was* looking a little frazzled when Sam walked in. She had two wedding cakes assembled in front of her. Two other decorators worked at the other end of the large table, one decorating cookies as fast as she could squeeze green frosting onto tree shaped ones, and the other piping a snow white border around a sheet cake.

"Let me hang up my coat and wash my hands," Sam said. "Tell me what's on the schedule while I reheat my belated lunch. Have you guys eaten?"

Becky nodded. "Yeah, Jen had sandwiches delivered a couple hours ago. We've got eight party cakes and four weddings this weekend. Most of the cakes are baked, so now—"

Jen bustled in from the front room, showing order forms in both hands. "*Why* do people wait till the last minute to order their wedding cake? I just do *not* get that— I'd have mine planned months ahead of time and on the schedule weeks out."

"That's just you," Sam said with a laugh, pulling her hot sandwich from the microwave. "And it's because you've worked here so long you know what goes into creating one. What have we got?"

"Three tiers, no pillars. I'm trying to get people to keep them simple when they spring this last-minute stuff." She held out the order sheet. "It's for a Sunday afternoon wedding, so we need it ready for delivery on Saturday."

"Make that five weddings," muttered Becky.

Sam looked at the specs and called out to Julio the sizes and flavors for the cakes.

"Got it." He spoke little but moved quickly, the ideal baker.

A small swatch of burgundy fabric was stapled to the wedding cake order form. "Matching flowers to the bridesmaids' dresses. Did you tell them I'll do my best? It's too late to order a custom tint from our supplier."

"Yep, I told her. The mother seemed pretty accommodating, but the bride threw a bit of a pout. I say, too bad." Jen suddenly looked contrite. "Well, I didn't say it to her face."

While the square cake tiers went into the oven, Sam pulled her gel food colors from the supply shelf. She could create a burgundy by blending a little purple and a little black into her standard red paste. She felt sure she could get it fairly close. She set about blending it and comparing to the fabric swatch until she had it just right.

"What was the other order Jen just brought in?" Becky asked.

Sam glanced over her shoulder to the stack of forms. "A party cake, square, two tiers, a six- inch and an eight inch. I could roll out some fondant and do one of our gift package designs."

"Good—that'll be easy."

Sam got out her flower nail and a bunch of precut parchment squares and began piping burgundy roses as quickly as she could. Each finished one went onto a baking sheet and she soon had about two dozen, both full-blown and half-open roses. Once the sheet was filled with flowers, Sam carried it into the walk-in fridge so they could firm up.

"What do we have in the way of extra cake layers

already baked?" Sam asked, not really expecting anyone to know offhand.

She surveyed the shelves in the large fridge. The procedure was that Julio kept the bake oven full at all times, so when they weren't making custom flavors such as poppyseed, lemon, strawberry, or spice he would fill the oven space with vanilla or chocolate layers in the most common sizes. The layers would be stored on shelves with the customer's order form taped to the rack in front of it, so no one would inadvertently use something that had already been promised.

Sam saw that there were easily six quarter-sheet vanilla and another six in chocolate, plus both chocolate and vanilla layers—round and square—which hadn't been committed for anyone yet. She pulled the six- and eight-inch squares for the gift package cake and carried them out. The helper who'd been working on cookies moved three large trays aside so Sam would have a little assembly space, and she quickly got the layers filled and rough-coated with a thin layer of buttercream in order to make the fondant adhere better.

"Okay, that's step one."

She put the other decorator to work kneading red paste color into a ball of pre-made fondant, green color into a second one. Sam fed a bigger ball of white fondant into the roller machine, over and over, until it was the thickness she wanted. The white fondant draped neatly over the larger, bottom layer and she trimmed it to shape. Same with the smaller tier, then she stacked them.

Eyeing it to be sure nothing was leaning or off center, she picked up the colored fondant balls and ran the red one through the machine. Flattened now, it would become ribbon. The green one would be cut into holly leaves. With a sharp knife, her new helper deftly cut the ribbons and handed them to Sam. Within fifteen minutes, the stacked 'packages' had vivid red ribbon and a bouffant bow on top. Green holly leaves were tucked into strategic spots for bright pops of color, and the cake went into the fridge.

"It's going to take those wedding cake layers a while to bake and cool," Sam said. "What can I help you with next?"

Becky was only too happy to turn over one of the other wedding cakes, and Sam studied the order form before she began piping intricate ivory lace over the bottom tier.

"I feel guilty that I haven't been here much in the last couple of days," Sam said as each of them worked on her projects.

"Normally, it's no problem," Becky said. "You love your work but you also have a life outside of it, as we all do. And I remember a bunch of times we went home at six and you stayed half the night."

Sam waved it off. She didn't really want to admit how many times she'd worked all night, almost always with the added energy boost she got by handling the wooden box.

"I'm helping the new librarian with a little personal matter," she said. "But still, the business comes first."

"That's Emily, right? Well, she started off as a customer, so it's smart that you're keeping a good rapport with her."

Sam thought of the painting, its ethereal beauty and the almost enchanted effects the artist had achieved with paint on canvas. She wished she had the same talent with dough and sugar and food color. The chocolate-making techniques she had learned from Bobul came close in magical qualities, but it had been a few years since she'd really applied her hand to that, not since she'd sold her chocolate factory business to a Swiss company.

She shook off the memories, pleasant as they were, and concentrated on the cake before her. There was something about having the boss on the premises that seemed to spur the others to greater output, as well. Becky finished the wedding cake she'd been working on and was already nearly half done with another. The seasonal helpers had turned out all the party cake orders that were due today and tomorrow, and four trays of cookies had been carried up front and added to the display case in the sales room. Sam put the finishing touches on the ivory lace cake, took a deep breath, and looked around.

Jen pushed her way through the curtain separating the sales room. "Don't shoot me—I come bearing no new orders for today."

The announcement was met with smiles.

"In fact, it's nearly six. I'm just sayin' since you tend to lose track of time back here."

Becky stretched and rubbed her lower back. "Yeah, I believe you. Don texted me to say he'd picked up the boys from school, but it's time for me to get home. It's gonna be takeout pizza in our house tonight."

One of the assistants offered to stay late, but Sam told them both to head home, congratulating them on their hard work. Two more helpers were coming in for the evening. They would work until ten and get all the standard breakfast items made and ready to go into the glass cases out front.

She could now safely break away for dinner with the family.

Chapter 12

Sam pulled up outside the Victorian to find Beau's truck already there. The beauty of dinner plans by text. Windows of the old house glowed with warm light, and tiny fairy lights twinkled throughout the garland that ringed the covered porch and pillars. She picked up the bakery box of snowball cookies she'd brought for dessert and walked inside.

Ana jumped out from behind the door and hugged Sam's thigh. "Come in the kitchen, that's where Grandpa Beau is."

"Oh my gosh, that sauce smells wonderful!" Sam exclaimed.

Scott was stirring the crockpot, Kelly was tasting a strand of spaghetti over a pot of boiling water on the stove, and Beau seemed content to observe while nursing a bottle of Heineken. Sam dispensed hugs and kisses and set the cookies on a countertop out of the way.

"What can I do to help?" she asked.

At that moment the oven timer pinged. "Pull out the garlic bread," Kelly suggested. She gave a nod to Scott, who came over with potholders to carry the heavy, boiling spaghetti pot to the sink. "We're all set up in the dining room so, Mom, you might help Ana wash up, and we're ready to sit down to dinner."

Talk of Christmas filled the conversational space, especially once Beau asked Ana what Santa was going to bring her. The list was lengthy. Sam and Kelly exchanged glances that meant, we'll-make-a-plan-later.

"That was a nice party at the Morton Library," Scott said. "The young woman who's running it now— did I understand that she's the granddaughter of David Plankhurst? You've gotten to know her pretty well?"

"It started with a cake order, and recently I've been looking into a few things for her."

"David was so helpful to me when I was researching my book on this house. I was really sorry to hear he's now in a care home," he said. "Eliza Nalespar was quite a character and a renowned writer, but the history of our house is interesting too. It's one of the few Victorian- style homes here in a town filled with adobe and the Spanish and Native American influences. So, what's Emily asked you to do?"

"This information doesn't go beyond this room," Sam said, making a point to establish eye contact with each person, including their brilliant little four-year-old. "It's something we can't talk about to our friends, right?"

Ana nodded seriously.

"Emily has found a painting by a famous artist, one that everyone believed had been destroyed in a fire. I'm just asking around, trying to find out what really happened twenty-five years ago."

"Is it possible the painting she found is a fake? That the real one actually was destroyed and someone created this one to look like it?"

Sam gave a half nod, half shrug. "Anything's possible." But not in this case. A person had to see the work of art as she had seen it in Emily's kitchen. There was no way anyone less than the brilliant JC Freeman had created that piece.

But she didn't say so, and the conversation turned to Beau's recent repairs and the myriad of ranch chores he and Danny were tackling in preparation for the real winter weather yet to come.

By eight o'clock Sam felt her eyes drooping, although Ana was lively as ever. After cookies and gelato, they all carried their plates to the kitchen. Kelly insisted she would handle the cleanup and loading of the dishwasher.

"You looked wiped out, Mom. Get home and rest up."

"I guess the afternoon did get a little intense at the bakery."

"And I'll bet you didn't ever eat any lunch …"

"Maybe not. I don't actually remember eating the sandwich you gave me."

Beau helped her into her coat and made certain her car started in the frigid air. "I'm following you home, just to be sure you don't doze off. You've had a very long day."

"Seriously, hon, it's barely after eight. I'll be fine." But she was glad for the sight of his lights behind her, and even more glad to peel off her bakery clothing, take a hot shower and fall into bed.

She was startled to see that it was well after nine in the morning when her eyes opened and focused on the bedside clock. Beau had been right—she'd needed the twelve hours of sleep. And this would be a good time to catch Susan O'Malley, the once-teen house sitter for the Crawfords, before she left to do her holiday shopping.

Sam hopped out of bed and dressed in jeans and a long-sleeved pullover with a fleece jacket for extra warmth. With a travel mug of coffee in hand, she walked out to her car. Heavy frost was melting from every surface the sun shone on, and Sam had learned from her first year of living in Taos that it was smart to park a vehicle facing east so the first rays of the morning would provide automatic windshield defrosting. She started her engine and let the car warm up, while she looked up the notes she'd made on her phone.

Susan's accommodating mother had let it slip that Susan lived next door, and it had been easy enough to find the senior O'Malley's address in the phone book. With that information at hand, she started out.

She caught Susan O'Malley at home, barely. She was slipping her arms into the sleeves of a heavy coat when she answered the door.

"Let me guess—Samantha … Sorry, I don't remember your last name."

"Samantha Sweet. Can you spare a minute or two? I just want to verify some of the things about that night at the Crawford home."

"Home? Well, maybe. The place was more like a modernistic museum. And the Crawfords barely spent a month a year there." Susan gave a sigh and stepped back to let Sam inside. "Come on in. We might as well do this now."

The living room smelled strongly of cigarette smoke, and a layer of haze seemed to permeate the air and the furniture. Overstuffed couches and a lone armchair filled the smallish space, but the real dominating feature was a big screen TV.

"I love my movies," Susan said, catching Sam's glance toward it. "It's how I fill the evenings."

Sam noticed the lines around her eyes, the downturned mouth that hinted at a deep sadness.

"How did you get the job of housesitting for the Crawford family?" she asked as they took seats at the opposite ends of a puffy couch of the kind you could sink into and have a hard time getting up.

"Mother was their housekeeper. Seemed strange, since she hardly did anything most of the time. Once a week she dusted the furniture, and now and then she would vacuum the rugs that still had the Hoover track marks from the previous visit. When they would show up—usually for a week of skiing in the winter and a couple weeks of fresh mountain air in summer—she was on duty to keep the beds made, laundry done, breakfast laid out. They went out for dinner nearly every night, so there wasn't much cooking."

"Why did they want someone staying in the house this particular time?"

Susan shrugged. "I was eighteen and didn't question anything beyond the fact that it was a week-long job that would pay more than I made in a month at the Dairy Queen. Once I settled in, though, I learned it was because they had brought their cat with them that year. It was a beautiful thing—some purebred Persian Phil and Camilla had just bought from God knows how expensive a breeder. Then they got invited to Mexico and couldn't take the cat with them, obviously, so they wanted someone to stay with it in the unfamiliar house. Mother couldn't do it because she's allergic."

She started to reach for a pack of cigarettes on the end table, glanced at Sam, and withdrew her hand. It was a courteous gesture for someone who was unexpectedly entertaining a stranger in her own home.

"The cat made it out of the burning house all right?"

"Yeah, when I ran out of the house, she raced out the front door so fast you couldn't believe it. I don't know what happened to her. I wasn't ever allowed back into what was left of the house. I got examined at the hospital and sent home. I really was only concerned about poor Mike."

"Your boyfriend."

She nodded. "I felt so much guilt over that. Inviting him there when I wasn't supposed to."

"You were only going to be there a week. Why did you invite him?"

She let out a hoarse sputter. "Because we were eighteen and horny, and parents back then didn't encourage boyfriend/girlfriend visits in our bedrooms at home. We had planned the most romantic night ever. He brought a bottle of wine and we lit candles, and we were going to spend the entire night together in one of the guest bedrooms. I would wash the sheets the next day and no one would ever know of our little tryst."

A tear slipped down her cheek and she brushed it roughly away. "I guess I still feel guilty about him."

"About those candles ... is it true they were still burning when the two of you went upstairs?"

"I honestly don't know. Of course I swore to the police officers that we had definitely blown them out, but I don't know. I still think about that night. We drank all the wine Mike had brought and then we got into Mr. Crawford's vodka. We were pretty blitzed. It was why neither of us heard the smoke alarms upstairs. I woke up feeling restless, and it was when I headed down toward the kitchen that I smelled smoke and heard the alarms. At first, you know, I thought maybe I'd left a cigarette burning, although that makes no sense. We'd been upstairs at least an hour at that point.

"But I went down the stairs to check it out, and that's when …" She coughed, at the memory. "I got to the bottom of the stairs and realized the whole living room, the dining room, and kitchen were filled with smoke. And most of that was filled with flames. The smoke and the smell were so horrible."

The tears were flowing freely now, and Susan stood and began pacing the room. "I screamed Mike's name a couple times, but I must have breathed in a bunch of smoke because suddenly I couldn't catch my breath anymore. That's when I ran for the front door. The very second I opened it, the flames got even hotter. Oxygen, obviously, but that's how little a teenager knows. It was all I could do to get down the front steps to the street. Somebody said I was screaming, but I don't really remember. I just knew I couldn't get back inside to wake Mike up."

Chapter 13

Sam reimagined the haunting scene Susan O'Malley had described, over and over, as she drove toward the center of town. She couldn't imagine the horror for a teenaged girl, or the fact that Susan had carried the guilt with her all these years. While the police were content to chalk up the fire as an accident so they wouldn't have to investigate a crime of arson, a young girl had spent her life believing a stupid mistake had cost the life of someone she cared about.

Sam had intended to ask whether Susan remembered the painting, *The Ghost of Christmas*, hanging in the living room, but after the story she'd heard she couldn't imagine a detail like that being memorable to a teen. If she saw Susan again, she might bring it up.

One person who might recall the painting would be

Susan's mother. On a whim, she turned around and headed back to their street. At the corner, she spotted Susan in a Ford pickup truck heading toward Paseo Pueblo del Sur. Susan didn't recognize Sam's vehicle, which was just as well. Sam parked in front of the mother's home and walked up to the door.

"Oh, yes, I saw your car in front of Susie's house a little while ago," Ida O'Malley said after they introduced themselves. She wore red sweatpants and a Christmas sweater layered over a collared blouse. "Well, come on in. It's chilly with the door open."

Once inside, Sam immediately unzipped her coat. It had to be eighty degrees in the house, which smelled of onions cooked yesterday and some kind of sickly sweet air freshener. She walked into a living room filled with collections—china figurines, Indian baskets, kachina dolls of the type found in tourist shops rather than the pricey ones from galleries. They filled two glass-enclosed cabinets and an entire wall of shelves. The riot of color and pattern was a little overwhelming, and there was so much that no one item stood out.

"Can I get you some coffee or maybe a nice cup of hot chocolate?" Ida must be perpetually cold.

"No thanks. I was just talking with Susan about what happened at the Crawford place all those years ago, and it occurred to me that you would be more familiar with the items in the house than she was. Specifically, I wonder if you remember a JC Freeman painting?"

Ida looked completely blank. "Oh, those people had lots of things in the house. I have to admit, expensive art isn't really an interest of mine."

Sam briefly described the winter scene, the snowy

forest and small house in the background. "It was done mostly in shades of white and gray, with small touches of color."

Ida was nodding. "That bland old thing. It hung in the living room. Never could see the appeal in that one. I dusted the frames of all the pictures, you know, and some of the bright ones in the other rooms were kind of okay. Although I never did understand modern art—all those blobs and slashes of paint." She made a face.

"But the snowy scene … it was different?"

"Yeah, different than what they had in the rest of the place, but it was so *plain*."

Clearly, either Ida hadn't taken the time to notice the finer details of *The Ghost of Christmas* or the painting had hung in an area of the room without good lighting.

"I need to ask about the days right before the fire. Did you notice anything unusual about that painting? Did it look different right before the fire than it had when they first bought it?"

Again, the blank stare, and Sam realized Ida hadn't cared enough about the artwork to pay any attention. Someone could have probably substituted a cheap print from Walmart, and as long as the colors were similar, the housekeeper wouldn't have paid any attention.

Ida was still talking. "I suppose everything in that house was expensive. It's the kind of people they seemed to be, you know, sticking a weird-shaped chair in the middle of a room. I heard Mr. Crawford sometimes bragging to his friends—Oh, that's a so-and-so piece. I guess the names of those designers and muckety-mucks meant something to that bunch. Never meant a thing to me. Are you sure you don't want some hot chocolate?"

Sam declined with a smile, saying she needed to get to work.

"Oh that's right … you're the lady that owns the bakery on the next street over from the plaza, aren't you?"

Sam nodded and edged her way toward the door. If she spent another minute inside the house, she would have to remove her jacket and that meant being stuck for another hour. The older woman seemed starved for conversation, but Sam wasn't the one to provide it, not today. She escaped and breathed deeply of the cold air outside.

The Finstadt Gallery was next on her list to visit. They'd represented JC Freeman during his lifetime and continued to feature his work since his death. Situated in a prime spot on Taos Plaza, it was on her way to the bakery, so she went in search of a parking spot. Every space at the meters in front of the shops was taken; she would need to go to the large lot north of the plaza itself. Might as well go on to the bakery and walk back; it was nearly as close.

She pulled into the alley behind her shop. Of course she couldn't very well park there and walk away without checking in. She decided to walk around to the front and observe the bakery from a customer's perspective.

The front window displays glowed in the morning light. She always designed the two windows from different perspectives during the Christmas season—one religious, one secular. To the right of the door was a desert scene with a couple of palm trees, a prominent star radiating beams toward the earth, and a manger scene complete with all the animals and people in their places. Cakes, gingerbread, and cookies went along with the color scheme and themes.

To the left of the window she'd created a village of gingerbread cottages loaded with candies and icicles made of royal icing. A snowy scene filled the window, and a marzipan Santa Claus stood beside his sleigh on the rooftop of one little house.

The overall effect was pleasing and Sam took in the minute details, making sure no decorations had slipped, nothing had melted. She stepped in the front door, enjoying the deep jingle of the sleigh bells Jen had added to the high tinkle of the normal small ones that hung over the door the rest of the year.

The shop was packed, with all the bistro tables occupied. Customers stood two deep at the counter, edging around each other to get a look at the offerings in the display cases, and Jen was scrambling to fill orders. Sam slipped off her outer coat and stepped behind the counter to assist. Her eyes skimmed over the boxes on the back counter, those with order forms taped to them. She recognized most of the names, and knew some of the faces in the crowd belonged to them. Picking up the first one, she called out the customer's name.

A lady stepped forward and Sam handed over the box. "You're all set," she said.

Two more of these prepaid orders were quickly dispatched, clearing the crowd somewhat. Sam continued to call out names and take payments, while Jen waited on those who were deciding which flavor muffin to get or what size cup of coffee.

Fifteen minutes later, there was enough breathing space that Jen could handle the front on her own, and Sam retreated to the kitchen. Becky's normal smile was in place this morning, and Julio already had the cooling racks loaded with cake layers, cookies, and scones. Sam picked up those items which could immediately go to the front, and took care of that.

"The evening crew did a great job of making a dent in the number of party cake orders," Becky said, her concentration on the new wedding cake from yesterday, the one Julio had baked in the late afternoon.

"Are we running on time with everything?" Sam asked, washing her hands.

"Close, but yes. We haven't been late with an order yet. We have almost everything made that's due this weekend. Next week … well, it's gonna get crazy again."

"It always does, this time of year."

Sam spent the rest of the morning on an elaborate groomsman cake, marveling at how complicated some couples wanted their weddings to be. Seldom did she see the days when the celebration consisted of family and a few close friends getting together for cake and punch and to wish the newlyweds well. She'd seen people spend enough on their one day of glory to put a down payment on a decent house. She shook her head. *Is this a sign that I'm beginning to think like an old person?*

One thing about working in a creative business, such as cake design, someone was always coming in with an idea that sparked her imagination, and it was easy to keep up with new trends by listening to her customers' ideas and trolling around on Pinterest.

"What do you think?" Becky asked, setting the topper in place on the cake she'd spent two days working on. The elaborate confection for the top had taken much of that time, fashioning poinsettia flowers, pinecones, and holly leaves from fondant and icing. The bride wanted every part of the cake to be edible, although Sam couldn't actually imagine guests requesting a pine cone with their slice of cake.

"It's amazingly beautiful," Sam told her. "Your skills are growing every day. I may just have to turn this place over to you."

"I thought you already did that," Becky said with a smile.

"True. Right after Beau was shot—I couldn't have made a wedding cake to save my life." Those were horrible days, and the months afterward had been no easy road either.

"But it all turned out fine, and you're back when we need you."

Sam held up the chocolate-on-chocolate groom's cake. "I think the newlyweds will be happy all around when they see these."

They carried the cakes to the fridge, where they would keep until the following afternoon when they would end up in the ballroom at the country club.

"It sounds quiet out front," Sam said. "I'm going to check with Jen, and then I have a quick stop to make at the plaza."

"Sure, abandon me now," Becky teased. She was studying the order forms with the baked cake layers on the refrigerated shelves, and she pulled a set of round fourteen-inch layers, which she carried to the worktable. "I'm kidding, Sam. Go. This design will be a cinch after that last one."

Sam slipped her winter coat over her bakery jacket and walked into the sales room. It seemed they were at a lull in the day's craziness, so she told Jen she'd be back in fifteen or twenty minutes.

"I've got my phone, in case things go all berserk again."

Jen laughed and assured her it would be fine. She was in the midst of organizing the trays of cookies and muffins, filling gaps so she could let Julio know which items they were running low on.

Sam walked out into the brisk air and looked up at the sky. The earlier solid blue was now broken with clouds, but these were the sort that formed over the top of the mountains, not the harbinger of an incoming weather front. So far, this December was proving to be a fairly mild one. She set out eastward, crossing the street in front of her shop, cutting around a church parking lot, and pausing at the crosswalk to the plaza. Cars passed in a steady flow and she had to wait for the lit-up Walk symbol before she dared walk on.

Taos Plaza hummed with activity. The holiday decorations had been in place for nearly a month now— electric luminarias lined every rooftop edge, a huge tree near the bandstand was covered in ribbons and oversized Mexican tin ornaments, garland draped the railing around the parklike area in the middle and around fronts of most businesses. Shop windows were filled with all the sparkly items to catch someone's eye as the perfect gift.

Parking spaces were non-existent. As soon as a car backed out, another took its place, and Sam was glad she had walked over now rather than battling that tangle earlier. She followed the covered sidewalk to the illustrious Finstadt Gallery, the place known as the dealer for JC Freeman's art and the one where she assumed the Crawfords had purchased *Ghost*.

A couple was browsing some smaller paintings along the west wall, while a lone woman stood before a roped-off easel with a framed JC Freeman piece on display. In her Taos-chic broomstick skirt, silk tunic, and angora wrap draped around her shoulders and neck, the customer was apparently worthy of notice, as a gallery employee hovered nearby.

Sam shamelessly eavesdropped on the employee's soft explanation about the Freeman legacy, how the artist's estate had been held up in probate for years, and it was only recently that a number of his paintings had been released to the market again.

The employee gave a down-the-nose glance at Sam's attire and made a quick judgment. "The prints and gift items are displayed on the wall over there," she said.

Sam held her ground and studied the piece on the easel. It was larger than *The Ghost of Christmas* by a few inches, but the subject was completely different, and not as well executed. The 'hidden' spirit was easy to spot, and although the painting was certainly beautiful, it lacked the hidden depths and layers that Emily and Sam had spotted in *Ghost*.

The customer's interest waned and she wandered to a different painting on an easel, the female employee trailing along like a hungry puppy.

"May I ask a quick question?" Sam asked, drawing another look of disdain and ignoring it. "Have you heard of a Freeman piece titled *The Ghost of Christmas*? I wonder if this was the gallery that originally sold it."

"I'm not familiar with that one," the employee said, "and I've worked here nearly five years."

A man stepped from behind a curtain at the rear of the shop and cleared his throat. He wore a thousand-dollar suit, a silk tie, and his smooth skin hinted that he got regular facials. His medium-brown goatee was perfectly trimmed. A silent signal passed between them, something like, *You take care of your prospect, I'll handle this one.*

He walked toward Sam. "Maurice Finstadt. Tell me, what do you know about *The Ghost of Christmas*?"

Chapter 14

Sam met his icy blue gaze as if she had the cash in her pocket to purchase anything she wanted. "I wonder what its value would be today."

"That painting doesn't exist. It was lost, many years ago."

"Was yours the gallery that sold it originally? I believe Phillip Crawford was the purchaser."

Finstadt's eyes narrowed. "I personally made that sale, but I don't see how that's connected to you, Ms. …?"

"Samantha Sweet. My husband, Beau Cardwell, was Taos County Sheriff."

"Let's speak somewhere more privately," the gallery owner said, tilting his head toward the back of the room. He led the way past the curtain, through an area where apparently packaging and shipping was done, and into a private office. He closed the door.

"How do you know the painting was destroyed?" Sam asked, once Finstadt took his seat behind the desk and she'd taken one of the two chairs in front of it.

"Did I say destroyed? I believe I said it was lost, although sadly, you are right. The homeowner suffered a fire that ruined a large portion of his fabulous home, a home in which I personally oversaw the delivery and hanging of the JC Freeman piece you mention."

"Did Freeman ever paint the same subject twice? Would he have created another *Ghost* after the first one was 'lost'?"

"Ah, no, that would never happen. Freeman was a creative genius, but also a decent marketer. He knew value came with rarity. Each of his works was one of a kind, and the originals were never duplicated. Now, I will admit that we had some discussion of it ahead of time, and I eventually convinced him to let us produce some limited edition prints of certain pieces—always signed and numbered—to appeal to those without the budgets to enjoy his originals."

"I saw your name on the police report," Sam said. "You were the one who certified that the painting lost in the fire was actually the real *Ghost of Christmas.*"

He straightened in his chair and his mouth became a thin line. "Are you questioning my integrity? Or my knowledge of the artist's work?"

Sam put on a neutral expression. "Not at all. Just verifying a fact."

"Yes, I examined the very scant remains of the painting and felt certain it was the same piece I had sold to the

Crawfords a few months earlier. It was Mrs. Crawford who loved the work. She said the snowy forest reminded her of their ski trips here. Mr. Crawford loved to indulge his wife and he wrote a check without a moment's hesitation."

"I saw from the insurance report that it had been insured for twenty-five thousand. Is that what he paid for it?"

Finstadt smiled and shook his head in wonder. "Yes, amazingly, that's what a Freeman went for back then."

"And now?"

"Oh, multiples of that. Large multiples."

"Give it to me in dollars."

"Freeman's simpler paintings, those created before he perfected his techniques of adding mysterious and hidden objects within the image—they easily sell in the six-figure range. His artworks with the hidden images, high sixes."

Sam gulped, hoping he couldn't read her thoughts.

"And let's say *if* the *Ghost* existed today … what would it be worth now?"

His eyes narrowed again and he studied her face. "Ms. Sweet, if it existed, *Ghost* would be easily in the seven, eight figure range. Again I must ask, what do you know about it?"

"Only what I read in the police and insurance reports. It's gone, and such a sad loss to the art world." She managed to keep her voice steady, but couldn't be sure the trembling in her hands wasn't noticed as she thanked Finstadt for the information and rose to leave.

Chapter 15

Sam walked away from the gallery, trying to shed the slimy feeling she got from Maurice Finstadt. When she asked about his certification of the burned painting, she'd gotten an edgy vibe.

"Dang, why didn't I handle the box before I went there?" she muttered to herself. "I would have at least seen an aura around him."

Two women with arms full of shopping bags turned to stare at her.

"Nothing—just talking to myself," she said brightly.

The man seemed slick, but would a gallery owner risk his reputation and that of his successful business by pulling a scam like that? And what would be the point, unless ... What if Finstadt had been friendly with Emily's grandparents back then, and perhaps he was the one who asked David Plankhurst to hide the painting in the secret niche?

Sam shook her head. But then why wouldn't the art expert have reclaimed the painting and hidden it somewhere he could easily get his hands on it, rather than leaving it with a friend? She was missing some piece of the puzzle.

The important thing, she realized with a jolt, was what lengths the man would go to in order to get the painting back. She may have tipped her hand just now, posing questions about *if* the painting existed today. Finstadt was in the perfect position to show up as the man who found it intact after all these years. He could claim he was duped, back when he certified the lost piece. Now, he could simply put the painting on the market and sell it for millions.

And that may have been his plan all along. Who was in a better position to drive up the price of Freeman's work than the gallery that sold most of it and therefore controlled much of the market?

Sam's pace picked up. Had she just now put Finstadt on alert? She had to get away from the gallery and the crowded plaza. And she needed to step up her warning to Emily, whose very life could now be in danger. She headed back to Sweet's Sweets.

Before she could get tied up with bakery questions or visiting with a customer, she walked around to the back of the building. Her car would be a private place for this conversation. She pulled out her phone and called Emily.

"Hey, Sam, how are things going? You're probably swamped with bakery business right now?"

"Oh yeah, definitely, but I'm still working on finding out some answers for you. Listen, I've learned more about Freeman's art, and … well, let's just say it's worth enough for someone to want to come after it. Please, *please* be sure you're keeping it hidden back in its safe spot, and do *not* show it or talk to *anyone* about it. Okay?"

"Um, okay …"

"I'll fill you in with more details later. There are people who were familiar with the painting when it was originally purchased, people who know what it would be worth today. If you should get a call from anyone in the art world—galleries, auction houses, anyone—don't admit that you have it. We need to do a lot more checking before we know who to trust."

"Got it."

"I'm doing the same. People know I'm asking around, but the only ones who actually know that the painting has been found are my family. I am swearing them all to secrecy too." Even as she said it, Sam wasn't entirely sure how she could keep asking questions about the fire and the painting without revealing anything about it. "Hon, your safety could be at stake. I'm dead serious about this."

"Sam, don't worry. I haven't shown it to anyone but you. My concern is for my grandfather."

Another possible target. "Can you contact the care facility where he's living, make sure they don't allow him any visitors other than family?"

"Do you actually think someone may go after him?"

Sam gave it a moment. Someone had asked David Plankhurst to hide that painting. "Yeah, it's possible."

"Okay then. I'll call the home right now." There were some fidgeting sounds in the background. "You know, people come in here all the time asking about my grandparents. I've been truthful, saying Grandma passed and Grandpa has Alzheimer's."

"It's fine, I'm sure. You shouldn't lie about that. Just stay a little vague about where he is. And let me know if anyone who asks about him gets pushy for more information or seems overly interested, okay?"

They ended the call and Sam could only hope that she'd impressed upon Emily the importance of keeping the secret. She raised her eyes skyward. "Grandma Valerie, if you ever wanted to send a warning message to your girl, now's the time."

Meanwhile, Sam had to think about anyone she had mentioned the painting to. Kelly, Scott, and Beau. Her rancher husband didn't know or care much about art, plus all his years in law enforcement had taught him to keep things close to the vest. She phoned Kelly.

"Hey, real quick. Have you told anyone about that painting I mentioned to you?"

She went over the reasons she'd just given Emily, and Kelly swore she hadn't given it much thought in recent days. "Mom, with Christmas coming up, there's a lot of other stuff on my mind right now."

"Good. Keep it that way."

Kelly laughed. "I will. Oh, by the way, I found something in the book—a potion that claims to help a person know if someone else is being truthful. I get the feeling it's mostly used in romantic situations, but hey—it might help with what you want it for."

"Is it something weird?"

"Not too weird. You'll need some cinnamon sticks and fresh peppermint leaves."

The back door at the bakery opened just as she was ending the call with Kelly. Out came Julio and Becky, carrying one of the wedding cakes Becky had finished yesterday.

"Need a delivery person?" Sam asked, grabbing her

things from her car and walking over to open the back of the delivery van.

"That would be wonderful," Becky said. "I could break away, but there's—"

"No problem. I've got this." Sam helped them set the cake securely in the van and checked the delivery address, the reception hall at one of the churches.

Fifteen minutes later, she pulled around to the side entrance of the building, where she spotted a priest walking quickly toward the door. When she called out to him, he smiled and propped the door open.

"Need a hand with that?" he asked, joining her at the back of the van.

"It's a big one," she told him. "Maybe I should take a peek inside and see where they want this."

"I'll just ask Mrs. Romero. It looks like she's running the whole operation with military precision." He trotted to the open door and came back a few seconds later. "All set."

Sam had loosened the clamps that held the open-topped cake box in place, and the two of them maneuvered it out of the van and into the building. The commander inside (presumably the mother of the bride) wore a purple dress that went along with the theme of purple and white decorations, which festooned the walls and topped the tables. Sam and the priest followed her hand signals and set the cake gently in place on a cloth-draped table at the edge of the room. Sam tucked the box beneath the table, made sure the cake hadn't sustained any boo-boos during transit, thanked the priest for his assistance, and then got out of the way.

Back in the van, she remembered she needed cinnamon sticks and fresh peppermint leaves for the potion she and

Kelly would work on later. She headed for the supermarket. Outside, the chief of police stood next to Santa Claus, beside a donation kettle. Passersby gave second glances—was Santa in some kind of trouble with the law?—until Santa handed Martinez his bell.

"Ho, ho, ho!" shouted the uniformed police chief. "Show your generosity this holiday season!"

A couple more ho-hos later and the chief handed the bell back to Santa. He recognized Sam and stepped toward her with his hand extended. When she got closer, she saw that he wore a sticker on his jacket that said "Elect Ben" and she remembered he'd recently announced he was throwing his hat in the ring for the office of mayor. She spotted another officer, a guy out of uniform, who was handing out the stickers to everyone who passed by.

"Campaigning already?" she asked.

"Never too early," he said with a wide politician's grin, "and there's a good crowd at the store today."

Sam took a sidestep, edging herself and the cop a little farther from the foot traffic heading toward the store's entrance.

"Ben, I got to thinking after we were at your office the other day. Is it possible something from the original case file is missing? I'd swear the insurance company's report had different information about the possibility of an accelerant being used. Could part of the investigator's report in your file have ended up elsewhere?"

He shook his head. "I don't think so. But maybe I should look into it. Reopening a cold case could be a good thing."

Sam felt tempted to say something about the painting, her suspicions that the burned one may not have been a real Freeman, but something held her back. She still didn't know who in this town she could trust with any hint that the real painting still existed.

Martinez turned away, greeting someone he knew, putting in a plug for his mayoral run, accompanied by an exuberant handshake and shoulder pat. Sam used the moment to duck inside the market. As she made her way to the spice aisle, she thought about what Martinez had said.

Was this truly a case where a crucial report had been deleted from an official file, or was it a politician wanting to create a controversy—one he would then solve—in order to look good to the voters?

Chapter 16

Okay, peppermint leaves and cinnamon sticks," Sam announced, handing over her small shopping bag to Kelly. "Now what do we do?"

Sam had hung her coat on a hook near the back door, and the two were on their way upstairs to the attic with Eliza the cat trailing along, as usual.

"I left the book open to the page we need," Kelly said, pulling the attic key from her pocket and opening the door. "It's pretty simple, as spells go."

She led the way to the heavy table in the center of the room where she had set out a beaker, a bottle of purified water, a clean jar, and a couple of other spice jars. As Sam read off the ingredients, Kelly added them to the beaker.

"You had coriander seed but not cinnamon sticks?" she teased.

"Yeah, well, the popular items go first," Kelly said as she concentrated on measuring from the small spice jar.

She set the beaker over a small burner and let the mixture heat to the point where the water was steaming but not boiling. Then she switched off the burner.

"Now we let it cool and strain the mix into the clean jar. You take this home with you. When you know you're going out to interview someone about the case, just drink a tablespoonful of it. If you don't like the taste, you can disguise it in your morning coffee or tea."

"Won't that just make my tea taste awful?"

"Maybe. I have no idea." Kelly set the beaker on a rack to cool. "At least it's all edible ingredients. I just have no idea how they'll taste mixed together."

"And I have no idea how I'll know, before I head out each morning, whether I'll be interviewing a suspect soon. Maybe I should just take a dose of it every day."

"Ha! Just don't go poking around with questions about your Christmas gifts—unless you really want to know ahead of time."

"I promise, I won't ask." Sam looked skeptically at the mixture, which now looked like a murky tea. "I do wish I'd thought to wait before talking to Maurice Finstadt at his gallery. I have to admit he's my number one suspect right now. He easily had ways to switch the real painting for a fake, and now that the values of Freeman's work have gone so crazy high, that could have been his motive."

"Crazy high prices which a gallery owner could have ways of manipulating."

"Exactly what I was thinking."

"The part that doesn't make a lot of sense—isn't twenty-five years a long time to wait for a payoff?"

"Yeah, true. And if he knows where Emily's grandfather

hid the painting, why hasn't he come after it?"

"Or after Mr. Plankhurst, for that matter."

"The other thing that bugs me is, if Maurice is so successful with his gallery, why would he take the chance of doing something so dishonest? At the very least, it's major fraud, and at worst he could have been involved in arson and murder. That's a long way to go, if you *hope* a painting will jump in value."

"I guess it all depends on his basic level of honesty. If he's dishonest enough to switch the paintings, maybe that's how he's made most of his fortune." Kelly touched the side of the beaker and judged it to be cool enough. She picked it up and strained the contents into the half-pint jar.

"I'll do some more research on Finstadt, certainly, before I toss out any accusations," Sam said. "And I have an idea who to ask. What time is it in Aruba right now?"

Kelly shrugged. "Close enough that you could call. Is Rupert who you have in mind?"

Sam had already pulled out her phone and was scrolling through her contacts. She tapped his number and smiled when he picked up.

"First off, I hope I didn't wake you or interrupt anything important," she said.

"You most certainly did—having mai tais on the beach under a palm leaf umbrella is my idea of the most important activity of our busy day. And now my dear friend's call has become the most important event of the day."

Sam could picture her writer friend, wearing a flowing shirt and breezy pants—most likely in a shade of purple—lounging back and staring out at turquoise water.

"I hope you two are having a wonderful time," she said. "We're expecting a snowstorm any day now."

"I love a white Christmas," he said, "but at this moment

where I am is perfect."

Sam asked after the new boyfriend, Mark, and then realized cell phone rates overseas could be super expensive.

"I called with an art-related question," she said, "and I'll try to keep it quick. You know Maurice Finstadt's gallery here in town?"

"Of course. I've purchased several good pieces from him."

"Do you think there's any possibility he could be involved in something shady?"

"Define."

"Maybe switching a genuine JC Freeman painting with a fake? Boosting values of certain works because he personally owns one?"

Rupert let out a low whistle. "Raising the values of certain works ... well, all galleries talk up their favorite artists and hope the prices will go up. But artificially raising prices? I ... no, I don't see Maurice doing that. And replacing a genuine with a fake—I'd stick my neck out and say there's no way."

"Locally, yes, I can see that. What about on the wider markets—nationally and internationally? Has there ever been a hint of wrongdoing around him?"

"Sam, what's going on?"

"I can't get into details, and I really don't want to trash someone who doesn't deserve it, so don't say anything about my suspicions."

"But ..."

"It's possible that a JC Freeman painting that was thought to be gone for many years may have turned up. I just need to know if Finstadt could have been involved somehow in its disappearance from the art scene."

"I can't very well phrase it that way without raising a lot of eyebrows. But I can check around with the major art auction houses, hint around that I'm looking to purchase something Maurice has certified, and see what comes out. Places like Sotheby's and Christie's don't take chances with dealers who could damage their reputations. I know some people. I'll get back to you."

She thanked him profusely and turned to Kelly. "Sometimes it pays to know people who move about in moneyed circles."

Sam took her jar with the potion, which she and Kelly jokingly called Lie Detector, and drove toward home. Her mind kept mulling over all she'd learned, trying to fit the pieces together. Unless she was missing something, Finstadt Gallery still seemed to be at the core of it somehow. Who else, outside of Crawford himself, had motive for wanting the painting to escape the fire and come back many years later, much increased in value?

On the other hand, she had to consider that maybe the art had nothing to do with the crime. People set fire to houses for other reasons than insurance payouts. If Ida O'Malley had been unhappy working for the Crawfords, she might have plotted some kind of payback and enlisted her daughter's help.

Sam shook off that idea. A disgruntled housekeeper would pilfer some jewelry, help herself to cash she found lying around, take up residence and enjoy the big house while the owners were gone. Setting fire to the place after taking a valuable piece of art didn't seem very smart at all. Of course, Ida hardly gave the impression of being the brightest bulb in the chandelier. For now, Ida and Susan would have to remain on her suspect list.

Poor Mike Miera had been a victim, any way she looked at it. Unless …

"I'd be dumb not to check him out. Sometimes wily criminals get caught in their own traps." She was nearly home now, and she felt her pulse quicken. She had bookmarked the newspaper accounts of the fire. Now, what about the aftermath?

Inside, she quickly shed her coat and turned on her laptop, which sat on the dining table. She brought up the articles she'd already read and began scanning through them for Mike Miera's name. His parents had declined to be interviewed, but one paper had listed their names anyway.

Sam jotted them down, then looked up issues of the paper published in the days after the tragedy, this time scrolling through the obituaries. Sure enough, young Michael Miera's name appeared, along with a full listing of his parents, grandparents, and siblings.

Once again, the good old-fashioned phone directory came in handy. No surprise that there wasn't a listing for the grandparents—it had, after all, been twenty-five years. The father's name was listed, but none of the siblings. Well, at least it was a starting point.

Sam debated calling but remembered the whole point of her interviews now was to determine whether a person was telling the truth, and she assumed she would somehow receive visual cues if she had taken the lie detector potion. She went into the kitchen for a tablespoon and decided to try a straight dose of the concoction.

The flavor was odd—a strange combination of savory and sweet, spices and herbs—not something she would care to recreate in her bakery, but not really horrible. She went back to the dining room, thinking it would be a good idea to hang around home a few minutes and make sure she didn't experience some adverse reaction to the mixture. If this thing was going to send her into hallucinations or something, better to know it before she got into her car.

She sat in front of her computer once again and clicked a news link to watch the video of a present-day headline story, accusations against a relative of the President who was supposedly skimming funds from a charitable trust. The earnest news anchor read the story in a somber tone, emphasizing certain words to make her audience believe the allegations were true. Sam had been focused on her notepad where she'd jotted the address she planned to visit in a short while, and when she looked up at the news story on her screen, she was jolted to attention.

The news anchor appeared to have a large purple X across her mouth.

Sam paused the video and the X went away. When it started, the crossed-out mouth showed again. Was this the effect of the lie detector serum? If so, did it mean the newscaster was purposely lying or that she was just reading untruthful words?

She switched to another story, a cute piece about an elephant at the Los Angeles zoo whose best pal there was a cockatoo. Everything on the video seemed entirely normal, including the on-camera comments by the reporter who was interviewing the zoo's trainer. No bright X over anyone's mouth.

Back to a different political broadcast, this one where some congressman was standing at the podium in the House chamber, railing on about promises the party had made to the people. This time the X over the man's mouth was bright red.

"Okay, interesting," Sam whispered to the empty room.

"I need to try this out on real people."

She put on her coat and walked out to the driveway. Beau and Danny were stomping mud off their boots, beside the front porch. Sam walked over to them.

"Hey, you guys having a good day?"

Beau told her they'd just finished stacking a load of hay and were about to tackle mucking out the two horse stalls. "My favorite chore," he said.

She saw nothing unusual about him until he made that statement. Apparently, the lie detector took a person's words literally because a faint black X showed across Beau's mouth.

"What?" he said, with a tilt of his head. "Everything okay?"

Sam chuckled. "Just great. You're cute when you're being sarcastic about your favorite jobs, that's all."

He reached out and touched her chin with his leather-gloved index finger. "Ha-ha. You're cute too."

The X immediately vanished, and when he bent forward to kiss her his face was clear and open in its honesty.

"I've got to run see someone," she said. "I should be back by the time you're done. Want something different for dinner tonight? I could pick up a pizza."

"Sounds great."

Sam got into her car and steered down the long driveway to the county road. "It works! Now I wonder how long the effect lasts." She may have driven a tad over the speed limit as she rushed toward town to see Mike Miera's parents.

Chapter 17

Jorge and Nina Miera's home was a small adobe on a quiet side street with arbor vitae flanking the front porch and crispy brown hollyhock stalks in the flowerbeds. Smoke billowed from a stovepipe chimney.

Sam had decided her approach would be the same she had taken with Susan O'Malley—she was looking into the facts of the old case and wondered whether the Mieras may have remembered anything they didn't bring up with the police at the time. Of course, their situation was much more touchy; they'd lost their son, and she couldn't forget that.

She tapped gently on the screen door frame and listened for sounds of movement inside. Thirty seconds passed before she heard a voice, then the door opened and she faced a woman of about fifty. Considering that

Mike would have been forty-three now, this couldn't be his mother.

"I'm looking for Jorge or Nina Miera," Sam said. "Do I have the right house?"

"You must be Samantha. I'm Roberta."

Sam felt momentarily thrown off base.

"Susan O'Malley called this morning, completely out of the blue. I think Mom and Dad are prepared for your visit." Roberta pushed the screen open and stood aside. "Mike was my little brother."

The front door opened directly into a small living room, and she could see a dining area in the L shape to her left. A tiled fireplace held a cast-iron insert, with a wood fire blazing quietly behind its glass doors.

"Mom's in the kitchen. I'll get her."

Roberta turned away, leaving Sam to notice the simple details of the home: a high-backed sofa upholstered in dark blue velvet, a low side chair, and a wooden rocker that must be a family heirloom. The corner nearest the fireplace held a little dresser with a picture of the Virgin Mary hanging over it and three votive candles in glass holders resting on the surface. Some rosary beads and a strand of some type of dried flowers were draped over one corner of the picture frame.

From somewhere around the corner where Roberta had disappeared came a gust of cool air and more voices, speaking rapid Spanish. A moment later, a stooped man with gray hair appeared, bringing with him the scent of woodsmoke and dead autumn leaves. He was brushing something from the sleeves of his quilted coat, which he then removed and tossed onto the arm of the sofa.

"Berta says you came to talk about Michael?" His dark

eyes held questions.

"Yes, and I am so sorry about the loss to your family. I hope to only take a few minutes of your time. Will your wife speak with me as well?"

In answer, Roberta came back into the room, leading a woman of about seventy whose straight, iron-gray hair fell just below her ears. She wore no makeup on her smooth brown skin, and her dark blue slacks and coordinated flowered top looked soft and warm.

Roberta introduced her parents and repeated the fact that they had heard from Susan O'Malley today.

"Have you stayed in touch with Susan during all these years?" Sam asked, as Nina indicated she should take a seat on the sofa.

"A few times. It's not possible to live in Taos without seeing people from your past. You live here?"

"I do. More than thirty years now."

"Our roots go back three hundred years in the shadow of this mountain."

"That's amazing." Sam shifted her glance among the three faces. All appeared clear and truthful. "I admire your heritage and sense of family."

"But you are really here to speak about our Michael. That is what Susan says." Jorge was clearly a man who liked to get to the point.

"I'm looking into the case files the police have from the night of the fire. It relates to the insurance claim on a piece of artwork, but I've felt there was more than the official report included. Since Susan O'Malley and your son were the only ones present, of course their names are in that report. I wonder if any of you may have thought of any small fact about that night, anything that might shed new light on how the fire got started or why your son didn't make it out. I'm sorry—I know this is painful."

Nina's eyes, which had a perpetual sadness about them, grew even more wounded.

Jorge spoke up. "I do not believe our son would have left candles burning so near the draperies, as the fire inspector says. We burn candles in our home. We burn wood to heat our home. Everyone is very conscious of fire and the danger. He would not have gone up the stairs with open flames in the downstairs room."

Truth. At least as far as Jorge's opinion went.

"This is a difficult question," Sam said, "but would there have been any reason for the police or fire officials to place the blame for the fire on the two teenagers?"

"Are you asking whether my brother was ever in trouble with the law? Because he wasn't." Roberta stood like a mama bear, protecting the elders from a predator.

"I'm not suggesting anything," Sam said calmly. "Other than wondering about the motives of the police. You do know that Ben Martinez has now decided to run for mayor?"

Switching focus to the police chief diffused the emotion somewhat, but not before Sam caught a hint of untruth in Roberta's statement. The faces of both parents closed, not necessarily in a lie, but in the concealment of something.

They talked a few more minutes, mainly about neutral subjects, and Sam didn't have the heart to bring them back to the horrific night of their son's death. What had she expected anyway?

She wished them well and apologized again for having brought the memories back.

"Memories are all I have of my Michael now," Nina said as Sam stood to leave. "I have made my peace, as much as a mother ever can."

Sam walked out to her car, thinking again of all the repercussions of that night, how many lives had been touched irreparably. The rich couple who'd lost their home were just the tip of the complicated iceberg.

Dusk was closing in as she pulled away from the Miera residence, and she remembered her promise to Beau to bring dinner home. She pulled over in a convenience store parking lot and phoned their favorite pizza place.

By seven-thirty that evening they'd gorged on the meat-lover's delight pizza and were settled in front of the fireplace. Sam had picked up a novel she'd started to read before the whole *Ghost of Christmas* drama started, but she found herself not concentrating very well on the story. When her phone rang and she saw it was Rupert, she happily set the book aside.

"Hey, you island-hopping traveler," she teased. She could hear Caribbean drums in the background.

"Don't knock it. We are sitting at an outdoor bar, with a warm breeze wafting through our hair. You're probably watching the snow pile up on your deck."

"Not yet. They keep predicting it but we seem to be getting passed by. The ski people aren't too happy."

"So, I made some calls …"

"Good. What did you learn?"

"As far as anyone tells me, Maurice Finstadt's reputation in the art world is sterling. I talked to contacts at the major auction houses, as well as some of the big galleries in New York and L.A. where I know Freeman's work is sold."

"No one has heard of him switching a painting with a

fake or pulling any kind of insurance scam?"

"Not a breath of it. If he did anything like that, it's the first time."

Well, there's a first time for everything.

"Okay, thanks, Rupert. I appreciate your checking into it. I owe you one."

"One of your fantastic amaretto cheesecakes would take care of the debt," he said. She could hear the smile in his voice.

"You got it." Sam hung up, thinking about Rupert's report. She hadn't specifically asked whether it was Maurice Finstadt himself with the sterling reputation, or whether that applied to his gallery and everyone there. Maybe another employee at the time had pulled some shenanigans.

She shook off the idea. Surely anyone Rupert talked to would have mentioned if they felt they'd ever been cheated by the Finstadt Gallery. When a person named their business with their own name, there was no getting away from the reputation that would follow everyone who worked there. If Maurice was as upstanding as everyone said, he would instantly get rid of anyone who might tarnish that shiny reputation.

It's not what everyone thinks. The words of Emily's grandmother came back.

What, exactly, *did* everyone think? Sam went back through the interviews she'd done so far. The media reporters thought the fire was sensational—big house, rich guy, possible arson. The police and fire investigator apparently thought the fire was accidental. At least they believed that strongly enough to have closed the case. Sam thought something was being concealed, on that front. Susan O'Malley thought it had changed her life and was something she'd rather forget, and the Mieras believed they would never recover—which was true. No one recovered from the loss of a child.

Sam, for the life of her, couldn't figure out what Valerie's warning could be about. *It's not what everyone thinks.* She glanced over at Beau, who was completely immersed in a basketball game on TV. They'd already discussed the case. Beau wasn't exactly thinking about it at all.

It wasn't until they'd gone to bed and turned out the lights that Sam remembered her final impression when leaving the Miera home. She'd gotten a distinct vibe when she brought up the fact that Ben Martinez was running for mayor. Someone in that household was concealing something—not an outright lie, but some type of secret.

Chapter 18

S am spent a restless night, with too many voices and a ghost with long gray hair floating around in her dreams. She woke with a start, realizing daylight was showing around the edges of the bedroom curtains. Beau's side of the bed was empty—no surprise, as he was always out at dawn to begin the ranch chores. She must have fallen soundly asleep in the early morning hours.

She shook off the vestiges of the oddball dreams, got up, and took a hot shower. Ten minutes later, with her hair sticking up in spikes, she felt ready for coffee.

"Too much input," she muttered to herself as she dressed in her black slacks and white shirt for the bakery.

She'd spoken with most of the people on her list of suspects, and could only imagine that the assortment of voices in the dreams came from some odd blend of all their stories. She shook off the feeling and went down to the kitchen. Beau had brewed coffee and the carafe was still warm to the touch. She poured a cup and nuked it to rewarm, thinking of her next steps in the investigation.

The experiment with the truth potion had been interesting, she decided, as she reached for a box of Rice Krispies on the shelf. She dumped some blueberries over the cereal and poured almond milk over it. To the snap, crackle, and pop of her breakfast she thought about those she'd not interviewed with the influence of the lie detector.

For one, there was Maurice Finstadt. But this was probably too early to confront him again. Plus, Rupert's research had given the gallery owner high ratings, so what would Sam say to him? She needed to think on this a bit more. If she went back to the gallery, she would make sure she was prepared.

One thing Beau had taught her over the years was to question the innocent as well as those you suspected. New information can always come out. So, as she rinsed her cereal bowl and prepared to leave the house, she swallowed another tablespoonful of the potion. Rather than growing on her, the brew was starting to be less palatable.

"I'm not keeping this up too long," she told herself as she grabbed her coat and backpack.

She pulled up at the library and spotted Emily out front, hanging a bird feeder from a hook on the tree nearest the west corner of the building.

"I'm starting to feel sorry for all the little birds," Emily said as Sam walked up to her. "Everything's so brown now, and with snow coming they're going to have a hard time finding something to eat."

The feeder was shaped like a small house, with spouts at each window and the doorway to dispense the seed.

"They will love you for it," Sam said. "They may also eat you out of house and home. Word has a way of getting around, especially if the stellar jays discover this little treasure."

Emily laughed. "We'll see. I may learn my lesson quickly. Want to come in for a cup of tea? There are no library appointments this morning so I've been using the time to organize my things in the house a bit better."

"If I'm not interrupting, sure."

Sam couldn't have hoped for a better opening. She followed Emily through the winter-bare back garden and into the house via the kitchen door. Emily draped her jacket over the back of a chair and picked up the kettle from the range top. As she filled it, Sam peeled off her own coat. She followed Emily's example and hung it on a chair, and when she looked toward the living room, her heart nearly stopped.

There, in the doorway, stood a gray-haired woman whose wavy curls were cut in a chin-length bob. She wore a long skirt of blue cotton and a short-sleeved yellow T-top. Strands of red and blue beads hung around her neck, and there were several beaded bracelets on each arm. As Sam watched, she entered the kitchen without appearing to touch the floor. She had a faint, enigmatic smile on her face, but something about her gaze made Sam believe the woman didn't see her.

"Emily ..." Sam edged backward toward the outside door.

"Yeah, Sam?" Emily was standing on tiptoes, reaching for a tea canister on the shelf above the stove.

"Who is this?"

Emily turned and dropped the metal canister with a

clang against the tile countertop.

"Grandma Valerie? What—it's daytime! How did you …"

The ghost spoke. "It's fine, Em. I don't sweat the daylight appearances. Although I think I'm less likely to be spotted if I visit at night."

Emily turned to Sam. "You can see her?"

Sam nodded, not taking her eyes from the wavering form in front of her. There was something so normal and human about her, and yet, something not quite real as well.

"You must be Sam," Valerie said. "I'm not sure we ever met, although I was in your bakery a few times."

"Seriously? I mean, thank you. And I hope you liked whatever you got there." Sam shook her head and chuckled.

Valerie laughed too. "I know. Feel a little crazy talking to a spirit from the afterlife?"

"More than a little," Sam admitted. "I have to say, there's no way I would believe this. And I halfway think I'll wake up in a while."

"You came to talk to Em about her grandfather, didn't you? To poke around and see if there might be some reason to suspect him of being involved with the theft of that painting."

That was uncomfortably close to the truth. "Can you read minds?"

Valerie shook her head in a way that appeared way too wobbly. "No. I actually can't even see into the past and tell you anything, other than what I witnessed."

"You saw your husband hide the painting in the secret niche?"

"Not exactly. But I did see him move the bookcase, so I knew the niche was there. When his mind began to get foggy, I went to that spot, hoping to find something that might jog his memory. Actually, I was hoping … Well, never mind."

"So, you found the painting. Did you know its history?"

"Oh, yeah. Seeing it here really shook me up."

"How did Grandpa get hold of the painting?" Emily asked.

"That, I don't know. I suspect a woman had something to do with it."

"What woman?"

Valerie slumped a little.

"I'd hoped you would never learn this," she said, "but your grandfather was not always the most loyal of husbands."

"What! He cheated?"

"I suspected several women over the years. I doubt he'd see it that way. Look, it was the '60s. People did lots of things and called it Free Love. And that's all I'm going to say."

Sam and Emily exchanged a wide-eyed stare. When they turned to face Valerie again, the ghostly image was gone.

Chapter 19

Sam felt a cold breeze in the room but when she turned, the back door was still tightly closed.

"I'm almost afraid to ask you to verify what I just saw," she said to Emily, who had stopped to pick up the canister and the dozen or so teabags that had scattered when the lid popped off.

"That's my grandma," she said.

"She always appears and disappears like that?"

"Yeah, pretty much. And the gliding into a room, and the kind of wavy lines around her. It's what I've seen each time. Those were mostly at night, in my bedroom. Other than that time in the corner of the library, this is the first time I've known that she roamed the house."

"Kind of disturbing."

"Yeah, I suppose. But, you know, in real life she

was quiet like that. I remember how I loved the way she dressed, all gauzy clothes and beads and stuff. Grandma Valerie wasn't at all like the other kids' grandmothers."

Sam relaxed enough to smile. "I'd say."

"So, was she right? About why you came here today?"

"Well, kind of." She briefly recapped the conversations she'd had with the Mieras, Susan O'Malley, and Maurice Finstadt. "I've been all over town, just trying to touch base with anyone connected with the fire, the burned house, or *The Ghost of Christmas*. Your grandfather came to mind, naturally, because we're fairly sure he's the one who put the painting into that hidden spot."

The kettle whistled sharply and Emily turned and removed it from the burner. "And you're wondering whether he knew it had been claimed as a loss in the fire."

"I don't know. It must have been taken from the Crawford home sometime in the days or weeks leading up to the fire. The gallery owner told me he was asked by the police to certify a burned painting as *The Ghost of Christmas*. To do that, he must have handled the burned remains of *some* painting, obviously not the real one. So we know that a painting hung on the wall where the *Ghost* had been. Someone substituted another one for the real one."

"You never knew my grandfather." Emily placed two mugs on the table, motioning Sam to take a seat. "And I guess, now, you never will. I mean, I could take you to the home he's in, introduce you, but you wouldn't be meeting the real *him*."

"I know. I'm so sorry."

"I may be looking at all this through the rose-colored lenses of a kid who loved her grandparents unconditionally ... but stealing something this valuable and then covering it up? That just wasn't Grandpa. He'd never do it."

Then how did the piece of art get into his home, in a place only he knew about?

But Sam didn't voice the question aloud. All of this, including Valerie's most recent revelation, was a bit much for a young woman to take in. Maybe after Emily processed it all, she would think of something that jogged a memory, something she didn't want to think about quite yet.

It wasn't until Sam was in her car later, heading toward Sweet's Sweets, that she realized she hadn't detected any sense of untruth either from Emily or the ghostly image of Valerie. Would she have been able to see the telltale X over the face of a spirit, the way she could with a human? She had been able to see the mark on the faces of television newscasters, so the power of the potion extended beyond live-and-in-person encounters. She pondered that as she pulled into the alley behind the bakery. Hmm. She would have to give this some thought.

She set the parking brake and reached for her pack, dimly aware that another car had pulled into the alley and stopped in front of hers.

"Grammy! Grammy!" Ana had managed to get out of her car seat and was running toward Sam's vehicle.

She opened her door and pulled the child into a hug.

"Grammy, you should have gone to Albuquerque with us. The *Nutcracker* was *so* cool. It's about this little girl, and she was about my age, and she falls asleep by the Christmas tree …"

"I bet you loved the music and the dancing and everything," Sam said.

"I did—I wish you had been there."

Kelly walked over in time to hear most of it. "Oh, darn. What was I thinking? I should have bought extra tickets and had you and Beau go along with us. I'm so sorry."

Sam raised a hand to pause her. "It's fine. You know what things are like around here right now, with the bakery and, um, what I'm working on for Emily. It would have been too hard for me to break away."

Kelly gave a little tilt of her head. "Yeah, but ..."

"Maybe next year. We'll see how everything's going by then."

Ana turned from Sam to Kelly. "Can we, Mommy? I really want to go see it again."

"We'll talk about it. That's a whole year away."

Uh-oh. Sam realized she'd opened a whole new obligation for Kelly, because it was unlikely Ana would forget this.

"Hey, I'm just happy you got to go and that you enjoyed it. Tell me more about what you guys did in Albuquerque while we go inside and find a cookie for you."

"Five minutes, Ana," Kelly said. "I'm just popping into Riki's shop to pick up my check, and then we have to get back home. Daddy has a really fun science experiment for you guys to work on today."

Sam had intended to ask Kelly if there was news on the pregnancy possibility, but this didn't seem the time. She took Ana's hand and they walked in the back door of the bakery. The little girl went around and said hello to each of the employees, and even Julio—who usually came across as silent or gruff—gave the little girl a smile.

"Go up front and ask Auntie Jen for a cookie," Sam said.

Ana skipped away and Sam turned to take a look at the order basket. It was fairly full, but everything was stacked in delivery-date order and it seemed nothing was running late. She admired the huge party cake Becky was working on for the country club's annual holiday soiree, and she complimented the other decorators on doing a great job with the cupcakes and cookies.

"You could carry those two trays up to the front," Becky said with a nod toward the cookies. "Jen said she was low on rugelach and brownies, in addition to the decorated ones."

"Will do." Sam balanced a narrow tray on each hand and backed her way through the curtain that divided the kitchen from the sales area.

Jen was waiting on a customer who looked familiar, but Sam had her hands full until she was able to set the two trays down. Ana stood behind the counter, dancing impatiently on the balls of her feet.

"Can I have a cupcake instead of a cookie—please?" she begged.

Sam gave her a sideways look. It would probably ruin her appetite for lunch. On the other hand, what were grandmas for? She told Ana to point out the one she wanted and she reached into the case with a tissue paper to pick it up.

"Take it over to that empty table to eat it."

"I'll be neat with it, I promise," Ana said, giving Sam her most winsome smile.

With a moment, finally, to greet her customer, Sam realized it was Mike Miera's sister, Roberta.

"Your visit to my parents' house reminded me of how much we love your pumpkin spice muffins," Roberta said with a smile. "They are the one thing I can get my teens to eat that somewhat resembles a vegetable. Otherwise, all they want is fast food. Ugh."

"Well, ours are made with locally grown pumpkin, which one of the farmers packs for us. We use it fresh in the fall, and freeze a bunch of it for our winter baking. I think we're down to the last few batches for the year."

Roberta upped her muffin order by a few more, and Jen boxed them up.

"Roberta, there was something about the conversation with your parents … Could I ask you something?"

"Sure."

Sam hoped the potion she'd taken earlier was still potent enough to ask a question or two and get honest responses. She waited until Roberta was finished, then steered their movement toward the door. Out on the sidewalk, she brought up the name that had triggered that secretive feeling she'd received in the Miera home.

"Something about my mention of Ben Martinez seemed to bring up a reaction. Any idea what that's about?"

Roberta opened the passenger side door of her minivan and set the box of muffins on the seat. She didn't immediately meet Sam's gaze. "I knew Ben in school. We were in the same grade, had lots of classes together as you can imagine between the first grade and high school."

The response didn't evoke any untruth. It also didn't answer Sam's question.

"Did your younger brother maybe have some issue with Ben as a cop? Sorry, you don't have to get specific about it, but I just wondered if some big family secret could possibly have been behind the fire. Maybe someone was targeting Mike, and the Crawford house was the place they chose to go after him." It was a thought that hadn't really occurred to Sam before this moment, but it could be a valid theory.

Roberta turned away, facing the street and staring at the busy entrance to the plaza.

Come on, turn where I can see your face ...

She took several long seconds before she responded. When she turned back to Sam, it was with a bright smile. "Sorry, Sam, I can't think of anything like that. Mike was the likeable kid with loads of friends, the kind that hung out at our house for Mom's homemade tamales and afternoons of video games."

"No enemies?"

"None that I know of. Mike was enough younger than me that I'd already left for college by the time he started high school. I did a couple of years at UNM in Albuquerque before I had enough credits to transfer to the campus here. I had my own set of friends, and I got married shortly after I came back to Taos. I really didn't keep tabs on my brother." Her face seemed clear, with no sign of dishonesty.

"And Ben Martinez? Where was he during that time?"

Roberta's image clouded although the smile kind of froze in place. "All that time? I wouldn't know. I assume he went to some police academy or something and then came back here to work. I don't keep track of what happened to everyone from high school."

In a town this size, kids you went through all twelve grades with? Sam would bet the ones who stayed local knew where most of their classmates were.

There was irritation in Roberta's voice, and an X flickered over her mouth. She circled the back of her car, leaving Sam on the sidewalk, and got into the driver's seat. She sent Sam a tight smile as she started the engine.

Well, darn it. Sam hoped she hadn't run off a good

customer by asking rude questions. But, clearly Roberta was hiding something, and if it was something related to finding her brother's killer, maybe the questions could later be forgiven.

The sun had gone behind a cloud and Sam suddenly realized she was chilled. Back inside, the warmth and sugary cinnamon smells greeted her. Ana had finished her cupcake in relatively good shape—only a smear of green frosting and some very sticky-looking fingers remained. Sam led her to the kitchen to wash up and found Kelly and Becky chatting at the worktable.

"Kel, I meant to mention," Sam said. "Beau and I still haven't decorated our tree yet. "I know. It's less than a week until Christmas, but things have been somewhat crazy. So, would you guys like to come over tonight and we'll make it a little social thing?"

"Yay, Mommy! Say yes, please say yes!" Ana, hyped up on that cupcake, was literally jumping up and down.

"Okay, yes." Kelly grabbed her kid's coat sleeve. "I've got a pot of posole on the stove, so we'll bring that. What time?"

Chapter 20

Beau had cut a tree on the property, but aside from setting it in a stand and making sure it had water, Sam had done nothing toward making it Christmassy, and she was glad of the help when Kelly's gang showed up a little after five. Their ranch hand, Danny, joined them and couldn't rave enough about the rich pork and hominy stew Kelly had brought, along with homemade tortillas. High praise, considering his mother was known as one of the best cooks in Taos.

Ana had come down from her earlier sugar high and, although she would have rather gone straight to the boxes of Christmas decorations than sit through a meal first, she made it through her bowl of posole before begging to be excused.

Beau and Scott cleared the table and offered to do

the dishes, so the others quickly congregated around the large boxes of ornaments Sam had brought out of the storage closet. Danny immediately climbed the stepladder and began stringing lights on the highest branches of the gorgeous blue spruce. Ana opened boxes of glass balls and exclaimed over the ones she remembered from the previous year.

"You look tired, Mom. Everything okay?" Kelly asked, sorting strands of garland.

"Nothing the after-new-year lull at the bakery won't solve. Even with extra help, I can't believe how busy we've been. Plus, I just wish I was coming up with some kind of answers for Emily Plankhurst. She's so scared that her grandfather could be implicated somehow in the theft of that painting." Sam kept her voice low, but the others were so absorbed in decorating the tree that no one was paying any attention to her.

"What will she do with it?" Kelly asked. "Personally, if it's as gorgeous as you described it, I'd probably hang it in my house and just stare at it every day."

Sam shook her head slightly. "I think she loves the piece, but there would be so many memories ... Well, I don't know. I guess it all depends on how it turns out, whether we can learn how the painting escaped the fire. Someone got it out of the Crawford house before that night, and that's what I'm trying to figure out."

She hadn't told Kelly yet about actually seeing the ghost of Valerie, or about what the wavery spirit being had said. That was probably a conversation for the attic, when they could be alone again.

"I used to ride past that house on my bike," Kelly said. "I guess I was about ten or so? Jen and I would make up stories about it. The place was so eerie—all stark lines and blackened window holes. We just knew it was haunted. We'd stop our bikes at the edge of the property and talk about the place for a couple minutes, then we'd zoom away down the street as fast as we could. Silly, I know. We were probably scaring ourselves more than the house actually scared us."

"Hm, that's right. After the homeowner received the insurance settlement, I wonder what happened to it. Most people would rebuild or make repairs and move back in. Or sell the house. I spoke briefly with Phil Crawford, and he said they moved into one of their other houses and never came back to this one."

"So, maybe someone else bought it and fixed it up?"

Sam nibbled at her lower lip for a moment. "I have no idea. Maybe I should check that out."

"How's this look, Sam?" Danny had plugged in the lights and stepped back from the tree. With that one addition, suddenly the whole holiday season began to feel more real.

* * *

The next morning, Sam checked in with Becky by phone. Things were ramping up for the final deliveries of the week.

"A lot of folks are planning to come by to pick up their cakes and pies for Christmas Eve and Christmas Day meals," Becky told her. "But there's a big multi-tray cookie order for a party tonight, a half-sheet office party cake, and there's an afternoon wedding. I can't even imagine getting married the same week as Christmas. The woman must be an expert planner, or she's insane."

Sam chuckled. "Set the delivery items aside so they

don't get mixed in with those the customers are coming in to pick up. I'll be there in a little while, and I can get the deliveries out of the way."

An hour later at Sweet's Sweets, Sam surveyed the orders. "Zoë ordered cookies? She knows I always bring by a tray for her to serve to the guests."

"Maybe she got a little panicky at how fast the holiday is sneaking up on us. Christmas Eve is only a few days away."

"I should have stopped by the B&B before now," Sam said. "Anyway, these are complimentary. And I'm going to box up a few of those cinnamon rolls as a personal gift for Zoë and Darryl."

She assembled one of her purple bakery boxes and filled it with the warm rolls that had just been drizzled with her special cinnamon glaze.

"I'm sad that we haven't had more time together this month," Zoë said, when Sam arrived at her place thirty minutes later. "We've been booked solid with skiers, and it looks like a full house through New Year's weekend."

"I know. Same at the bakery. Is this the most popular year to get married or what? I can't believe how many wedding cakes Becky has finished in the last two weeks alone."

Zoë accepted the box of cinnamon rolls, mocking a swoon when she peeked inside and took a whiff. Sam set the cookie tray for the B&B guests on the kitchen counter.

"Stay for coffee?" Zoë asked.

"I wish. But I've got several more deliveries, and who knows how many more there will be by the time I get back to the shop. I know you're busy Christmas Eve, but maybe we can all get together the next day when your guests are out on the slopes."

"We would love that. Darryl was just saying it's been ages since he's seen you guys."

"Deal."

Sam went back out to her van and checked the next of her deliveries. She'd planned to basically make a loop, taking the most fragile item for the wedding reception first, then circling back toward the middle of town for the smaller cakes and the cookie trays. The last of those would bring her back to within a few blocks of the bakery, where she would check in and see where her help was needed most.

Two hours later, she was down to one—admittedly gigantic—box of assorted cookies destined for one of the sprawling adobe homes on a couple of acres in the shadow of Taos Mountain. It was on a side road that meandered toward the center of town, so after she'd dropped off the goodies, Sam decided to follow that one rather than getting back out on the more congested Kit Carson Road and into the plaza traffic.

It was one of those streets, she discovered, that went by one name for a while then changed, seemingly without reason, to a different name. And this one she recognized— Vista del Reyes. The street where the Crawford's massive house had been located.

"Well, I told Kelly I should drive by and check it out," Sam said to the empty van. It would be interesting to see if anyone had rebuilt, or if the big house had been bulldozed to make way for something even bigger and more ostentatious. After all, when your street purported to be the view of the kings, it stood to reason that the homes there would be flashy. She started eyeing the addresses of the widely spaced houses.

And there it was.

People had described the house as ultra-modern, blocky, concrete, some said ugly, and not in keeping with most of Taos architecture, in which adobe dominated, with a few ranch homes and the occasional Victorian with a pitched roof. They were right. If the huge house had been borderline acceptable in its glory days, it was way far gone now as a shell of a building.

It consisted of a center section that rose three stories high, a wing to the east that was a single story, and one to the west that was two stories. The designer was probably going for style and innovation, but the effect was so asymmetrical as to be jarring. The two-story west wing was obviously where the fire had occurred. The window glass was missing and black soot still rimmed the openings that stared into the even blacker maw of the rooms. As far as Sam could tell, the place was empty of furnishings and completely open to the weather.

The grounds were overgrown with trees and shrubs in desperate need of pruning, if one could actually tell which parts were still alive. A pathway up to the front door was partially blocked by thorny branches from a pair of untrimmed pyracantha bushes, and many of the stepping stones were tilted precariously. The entire property had been fenced off with chain link and notices posted to keep out.

Boy, the neighbors must love this place. Sam was surprised they hadn't raised a fuss and started petitions to have it torn down. Or maybe they had. Getting things like that done often moved at a snail's pace around here, and this amount of damage had taken years to accumulate.

Sam's van had coasted to a stop as she stared at the building, and she almost didn't notice that there was a woman standing at the fence, staring at the ruined house. A black BMW was parked twenty yards farther down. She pulled to the roadside and the woman glanced over her shoulder.

Something seemed familiar about her, and Sam realized it would be rude not to at least say hello. She powered down the window on the passenger side of the van. The woman didn't notice and turned back to stare at the house again, her fingers linked through the wire fencing. Something odd about her behavior, Sam thought. She'd taken to carrying a small vial of the lie detector potion in her pocket, and she took a swig of it now. Anyone this obsessed with the old Crawford place would be worth talking to.

Sam got out and walked around to join her. "It must have been quite a place," she said.

"Oh it was. So beautiful. I had hoped …" She turned to face Sam fully for the first time. "Camilla Crawford. This is my place."

Chapter 21

For a very long moment Sam found herself completely speechless. "Yours?" was all she managed to croak out.

She took in the woman who, now in her mid-sixties, had clearly once been beautiful. The years hadn't been kind—evidence of too much partying, drink, drugs maybe, and definitely too much cosmetic surgery. With her face in repose, Camilla's features were those of a much younger woman, but the moment she smiled, the stiffness of Botoxed muscles and cortisone-plumped lips was so evident as to be nearly hideous.

She wore skinny jeans on much-too-skinny legs and a faux fur jacket in what had probably been the top fashion purple a few years back. An expensive designer bag hung in the crook of her elbow, and a pair of some other designer's sunglasses were pushed to the top of her head, holding back red hair that was both too bold for her aging face and had just a fraction too much gray root showing. The whole picture made Sam feel sad.

"Yes, I know," Camilla continued, looking again at the burned out house. "I need to either fix it up to its former glory or make plans to sell it. I only get out here once every few years, and it pains me to watch what's happening. I'm not fond of the angry calls from the other property owners either."

"Well, I can imagine—"

The woman gave an oversized sigh. "Well, it's not going to happen this trip. I'm just in town for the holidays with good friends who have a place up at the ski valley. You may know of them?" She dropped the name of a top Hollywood producer and his wife, a celebrated actress.

Sam felt the potion beginning to kick in and, amazingly, didn't sense any deceit as Camilla rattled off those and a few more celebrity names.

"Is that where you live now—Hollywood?" Sam asked.

"Brentwood Hills, actually." Which was a lie.

"So, you said you had hoped … something?"

"Did I?"

"Something about the house, about living here again, maybe?"

"Oh, yes. It's just one more thing on my huge to-do list, getting this place fixed up so I can be the one entertaining friends instead of always tagging along with them." She gave a feathery laugh. "You know how it is. So much to get done and only so many hours in the day."

"Well, I can imagine there's only so many dollars in the bank, too," Sam said. "I mean, that would be the case for me."

The laugh turned bitter. "Yeah, well, my ex. Guy has, like, all the money in the universe and can he share any of it with me? Hell, no."

Now that emotion certainly rang true, as far as Sam could tell.

"Back when this happened? He's got a net worth of somewhere north of a billion and I get a lousy two mil. Do you have any idea how quick a person goes through two million measly dollars?"

I could easily retire for life on that much, as long as I didn't pretend to live in Brentwood Hills.

"You were married to Phillip Crawford, right?"

"You aren't friends with *him*, are you?" Camilla said with narrowed eyes.

"Oh no. I just remember reading about all this in the papers."

"And I'll bet they made it sound like the woman who divorced him made out like a bandit and continued to enjoy the same lifestyle. Do you have any idea what it costs to keep up with my set of friends? Renting in the right neighborhoods, keeping up the old body, dressing the part for every social occasion, the spas, the clubs, shopping at the right stores." The designer handbag twitched a little when she said this last part.

"Yes, it must be tough," Sam said, actually feeling sorry for anyone this obsessed with the outer trappings of that lifestyle.

"I've got resources, always got resources," Camilla said, giving that plump, scary smile again.

Sam sensed something deeper. Not a lie, exactly, but not a truth Camilla would be willing to share. Everything about the woman was so superficial, so fake, that it was hard to determine whether anything she said was genuine. The lie detector gave off mixed signals—sometimes a bright X shape, other times little wavery signals that floated around her head. It was all making Sam feel a little dizzy.

"I really need to …" she nodded toward her van. "I was just curious about the house, since I haven't driven down this street in a long time."

For the first time, Camilla actually looked at Sam's vehicle. "Oh, cute! I love your paint scheme."

Sam had become so used to driving the van she tended to forget that the artwork on it—a huge pastry box filled with goodies—was something of a traffic stopper. She reached into her pocket and pulled out a business card.

"We're only a block off the plaza. Come by anytime." Why not? Another conversation with the poor little rich woman could be interesting. But first, Sam wanted to verify some of what she'd just been told.

* * *

After checking in with Becky and Jen and learning there was no urgent need for her assistance at the bakery, Sam's next stop was the county courthouse. She'd received such mixed signals from Camilla Crawford, Sam just wanted to verify that the shell of a house really did belong to her. She could have done a property search online, but didn't want to run into the hassle of paying a fee and getting her name on a bunch of mailing lists. Plus, the courthouse was only five minutes down the road.

She made her way to the property records division and gave a clerk the address of the property on Vista del Reyes. In less than a minute she had a view of the details. Yes,

Camilla was the legal property owner—her address was a post office box in Los Angeles.

"Are the taxes up to date?" Sam asked the clerk, who turned the screen back to face herself and scrolled down.

"It looks like the November billing hasn't been paid yet ... Last May's payment came in a few months late, but it's technically up to date."

"Okay, thanks."

As she turned away, Sam had to wonder, if Camilla was down on money why was she bothering to pay the taxes on the place? She could have surely found a buyer to take it off her hands. She'd be done, and someone else could deal with the expense and hassle of renovating. It certainly didn't sound as though there were fond memories of her time with Phil Crawford.

She retraced her steps down a corridor, turned a corner, and literally ran into Ben Martinez.

"Whoa, sorry!" she said.

"It's okay. Samantha Sweet, right?" The police chief was in uniform, although hatless, and he carried a couple pages of white paper in one hand. He held them up. "Forms for filing my candidacy. We can officially file in January, so I'm just getting a head start by picking them up now."

Sam smiled, hoping he didn't see how little she actually cared about that.

He glanced up the hall. "Can I help you with anything?"

"I was just at the county clerk's office, looking up a property record. I found what I needed. It actually pertains to that old case of yours, the house that burned. Did you know Phillip Crawford's ex-wife still owns it? She's here in town for the holidays."

"Oh? You met her?"

"Completely by accident. I had pulled over to take a look at the house and she was standing there. You know, seeing that huge place, with the sooty window frames and all blackened inside, made me realize just how fast and furiously the fire must have spread. Amazing to think it all started from a few candles."

"Well, that's what the final report said." Ben shifted a little from one foot to the other.

Sam sensed there was more, but the potion's effects had worn off, and she couldn't tell whether he was hiding information or simply getting impatient to move on. She needed to keep him here and ask a few more questions.

"The final report," she said, "but didn't you say something the last time we talked about there could have been an accelerant used?"

He tucked his head and moved closer to her ear.

"I think I said it was rumored."

Actually, the media had used the word 'rumored' but Sam was sure Martinez had said something else.

"No, I'm pretty sure you told me it was in a report," she bluffed.

"Hey, I was a rookie then. People on high didn't actually tell me much of anything."

He switched out of serious mode, flashed her a smile, and wished her a good day as he walked down the hall.

Hmm, someone on high? Who would that be?

His words tumbled around in her head as Sam walked out into the chilly afternoon and got into her van. Who would have been high enough to quash a vital piece of information in a police report? She immediately thought of Phil Crawford, who was certainly rich enough to pay off whoever he needed to. Maybe Crawford had become tired of the place and simply wanted out. Would he have gone so far as to hire someone to torch the place while he was conveniently away on a side trip to Mexico? And rather than risk that person turning on him and revealing the plan, he'd found it more convenient to get the authorities to drop the single word *accelerant* from the report?

She drove toward Sweet's Sweets, her mind churning. There were a couple of faults in her theory. One: It would be iffy to hope that no one who'd seen the report would blab about it to the media. Reporters could be relentless, and could have gotten someone to talk. And two: Phil Crawford was an outsider—why would the police bow to his wishes to keep a certain fact quiet?

The more she thought about it, the more Sam became convinced that whoever got the police to drop the reference to the fire being purposely started, it must have been a local.

But Martinez said 'people on high.' How high?

Chapter 22

Sam parked behind the bakery and went inside to see how everyone was doing. All under control, according to Becky, who was boxing up a finished party cake.

"The customer is picking up this one tomorrow, the evening crew will be in soon, and I'm going home to—oh goodie—bake cookies with my kids. We need to show up at grandma's with something the boys contributed to, and my mom is a complete fan of your world-class thumbprint cookies."

"Gonna snow," Julio said.

Sam peeked at the app on her phone. "Yep. Starting later. Everyone, be safe out there."

She thought of her new, young friend who didn't have a lot of snow experience, so she tapped Emily's number.

"So exciting!" Emily said as soon as she picked up. "We

never got enough snow in Albuquerque, and I'm really jazzed about having a white Christmas."

"You have some food in the house and plenty of firewood, in case the electricity goes out?"

"I do. I'll bring in some more from the woodpile, just in case."

"Well, enjoy! And you can call me if you need anything." Sam hung up, smiling and wondering whether Emily would be this enthusiastic about snow by the end of the months-long mountain winter.

Dusk was coming on fast—these were the shortest days of the year—and Sam realized on the way home that she'd never paused long enough to eat any lunch. She needed something quick, warm, and filling for dinner and her taco soup recipe came to mind. It could be made from pantry items and a pound of ground beef, so she hit the kitchen the moment she walked into the house. While the meat thawed in the microwave, she dumped everything else into her big soup pot. She browned the meat in a skillet, added onion, and within a few minutes the whole mix was beginning to simmer. The beauty of this recipe was that it could cook for twenty minutes or two hours, and it would be equally delicious.

She found Beau upstairs, just stepping out of the shower.

"We never did get the stalls mucked out the other day," he said, "so that was this afternoon's chore."

"Well, I appreciate your showering afterward." She stretched up to kiss him.

"You smell like sugar," he said, nuzzling her hair.

"Don't I always?"

"Yeah, actually." He shivered. "It's chilly in here. Gotta

find my flannel shirt."

"Soup is in the pot and will be ready shortly."

"And maybe some cornbread?" The man definitely had hope in his eyes.

"Sure. I can do that." She turned away from her plan to change her clothes, and went down to quickly stir up a cornbread mix. Even bakers, once in a while, can resort to using mixes, she decided.

While the soup bubbled and the cornbread baked, she put on her own soft flannels and a pair of fuzzy socks. Grabbing her laptop, which she'd left on the bedroom dresser, she went back downstairs. Several things about her conversation with the odd Camilla Crawford had nagged at her, and she decided she might go online and troll the social media sites, as well as looking back through the old news stories, to see what new clues she could pick up.

Camilla said she had resources. What, exactly, did that mean? At the time, she was talking about having the money to keep up her California lifestyle, so did that mean she had friends who helped her out? Sam couldn't imagine someone who carried a designer purse going around to her acquaintances to beg money. Something didn't fit.

Beau was dipping a spoon into the soup when Sam walked into the kitchen. "Just thought I'd see if it's getting close."

"By the time the cornbread comes out, it'll be just right," she promised. She picked up silverware and napkins and headed toward the dining table.

The soup turned out perfectly and was just the thing for the chilly night. As soon as they'd cleared the table, Sam put away the leftovers and Beau brought the dogs in from the porch and fed them. Everyone soon settled in front of the fireplace, Beau with a book, Sam with her laptop, and the dogs doing what dogs always do in the evenings— stretched out in complete contentment.

First on Sam's search list was to simply google Camilla's name. It came up, but not with prominence. Coverage of the Crawford divorce was old history, but that was exactly what Sam was after. It seemed Camilla had been quite candid with Sam this afternoon. The gossip on the settlement and disbursement of property was remarkably close to what she'd said.

Later social news stories placed her at several movie premiers and at parties hosted by the Hollywood elite. Maybe this was Camilla's way of rubbing her own happiness in the face of her ex, since Phil said he had moved to New York, into one of his other homes. *See, I can be just as successful on my own*, seemed to dominate the tone.

So, who's the *resource*, Sam wondered. A man, she guessed, would be the simplest way for Camilla to attract the kind of money she needed. Sam found many pictures with the attractive redhead on the arm of someone famous, but none that ever developed into a big romance. So, maybe her story was true—she'd blown through the divorce money and was now short on cash.

Reading between the lines, it appeared to Sam that Camilla had become one of those hangers-on, the people at the fringes of the Hollywood crowd. Interesting *enough*, attractive *enough* to be a filler guest at a party or for a ski weekend. But she wasn't really one of them.

Sad, really. She might have gone back to school in the after-Phil era, learned a skill, built a business of some kind based on that skill, and earned her own accolades instead of living in the shadow of everyone else's glory.

Oh well. Back to the news of the fire in search of some clue she may have overlooked the first time. Sam performed a new search, to see if there were articles she hadn't already read. A reporter's name stood out. Sandy Greene, who had been here in Taos a few years ago to cover an election scandal.

Sam read the piece in detail and found it to contain mostly the same information the other articles had covered. But there was something about this one, something she couldn't pinpoint, which hinted at more. Somewhere, in an old address book, she had Sandy's number. She found it and dialed. It actually reached her, and the reporter seemed pleased to hear from Sam. She carried her phone into the kitchen on the pretense of making a cup of tea, but really to leave Beau to read quietly.

"Sandy, I came across a story you wrote on one of the anniversary dates of the big fire here in Taos that destroyed Phillip Crawford's house. Do you remember that?"

"Of course. It was one of the first times my editor sent me outside Santa Fe to do a story. I drove by that house, surprised to find it had never been rebuilt."

"It still hasn't. I was by there earlier today. And guess who was standing there, staring up at it—Camilla Crawford."

"No shit. Wow. Well, I seem to remember that she owns it now."

"That's right. She was looking kind of wistfully at the place and told me she planned to fix it up and move back. I got the feeling that wasn't really going to happen. She's gone through the insurance money and what she got in her divorce settlement." Sam paused. "So, I'm kind of looking into the old case on behalf of a new friend here in town."

Sandy's journalistic ears must have perked up. "Who's that?"

"For now, I need to protect my source. I'll just say that it has to do with the JC Freeman painting that was lost in the blaze, and whether the fire itself was arson or not. The official report says not."

"Oh, wow. You know, I always wondered about that."

"I thought you might have. Everyone else covered it in nearly the same words, leaving the public perception that both the fire and the death of the young man were accidental. But your story rang differently somehow. Can you tell me why?"

"I can tell you what I heard. Can't put any of it in print. And neither can you."

"Don't worry about that."

"Well, the inside gossip was that the governor was the one who pressed—pressed hard—for the 'accidental' ruling. Supposedly, it was because Phillip Crawford wanted it that way and he'd donated hugely to the governor's campaign."

"No kidding?" Sam remembered her own conviction that it had to be someone in New Mexico who'd put the pressure on the police.

And if Crawford's business managed funds for, say, the state employees' retirement fund or some such … maybe Phil Crawford actually could have had the ear of the governor. Important people traded favors all the time. It might not be as implausible as she'd first thought.

"But—" Sandy continued, "there was no way my editor would print that. 'Not if you want a journalism career in this state' was how he phrased it. Okay, I get that. You don't piss off the governor."

"But people write unsubstantiated exposés on politicians all the time. It's practically the backbone of the news today."

"Right. But not so much then, and not with my old-school editor. He insisted on verification, not speculation. We never used phrases like *some say* or *it is believed that* ... No way. He came from that Walter Cronkite era where you verified everything from three sources."

"I wish it was still that way."

"Yeah, well, I railed against it silently to myself. But now, older and wiser, I can't disagree. It *was* gossip, and although I heard the rumor from several people, I couldn't verify it. I tried, believe me. It was a good education in ethics for me, and I'm glad I listened to the old guy."

"So the governor wasn't involved?"

"Not as far as I could ever prove."

"And the fire—arson or accident?"

"All I know is the official ruling. Even if I'd wanted to dig deeper, as soon as my first story was filed, I was asked for all my notes and sent off on a completely different assignment."

"And you didn't find that suspicious?"

"Well, of course. But, as my editor reminded me, I really did want to keep my job. Plus, you know, I never really had any proof. I had to drop it and move on."

"One last question," Sam said. "Some of the news stories mentioned a 'person of interest' who was interviewed in the beginning as the possible arsonist. Did you have access to that person, or did you ever get their name?"

"Access, no. He was a minor, and the police are very protective. I did hear the name, and I'm sure I won't forget this one. Bearcat Sowlow."

Sam chuckled when Sandy spelled it for her. "Yeah, that would be a hard one to forget."

Chapter 23

Sam had no trouble finding Bearcat Sowlow. It seemed she'd taken up a trade as a welder. Looked as if he still liked to play with fire.

She'd peeked out the window first thing this morning. Last night's snow hadn't amounted to more than a couple inches so that was good news, considering how much she needed to get done in the next two days. She wasn't sure why she felt this urgency to put together the answers in this case—after all, it was old news. She sighed as she stared at the jumble of notes she'd made. If she didn't get around to see him before Christmas it wouldn't be the end of the world.

She looked up the address of ABC Welding and since it wasn't far from her home, she put a visit to the shop on her to-do list. But first, she took a spoonful of the lie detector potion and refilled her little vial. Kelly's concoction had, so far, come in handy.

The welding shop sat on a short side road off Highway 64, a metal building surrounded by non-working vehicles and piles of scrap metal, now nicely disguised by the thin layer of snow. She pulled into the dirt parking area, next to a pickup truck with pipe racks over the cab and the company logo on the doors.

A forty-something man wearing a brown Carhartt coverall was poking through some tools on a workbench with his right index finger while holding a steaming mug in his left hand. He looked up when she closed the door behind her.

"Bearcat Sowlow?" Sam asked.

"Nope. I'm Randy, his boss. He's not here yet. Something I can help you with?" He set down the coffee mug and turned to her.

"Oh, no, just some personal chit-chat. I can wait, if he'll be in soon."

Randy shrugged. "No idea." He drew out the phrase, a resigned look on his face.

Sam raised her eyebrows, hinting for more. "I hope he's not ill."

The man shook his head, resigned. "You got employees?"

She nodded.

"You know, Bearcat's a good worker, a *great* welder. When he shows up. You got any of those? Great at the job, but iffy as an employee?" He didn't seem to expect an answer. "I wanna rip my hair out sometimes. I don't know what his story is, but he takes it out in the bottle. I'd fire his sorry ass but he's the best welder in town. I need him—I just don't need the b.s. he brings to work with him."

Sam nodded, quietly thanking her lucky stars that she didn't have to deal with many personal issues with her own crew.

"I'm sorry." It was the only thing she could think of to say.

Randy looked up at a clock on the wall. "He's an hour late already. I called. No answer. If you want to go over to his house, roust him out of bed, and get him over here, at least maybe I can get him to finish the project we promised by tonight. Chit-chat with him all you want, just let him know he'd better get in here."

He picked up a helmet-like thing with a flip-up face shield.

"Where—"

"Go a mile out toward the airport, right on Tapia Road. It's a trailer with a blue awning and you'll see his red pickup out front."

Sam could tell Randy had indulged his employee quite a lot already. She agreed to drive out to the trailer and see what she could do. When she walked out, Randy was donning heavy work gloves and turning toward some kind of angled metal thing clamped onto a stand.

"Okay, not exactly how I envisioned spending time this morning," she muttered to herself as she got into her car.

But she'd kind of promised Randy, and the place he described was no more than two miles away. She turned around in the parking area and headed out.

The single-wide trailer clearly had not seen any of its occupant's repair skills. The railing beside the two steps leading to the door was leaning at a precarious angle and half the skirting around the bottom of the dwelling was either missing or hanging loose. Thick weeds had grown around the place, filling in around a cast-off wooden pallet and a car engine that sat on a couple of cinderblocks. The weeds were crisp and frozen now, and the morning sun had already melted much of the overnight snow, so every depressing thing about the place stood out.

She approached the front door and knocked. A couple of thumping sounds came from inside, then it went quiet. She knocked again and called out. "Bearcat? Can you open up?"

She could smell alcohol the moment the door opened. Before her stood a man who hadn't shaved in a couple weeks, wearing a set of long underwear and a rueful expression.

"Oh, god, sorry," he said. "You from the child support place? Cause really, I was gonna get caught up."

"No, um, that's not it at all. I got your name from Sandy Greene and … this may be a bad time …"

"It's okay," he said. "I need to get ready for work anyhow. It's—oh shit—it's late." He grabbed a pair of jeans from the arm of the couch that sat only inches from the door. "Look, come in, if you don't mind talking while I get ready."

Sam wanted, mother-like, to grab him by the shoulders and tell him to straighten up his act, to start reporting to work on time, and to get his life together. If he didn't manage to do it soon, he would lose the benefit of an understanding employer, and did he envision spending the rest of his life in a crappy trailer while his paycheck all went to the bars or the liquor stores? But she didn't.

She stepped inside, closing the door against the cold outside air, and stood beside the couch. Sowlow had disappeared into the bedroom to her right.

"So, who's this Sandy person that sent you?" he called out.

"Um, she's a journalist. Some years ago she covered the story of the fire at the Crawford house, and she told me you had spoken to the police at that time."

He appeared in the doorway, his face drained of color. "What?"

"The fire. I get the feeling it wasn't your idea to just go into some rich guy's house and start a fire. So, can you tell me what happened?"

"And you'll write it up in the papers and bring my name into it all over again? No thanks."

"No, no. I'm not a reporter and I have no reason to bring your name up to anyone else at all."

"So? The cops let me go."

"But you did start the fire, didn't you? Maybe it was an accident? Were you there with Susan and Mike, a friend of theirs? Or did they just sit back and let you take the blame?"

He swayed against the doorframe, then stumbled to a recliner chair and flopped down on it.

"The cops let you go because you were a minor at the time—fifteen, I think—and they didn't quite have enough evidence to convict you. Or maybe because you were a kid, they decided to cut you a break."

Sam watched him rake his fingers through his long hair. She decided to toss in her own theory. "I believe someone paid you, and I'm trying to figure out who that was. That's the person who should have been questioned, the person who should have gone to jail."

Her words hit the mark.

"I didn't even get—" His shoulders slumped, the

argument gone out of him.

"Who paid you?" she said gently.

He looked up, and the rims of his eyes were red. "I don't know. It was an envelope in the mailbox with my name on it. There was five thousand dollars and a note that said to go to this place during these certain days, make sure the place would burn. I had no idea somebody would be there, honest, I didn't."

"Did you keep the note, show it to the police?"

"No. I burned it. I hid the cash in my room 'cause I was afraid to start showing money around."

"How did this person know you wouldn't just keep the money and not start the fire?"

He shifted in his seat, fidgeted with the laces on his boots. "I guess I had a little bit of a reputation? From the time I was pretty little I liked to play with fire. I'd fiddle with candles, take sticks out of the fireplace and wave them around. My mom never caught me, so I got braver about it. Set a fire once in some guy's barn. Whoa—hay burns really quick. I was showing off for some buddies from school. We ran out of there and got a hose to put it out. After that, kids would ask me to light something, you know, just fooling around."

"So, lots of people could have known … if someone wanted a fire started, you were the guy to ask."

"I suppose. I didn't really think about the money in the envelope. It was just like, wow, look at this."

"You were still living at home then. Didn't your mom notice you suddenly had money to spend?"

"When the police let me go, they called her and she picked me up. She took me to this overlook by the gorge and I guess it was what you'd call a Come to Jesus meeting.

She told me I'd better get my act together, and quick, or I'd be spending my life in prison. She moved us to Albuquerque where I got my GED to finish school and then she put me in a trade school where I learned welding. I guess she was a pretty smart mom, huh. Being that my dad had skipped when I was way young."

Sam nodded. "She was."

"I was so stupid. Still am, I guess, or I'd be living better than this." He looked around the messy trailer, as if seeing it for the first time. "A guy died in that house fire. I can't let go of it."

"Confession is good for the soul. Maybe you could somehow make amends." Although she couldn't think what that would be. Nothing was going to erase the Miera family's pain.

Sam stood. "Look, you remade your life once, and you can do it again. Randy seems pretty understanding. If you can get your drinking under control and just be responsible at work, you at least have a future there. The rest of it, well, I think you'll figure it out."

She walked to the door and opened it. "I'll let you get ready for work. When you get there, apologize to Randy. He's on your side if you'll just get your act together."

Sowlow nodded solemnly. That was the last she ever saw of him.

Chapter 24

Emily was walking out the front door of Sweet's Sweets, a purple box in hand, when Sam arrived and parked her car out front. She reached out with her free arm and gave Sam a hug.

"My parents want to drive up on Christmas Day. I wasn't sure if you'd be open tomorrow, and I had to have some breakfast muffins," she said. Her honey-blonde hair hung in loose curls past her shoulders, and she smiled at the thought of a visit from home.

"We're open a half day tomorrow, closed the next. I like to do a little employee gathering the afternoon of the twenty-fourth, just a thank-you to the crew for putting in the extra hours." She also handed out holiday bonuses, they did a little gift exchange, Secret Santa style, and then delivered any remaining pastries to the homeless shelter.

Emily looked around. "I'm sad that there wasn't more

snow. Look how bright the sky is—it's melting off already."

"There's more on the way," Sam assured her. "According to the weather app, we'll still have a white Christmas for you."

The young woman's smile widened at the news as she opened her car door. "I hope it's a ton. Well, not so much that my parents can't get here." She slipped into the driver's seat. "I need to get home and get things ready for company. I want Mom and Dad to be impressed with what I've done at the library. Family legacy and all that."

Sam watched her drive away, reminding herself she still had errands and had hoped to put together notes about the case. She had a feeling she had learned something important in the past couple of days, but the nagging feeling in her head wasn't spelling out what that important thing might be. For the moment, though, she needed to check in with Becky and see if she could help with deliveries today.

She was debating whether to move her car to the alley or leave it in place—sometimes it helped bring customers in when a place looked busier—when another vehicle pulled in beside hers. Camilla Crawford's black BMW—interesting.

"We meet again," Sam said as Camilla got out of the car. "I'm glad you came by."

Camilla's face took a moment to rearrange itself into a smile after she remembered Sam.

"Yes! Well, I just had to come and see why this is the most popular bakery in town. If you have something elegant in the way of a coffee cake or something, I'll take it to my hosts. They're having a huge brunch tomorrow."

Again, she couldn't resist dropping the names of both hosts and several of their guests, all Hollywood A-listers. Sam kind of felt sorry for the woman whose whole identity seemed so wrapped up in knowing and hanging out with the rich and famous. It didn't seem as if she'd made a life for herself at all after living in the shadow of Phil Crawford all those years. Whole psychology studies had probably been written about people like this. Sam shrugged off the feeling.

"I think we can accommodate that," she told Camilla. "And if something in the display cases isn't quite fancy enough, we can add little touches or we can bake something you could pick up in the morning."

They walked to the front door and Sam held it open for her guest. "How about a cup of our signature blend coffee while you decide about the brunch items?" At Camilla's nod, Sam headed for the beverage bar, sending a secretive raised eyebrow toward Jen. "Who told you we're the most popular bakery in town?" she asked, handing her the coffee mug.

"Oh, I was over at the Finstadt Gallery yesterday afternoon. Maurice remembered me, of course, since he sold us *The Ghost of Christmas.*"

Twenty-some years ago. What a memory.

"And, naturally, we started chatting about the painting. I loved that piece," Camilla said with a wistful look on her face.

"You must have been heartbroken when it burned beyond restoration."

"I was. So, so devastated." Camilla was eyeing the croissants in the case. "But the most interesting thing happened at the gallery. Maurice told me there's a rumor that the painting may have turned up."

Sam's heart thumped. "Where would he hear a rumor like that?" She hoped her voice wasn't shaking.

"Oh, I don't know. He didn't actually say."

And Finstadt moved once again to the top of Sam's suspect list. He certainly had motive, and probably had the opportunity to get the piece. But that still didn't explain how it ended up hidden in Emily's house.

Camilla pointed to the amaretto cheesecake in the case and Jen pulled out a whole, uncut one and began boxing it up. When Camilla turned back to face Sam her eyes were sparkling. "It would be very exciting if the picture actually did turn up. It's mine, you know. I was awarded the house and all its contents."

"I'm not so sure about that," Sam told her. "The insurance company paid for it, so it seems technically it's theirs."

Camilla abruptly turned back to Jen. "Add a dozen of those croissants, half with the almond filling, half with the chocolate, will you, sweetie?"

"If you'll excuse me …" Sam said, heading toward the kitchen, her mind in turmoil.

Camilla barely responded. Every word out of her mouth had resonated as the truth.

Chapter 25

How could she know about *The Ghost of Christmas* showing up again?" Sam fumed. She was repeatedly dunking a teabag into a mug in Kelly's kitchen, while her daughter sat at the table, paging through a recipe book. The book of spells sat nearby.

"Mom, just because you saw evidence that Camilla's words were truthful, doesn't mean the words were *true*. It meant she *believed* them. Finstadt might have lied to her, right?"

Sam stopped in place. "Yeah ... and she did say she'd heard a rumor. Maybe Maurice tossed that out, like a tasty morsel to keep her coming back. The more often she comes into the gallery, the more likely she is to buy something new."

"Speaking of tasty morsels ... aren't we supposed to be planning our Christmas dinner?"

"I just feel like I should have a better idea of who the guilty party is by now," Sam said. "All these people I've talked to, and it's just not coming to me."

"Dinner, Mom. You're so busy right now, I'm thinking we should have it here. It's kind of late notice, but I'll see if our friends want to come. Riki hasn't said anything—maybe she and Evan don't have plans. And you could invite Zoë and Darryl if you want."

Sam had paced over to the kitchen window and back. "Of course, *I* know where the painting is … Maybe we could somehow use it as bait to draw out the real culprit."

"Mom! Focus!"

"Sorry, Kel. Christmas dinner. I agree, having it here would be lovely. I'll run to the store this afternoon for anything we don't already have. Just tell me what to bring." Although the idea of walking into the holiday crowd in any supermarket two days before Christmas made her cringe.

"How on earth would you use *The Ghost of Christmas* to lure out the suspect?"

"Ha—you *were* listening. Actually, I have no idea how I would do that. I'll give it some more thought."

"Okay, good." Kelly had pushed aside the cookbook and picked up a pen and scratchpad. She jotted down the basics for the holiday meal. "I've already got a huge ham, and there are sweet potatoes in the pantry. The guys will want green bean casserole—they love that dish."

"Cranberries, dressing, a salad of some kind."

Within a few minutes they had a menu, and Kelly walked into her pantry to check supplies. Sam pocketed the list of needed items they compiled, but her mind was already back on her suspect list instead. She eyed the leather-bound book with the rune-like writing inside.

"Too bad there's not some magical way to categorize a person's motives, and whether they had both means and opportunity to have done the crime. I'm talking about the forgery and substitution of the real painting with a fake one. I did learn who started the fire. Now I just need to know who paid him to do it. Is there any way we have a spell for that?"

Kelly pulled the spell book closer. "It sounds more like you need a spreadsheet. Or what do they call it on the cop shows on TV, the bulletin board on the wall where they paste up pictures of all the suspects and draw lines between them and the weapons and all that stuff?"

"A murder board?"

"We could rig up something like that."

"Maybe. I don't know. It seems like this should be easier to figure out," Sam said. "I guess I got spoiled to having inside info at Beau's office."

The back door opened and in bounded Ana, glowing with rosy cheeks and bursting to speak. "You'll never guess what we got!"

Scott spoke up. "Uh-uh, no talking. Christmas and birthdays are the acceptable time to keep secrets. You can't tell what we bought."

He held several shopping bags above his daughter's head. "Let's go straight upstairs to my office and you'll help with the wrapping." He sent a slightly weary smile toward Kelly.

"He's such a good dad," Kelly said, once the two were out of earshot.

"And is there going to be another …?" Sam asked.

Kelly shrugged. "I haven't got around to doing the home test yet. I'll go out tomorrow and buy the kit."

"I have the grocery list," Sam said. "I could pick up a test for you."

"That's okay. Emily and I have lunch plans tomorrow, and I need to get some shopping of my own done, stocking stuffers and things like that. Maybe that's the way to break the news to Scott—a test stick in his Christmas stocking."

"Whatever you think." Sam was already pulling her jacket on. "I'd better hit the supermarket soon. The crowds won't get any smaller later in the day."

It turned out she was right about that. She had to circle Albertson's parking lot twice before someone backed out and left her a spot. She gathered her phone and pack and the shopping list, snagging an empty cart out in the lot rather than taking her chances on whether there would be any available inside. The wind had picked up and a frigid gust went down the back of her jacket. The storm was on the way.

Inside, the huge supermarket was a madhouse. The floral department just inside the door had stocked about a thousand poinsettia plants, so every new patron came to a halt to browse through them, causing a massive traffic jam. Sam gave up and bypassed the check stands on her way to the opposite end of the store.

She grabbed the items Kelly wanted for a relish tray, and was trying to remember whether she had all the ingredients for her cheese puff appetizers when she spotted Maurice Finstadt, standing at the deli case. He was right in front of the gruyere, of course, the item she wanted. In his cart sat three huge party platters—meats and cheeses, sliced fruits, and veggies with dipping sauces.

He looked up and recognized Sam, just in time to catch her staring at the food.

"My regular caterer reneged at the last moment," he said. "But they do a nice job here, and I had to come up with *something* for our holiday customer appreciation party."

"It all looks great," Sam said. "I saw Camilla Crawford earlier. She stopped in at my shop. I supposed she'll be attending?"

Finstadt fidgeted a little. "I'm not certain. She was in the gallery this week, too. I was under the impression her social calendar was fairly booked."

"She somehow got the impression that *The Ghost of Christmas* had turned up. I wonder where she got that idea?"

Maurice shrugged. "Not from me. You know where I stand on that particular piece."

Yeah, you certified the destroyed painting as the real one. Can't very well back down and switch opinions now, can you? But she merely smiled and wished she'd swigged a little of the potion before she'd left for this errand. But who knew she would run into her number one suspect in the supermarket?

She wished him happy holidays as he steered his cart away, then she grabbed her wedge of gruyere and headed for the checkout stands. The queues were long and she had no choice but to join one and wait. Spotting Maurice at another of the lines, down the way, started her thinking about her list of suspects. In terms of motive, means, and opportunity, what did she really have to go on?

The gallery owner already filled the criteria, but there was also Susan O'Malley (although her motive was a little murky). And Susan's mother could have filled the bill—except where would she come up with the extra money to pay Bearcat Sowlow to set the fire, and what motive would she have?

The homeowners didn't seem motivated enough.

When they tired of the Taos home they would have simply sold it, rather than taking the risk of paying someone to set it on fire. Insurance-based motives usually revolved around someone deeply in debt who needed to get out of an overpriced mortgage—that simply didn't seem to fit the Crawfords at all. Maybe a crooked cop or bribable inspector—again, where would one of them get the cash? And what was with the secretive feeling she'd gotten around the Miera family?

Of course, there was still David Plankhurst. Emily's grandfather *had* ended up with the painting, after all. But why would he go to such lengths?

Sam decided she needed to know more about David's relationship with the Crawfords. He had known them and done some research, according to Emily. And sometimes, he who possessed the missing property truly was the guilty party. Emily would never believe this of her grandfather, and Sam didn't want to believe it either. And since David couldn't remember anything, it might just remain one of those mysteries that would never be solved.

By the time all this ran through her head, she'd gone through the checkout process and was on the way back to her car.

To be on the safe side, knowing that *The Ghost of Christmas* was fresh in Finstadt's mind, and Camilla's, Sam decided to phone Emily and reiterate how important it was that she keep the painting hidden away, and especially not to mention anything about it to the gallery owner, should their paths cross.

Chapter 26

Sam awoke the next morning with the words to *White Christmas* running through her head. Despite the fact that it was going to be a busy half day at Sweet's Sweets, and she hadn't yet written the bonus checks to hand out during the employee party after closing, she found herself anticipating the next two days almost as she had done as a child.

The sky was white, the clouds low and heavy, and there was a half-inch of new snow on the ground when she looked out. Perfect.

Her phone rang as she finished toasting English muffins for eggs Benedict. A hearty breakfast should tide her over until the late-afternoon party, and it was one of Beau's favorite dishes.

"Hey, Kel," she answered when she picked up the phone. "Merry Christmas Eve. What's up?"

"Well, I was wondering … Do you suppose you could take Ana with you to the bakery today? I know it's super busy, and I wouldn't ask except that Scott has a book deadline and is scrambling to finish editing the last few pages of his new one so he can email it out to his editor this afternoon. And I'm trying to carve out some time alone this morning to wrap gifts and then I'm having lunch with Emily."

"Sure, no problem. Can I stop by and pick her up in about half an hour?"

The plan was set. Ana loved 'working' at the bakery, and Sam could surely find things for her to do. Her small hands couldn't manage the pastry bags just yet, but she loved it when she could meticulously add little touches to cupcakes and cookies. Anything involving sprinkles, edible glitter, or cinnamon candies—she'd be on it.

Sam headed toward the Victorian as soon as the breakfast dishes were loaded in the dishwasher. Little sleety granules had begun to fall, and she was using her windshield wipers by the time she arrived to see Ana, bundled in her winter gear, rushing out the front door toward her car.

Kelly waved from the porch, then wrapped her sweater more tightly around her body and went back inside. At the upper turret window, Sam could see the golden glow of Scott's desk lamp and knew he was completely immersed in his newest Maddie Plimpton children's mystery. She gave a wave, but wasn't sure whether he saw her.

"Okay, are you ready for a busy bakery day?" Sam asked as Ana buckled herself into her seat in the back.

"Can I make snowman cupcakes?"

"Probably. We'll have to see what orders we've received, and we'll play it by ear." She glanced at Ana's face in the rearview mirror as she backed around to exit the driveway. "But I imagine we can figure out a few extra cupcakes. They'll be your contribution to the nice Christmas dinner your mom's cooking tomorrow."

The child's face lit up. "Is Auntie Jen working today? And Auntie Becky?"

"Everyone is. It's one of our busiest days of the year." Sam did a mental wait-a-minute. Everyone was exchanging little gifts this afternoon. What could she come up with for Ana? She would give it some thought. If the last gingerbread house in the display hadn't sold, that would be something she knew would delight her granddaughter.

The tiny snowflakes gradually became larger as they neared the center of town. For fun, rather than taking the back street directly to the bakery, Sam turned in at the plaza. In the dim morning light the decorations were all lit—brown bag electric luminarias edged the tops of all the buildings, and the huge Christmas tree in the center of the square was lit in blue lights. More blue lights were swagged along the storefronts, and garland with red bows was draped along the short iron fence that edged the bandstand.

"It's so pretty!" Ana exclaimed.

"It is. We're really lucky to live here, aren't we?" Sam circled the plaza once, then took the narrow street that exited toward the bakery.

When she glanced over, she saw the cheery light glowing from her windows, and noticed the parking lot was full. Mysterious Happenings, the bookshop next door, was equally busy. She drove to the end of the short block and pulled into the alley behind Julio's Harley.

Ana was out of her seat and dashing to the back door before Sam had gathered her things.

"Grammy, I hope it snows a mile."

"Um, maybe you mean a foot?" *And hopefully most of it comes down later, after we're all tucked in at home.*

They walked into the warm kitchen, redolent with the scents of sugar and cinnamon, butter and almond. Ana dashed over to hug Becky, who immediately understood she now had an assistant.

"Hang up your coat and wash your hands. You're just in time to help set decorations on these tree shaped cookies."

Sam mouthed a thank-you to Becky, as she turned to check the order basket. Only two items hadn't been completed yet, and she saw that Marcie and Christopher were working on those.

"Julio, you may want to put the cover over your bike. Snow's coming down out there," Sam said.

Her chief baker was stacking empty pans near the sink, and he paused to step out back and check the Harley. He came back five minutes later, shaking the melting flakes from his jacket.

"I heard there could be pretty significant snowfall tonight," Christopher said. "My mom is so excited about a white Christmas, but my little sister is worried Santa won't get through if the reindeer can't see the rooftops."

Ana paused in setting silver dragées on a green frosted cookie. "It'll be okay. The presents will get here."

Sam smiled and tickled her head through the hairnet Becky had placed over Ana's bright red curls.

"Since we may have a weather situation, I vote that we finish up what's in progress and shut down the kitchen right after," Sam said. "All the baking is done, right?"

Julio gave her a thumbs up as he ran hot water into the deep sink.

"And there are only these two orders and the cookies?"

"There are a few baked cupcakes in the fridge," Becky said. "Shall we decorate those and set them out in the cases, or do you want to freeze them?"

"Decorate them!" Ana voted.

Sam took a look and decided there weren't enough to be worth saving for another day. She brought them out, along with a big tub of white buttercream, and told Ana she could make snowmen if she wanted to.

Sam walked out to the sales room, where Jen was filling orders and taking money as fast as she could. No one sat at the bistro tables. It seemed everyone was dashing in to pick up their orders, or a few last minute treats, and then heading home. There was a lot of chit-chat about the weather.

She wiped down the tables and cleaned up the beverage bar. Through the front windows she could tell there was already more than an inch of snow on the parked cars. Back in the kitchen, she sat at her desk and pulled out her checkbook. She should have written the bonus checks yesterday, or earlier, but she most certainly couldn't put them aside now. She hastily filled in the names and amounts and tucked each check into a Christmas card and sealed the envelopes.

By the time she finished, the snow was two inches deep outside.

"Julio," she said, handing him his envelope. "Unless you either want to stay here overnight, or get a ride with someone else and leave your bike parked out back, I think you need to head home. Don't worry about the pans—I'll finish them."

He took a look out the back door and agreed. With a quick Merry Christmas to everyone, he donned his winter coat, cap, and goggles and headed out.

"Same goes for anyone who doesn't have four-wheel drive or doesn't want to hang around," Sam said as she walked around, handing out envelopes. "I can finish up whatever's left. I hate to cancel our little gathering, but I'd rather you all were safe."

Since Marcie and Christopher often rode to work together in Marcie's compact car, they handed over their finished projects and bade everyone a happy holiday. Becky's husband called right after the others had walked out the door, informing her that their house partway up the ski valley road already had six inches of snow. He asked if she wanted him to drive down and pick her up, but she assured him she could make it if she started out now.

Sam looked out back. Three inches shouldn't pose a problem for her all-wheel-drive vehicle. She called Kelly.

"Are you and Emily still going out to lunch?" she asked.

"I'm at Em's now, and we changed the plan. She's making soup here so we'll just stay in. As long as you can keep Ana with you, we're fine."

"That's not a problem at all." Sam hung up and walked back up front to check on Jen's situation.

The crowd had thinned. Only four customers inside, and two of them were here to pick up the cakes Marcie and Christopher had just finished. Sam boxed those and got them into the customers' hands, wishing each of them a wonderful Christmas as they left.

Outside, the snowfall had abated. Maybe this would be all of it, Sam thought.

"I'll stay until one o'clock," Jen said, "just in case there are last minute customers. My Jeep will make it home through nearly anything."

"If you're sure. If you get uncomfortable with this, feel free to head out. I can watch the front and get the baking pans washed."

She realized she also needed to clean the walk-in fridge—this was one of the only afternoons of the year it was completely empty—and she should inventory supplies so she could place an order quickly on the twenty-sixth, in preparation for the New Year's Eve orders that were already coming in.

Ana was perched on a work stool, happily making a huge pile of white icing on top of each cupcake. Sam turned to the pans Julio had left soaking in the sink, washing and rinsing them as she heard Jen out front chatting with the last few customers of the day.

"I turned over the sign and switched off all the front room lights except the small lamp and the Christmas decorations," Jen said.

"It's one o'clock already?"

Jen eyed the stack of pans in the drainer. "One-thirty. Time flies when you're having fun."

"Be safe going home," Sam said. "And have a wonderful Christmas day with your family."

"You too." Jen gave her a hug.

Christmas day with family, Sam thought. It really would be beautiful tomorrow at Kelly's house. She could picture the blue Victorian, with all the fancy trim now wearing a lacy edging of white.

Chapter 27

Sam pushed back from her desk and rolled her shoulders to work out the kinks. She realized with a start that it was already after four-thirty. The fridge and kitchen were spotless, the supply order was ready to send, and Ana had curled up beneath the desk with a cookbook to read. Surely Kelly would be home from her girls' lunch out.

"Let's get you home, Miss Anastasia, and I'll make sure Grandpa Beau is tucked in for Santa's visit tonight."

Ana gave her an indulgent smile from her cozy cubbyhole, but she crawled out and handed the cookbook over to Sam.

"Grab your coat. I'll go out and get the car warmed up."

Sam pulled the back door open and came to an abrupt halt. The snow packed against it came up to her knees.

And looking down toward her car, the vehicle looked like a lump of marshmallow crème.

"Whoa!" The word whooshed out of her.

Ana immediately appeared at her side, and for once the child seemed speechless, her eyes huge and round.

"Stay inside," Sam instructed. Where had she stored the snow shovel? *Silly me, there's no way to shovel enough to get that car moving.*

They would be spending Christmas Eve in the bakery.

She closed the door and picked up her bag, digging into the side pocket for her phone. She had missed more than a dozen messages. Apparently, she had somehow switched off the phone without realizing it. She began going through them.

Voicemail, Beau: Snow's really picking up. You on the way home?

Voicemail, Beau: Sam? Pick up.

Voicemail, Beau: I'm coming with the truck to get you.

And five minutes later: Even with four-wheel drive, I can't get the truck out. *Sam, call me!*

Text, Kelly: OMG, Mom, have you looked outside? Em and I got busy. I'm stuck here at her place. Will call Scott. Don't worry, I'm safe. Are you?

Text, Kelly: Mom? You and Ana okay?

Voicemail, Kelly: Mom, I'm getting worried. You never ignore calls. Are you and Ana all right?

Voicemail, Kelly (shaky voice): Mom, I called Beau and he hasn't heard from you either. He's calling out the sheriff's department. Please be okay. Please don't be stuck out there somewhere.

Oh, crap. How could she have missed all this? Sam shot off a quick text to Kelly. We're fine, I'll call you in a minute. Then she phoned Beau, apologizing and explaining the situation.

"I'm relieved, darlin'. You had us all worried. I'll call Evan's men and let them know."

"Yes, don't let anyone come out in this weather, including you."

"We couldn't drive in it if we wanted to. They're saying on the radio that most of the roads are closed now. Stay where you are. At the rate the snow's still coming down, it could be a couple days before the plows can handle it. Do you have food?"

Well, most of it might be sugar and flour and butter, she thought. But she assured him they would be fine.

When she got Kelly on the phone, her daughter asked the same question.

"We'll eat the cupcakes I made," Ana piped up.

"Uh, not only cupcakes, please," Kelly said. "Mom, you do have other stuff, right?"

"I do. Don't worry. You girls stay inside and keep warm. Everything going okay?"

"Oh yeah. Emily's been telling me ghost stories and I swear now she's got me hearing scratching noises at the windows."

"Tree branches, I'm sure. Beau says this could take a couple of days before they're able to plow us out, so just enjoy your little slumber party." She ended the call.

Ana's expression fell when she heard that part. "But what about Christmas? How can it happen if we aren't home?"

A flashback to an earlier Christmas, the first year when she'd opened Sweet's Sweets, and the chocolatier who showed up to make his lovely handcrafted chocolates for her. She blinked and the image went away.

"Christmas happens no matter where you are," Sam said. "As far as the presents and the big dinner, we can have all that after we get home."

"You're sure?"

"I'm sure." Sam's mind was whirling. She couldn't feed the child cupcakes and cookies for two solid days. Then she remembered the emergency kit in the back of her car. Beau had insisted they each carry one during the winter months, especially given the fact that the ranch was miles outside town, off a less-traveled county road.

Granted, she and Ana were safe indoors with heat and light and food. But still, if something should happen, it would be better to have the kit with her than twenty feet away, out in the car. She grabbed the push-broom and put on her heavy coat, instructing Ana to remain exactly where she was.

With a mighty shove, she created a very slight indent in the snow against the back door, but it was quickly evident she'd never be able to make a path through it. She plowed on foot through the light powder, feeling her way down the steps and to the back of the car.

In the faint glow of the streetlamp at the end of the alley, she saw what Beau meant by how fast it was coming down. Dollar-sized flakes filled the air. They landed softly, adding to the fluffy layer that made everything—from the trash dumpster to the buildings to the electric poles—beautiful.

No time for snow gazing. She used the large broom to shove enough snow off the back of her car so she could open the hatch. From it she pulled the duffle, a sleeping bag, and her heavy Sorel boots, hanging straps over her shoulders and tucking things under her arm. Now, to get back inside without dropping anything down into the white that would swallow it up.

She managed to slam the hatch, even as handfuls of snow fell into the car. She couldn't worry about that. She got a firm grip on all the items and turned back toward the steps, where her footprints and the channel made by her legs had already become fuzzy around the edges.

When she looked up, a man stood there. A large man, one she recognized.

Chapter 28

Bobul, my gosh! What—how on earth did you get here?"

"Hello, Miss Samantha. Bobul coming to help you."

Words failed her. The oddball Romanian wore the same brown pants and boots, the spacious old coat, and the floppy hat. Slung across his shoulder was the canvas bag he always carried. And he didn't appear to have aged at all, at least from what she could tell in the translucent light of the snowfall.

He reached out and took the push-broom.

"Come inside, Bobul. You must be freezing."

He gave a slight shrug and followed her. He'd always been the untalkative type.

"Ana, we have a visitor," Sam called out, thinking of the fright this hulking man with his thick boots and mangled

English might give her granddaughter.

Ana stepped forward, extended her hand. "Hello."

For the first time in memory, Sam saw Bobul smile. It was the sweet, indulgent smile a grandfather would give to a child. Ana rushed forward and hugged him around the legs. It was almost as if she'd met him before. And, in a way, maybe she had. Kelly had been pregnant when, in England, she encountered Bobul sitting on a park bench, and he had handed over the leatherbound book. Could the then-embryonic Ana have somehow established a connection?

No, Sam thought. That was way beyond weird. She dropped the duffle, boots, and sleeping bag near the back door and brushed a thick coating of snowflakes from her jacket. Her pants were cold and wet and her street shoes sodden.

"I need to get into something dry," she said. "We'll round up something for you, too, Bobul. You must be chilled all the way through."

"Is not problem," he said, reaching into his bag and pulling out a white baker's jacket. He shook out the wrinkles and, after shedding his outer coat, put it on. Sam noticed that, miraculously, his boots and pant legs did not seem very wet.

Okay … how did that …? She dropped the thought and unzipped the duffle bag.

Inside, she kept a quilted snowmobile suit, a change of socks, pants, and shirt, heavy gloves, and a knitted balaclava. There was a plastic container of matches and a couple of fatwood sticks, along with protein bars and trail mix. The idea of the emergency kit was that if she found herself in a broken-down vehicle at the side of the road, she could bundle up, build a fire if necessary, and survive. If she had to walk out for help, she had the Sorel boots and the snowmobile suit.

She pulled out the clean but wrinkled clothing and went into the bathroom to get out of her wet things. When she walked out, wearing the comfy sweatpants and dry socks, Bobul was standing by the stove where a pan of milk was warming over a burner.

"We're making hot chocolate," Ana announced.

Sam thought of the packets of instant mix on the beverage bar in the sales room, but she knew from experience that Bobul's made-from-scratch cocoa would taste much better.

The thought of the warm, sugary drink reminded her that she really needed to come up with something more substantial for their dinner. As she'd assured Kelly, they would not live by cupcakes alone during their enforced confinement. While Bobul stirred the contents of the pan, she went back to the regular refrigerator to see what supplies they had on hand.

Eggs, cream, milk, butter. The crisper contained a few remnants of the produce items they used in baking—some carrots and lemons, mostly. There was a partial bag of fresh spinach and a couple of mushrooms, which she'd intended to take home since they wouldn't keep long. She had her dinner plan.

She lit the bake oven and pulled a small stainless steel bowl from the shelf. Blending shortening and flour together, and sprinkling in water, took her mind off the things that were really pressing—the fact that her little family was so spread out and didn't know when they would all be together again.

Within a few minutes she'd rolled out the pastry crust

and deftly lifted it into a springform pan. She filled it with chopped spinach, sliced mushrooms, and the grated remains of a chunk of cheese she'd found. Eggs and cream, seasonings, all beat together got poured over the top of it.

"Quiche will be ready in forty-five minutes," she announced, raising her cup of cocoa to the others.

"Bobul says we can make chocolates later," Ana told Sam as they set one of the bistro tables with napkins and flatware for three. "He told me he knows how to make chocolate pinecones and little fairy castles and all kinds of things."

"He told you that?" Surprise, surprise. "Well, I happen to know he can. He's a very talented chocolatier."

The quiche turned out perfectly, and they kept the bright shop lights off, dining by the ambience of the small table lamp, the Christmas lights in the windows, and the sight of heavy snowflakes floating down. A hot dinner, a pleasant setting, and knowing her family was safe. All things considered, she had to feel grateful. She thought of the homeless shelter and silently prayed that others around town were also being kept snug in safe places. The storm had come on so quickly, Jen had not had the chance to take the last of their baked goods over there. But despite her worries, Sam felt happy in the moment.

She glanced over at Bobul, wondering for perhaps the hundredth time what his story was. She would never know. He ate with little comment, and she realized this was the first time they had sat down to a meal together. In all these years, had she actually ever seen him eat anything, other than taking a quick taste of one of his chocolate mixtures?

"We shall have snowman cupcakes for dessert," Ana said. She turned to Bobul. "I made them myself."

"Well, then we shall," he said, mimicking her formality.

True to his promise, as soon as they had put away the leftover quiche and washed the few utensils, Bobul pulled out the double boiler and started the chocolate-making process. Sam went online to check the progress of the storm and forecast. Newscasters were advising everyone, statewide, to stay in. There were reports of those who'd attempted travel and were now stuck—notably on I-40, the main east-west corridor across the state. Ranchers were doing their best to protect their livestock. It was a record snowfall everywhere in the Rocky Mountain region.

The news became repetitive and Sam decided she'd had all she could handle. She made a quick call to Kelly. "Still hearing ghosts?"

"Probably not. We opened a bottle of wine and found chick flicks on TV. It's turning into a very fun girls' night out. Although I really miss my family on Christmas Eve." She actually didn't sound terribly sad about that.

Sam told her how Bobul had showed up and that he and Ana were hitting it off.

"I wonder which of them will teach the other one the best magic trick," Kelly said.

Sam glanced toward the worktable, where the chocolate was now tempered and the two chocolatiers were working with it. "I'd say it may be an equal match."

She hung up the phone in time to overhear Ana's words.

"Kids will be surprised when Santa gets through the storm and leaves their gifts tonight." She gave Bobul a grownup look. "That's because it's really the parents who leave the presents. Personally, I go along with the game. It makes Mommy happy to think I believe that Santa really lands his sleigh on the roof and comes down our chimney. And Daddy really likes it that I always choose his favorite cookies as the ones we leave out by the tree."

Ana glanced toward Sam, who gave her a wink.

"Look, Grammy, I made a tiny chocolate butterfly." She held out her palm with the delicately formed piece.

"You did this by yourself?" Sam glanced at Bobul, who was busy dusting gold powder over a miniature replica of her carved wooden box, which she wasn't sure he'd ever seen.

"I did," Ana said. Then she popped the butterfly into her mouth.

"No more sweets tonight," Sam said, realizing the child could easily be awake with a sugar high for hours. "Make them, but then we'll save them to take home tomorrow."

She phoned Beau next, and he immediately wanted to know that she and Ana were all right. She assured him they were and was about to mention Bobul's unexpected arrival, but he seemed distracted.

"The power went out about a half hour ago," he told her. "Danny and I need to figure out how to keep the horses warm enough. He's here now. You probably won't be able to call me again tonight. My phone battery's nearly dead, and Danny's down to ten percent with his."

"Beau—my gosh. What can I do?"

"Nothing at all. Just stay where you are and have some candles ready in case your electricity goes out too."

"I will. We have the oven, so we can close ourselves in the kitchen area and turn that on if we get cold. We'll be fine. Don't worry about us. You have enough on your plate."

"I do. I love you, Sam."

She hated the way his goodbye had a finality to it. Then the electricity in the bakery faltered and went out.

Chapter 29

Without so much as the lighted clock on the microwave to serve as a guide, the kitchen sank into deep black. Bobul produced a match from somewhere and struck it. Held high, it gave Sam enough light to make her way to her desk, where she pulled a flashlight from a drawer.

"We'll have this in a second," she said.

The shelf with cake accessories held a number of birthday candles. Unfortunately, those wouldn't light the room for long. Then she remembered pillar candles Jen had bought for the bistro tables but ended up stashing somewhere in the sales room instead.

She made her way by flashlight to the front. Staring out the front windows, she couldn't see lights at any of the other businesses or toward the plaza. All was dark. Of course, such a curtain of snow was still falling, she might not have seen a bonfire in the parking lot. The snow was up to the bottom of the display windows now. With the furnace off, the room had begun to chill already.

The three pillar candles were on a shelf below the cash register, and Sam gathered them into her arms. Back in the kitchen, Ana was seated on her stool at the worktable. Bobul had lit a stove burner and the blue light kept the room from being in total darkness.

"Okay, let there be light," Sam announced as she handed him each candle so he could stick the wick into the gas flame.

The room soon had a cozy glow—not enough to read a recipe or decorate a cake, but enough that they felt warm and secure.

"Looks like it's time to wind up the chocolate production for tonight," she said.

Ana looked crestfallen, but Sam explained that the tempered chocolate could be re-melted and used again later. She finally convinced the little girl to take off her shoes and crawl into the sleeping bag Sam had laid out beside her desk. Bobul prepared himself a little nest with his coat near the stove, using his bag as a pillow.

"Are you sure you'll be comfortable there?" Sam asked. There was no way her snowmobile suit would fit his large frame, but she thought of gathering whatever towels and tablecloths she could come up with, to use as extra blankets.

"Bobul very comfort."

Sam blew out the candles and crawled into the sleeping bag with Ana, rolling the snow suit into a rather lumpy pillow. It wasn't an ideal way to get a night's sleep but, she reminded herself, it certainly beat being stranded in the car as she might have been if she'd headed home earlier.

Without the hum of the refrigerator or the furnace fan as background noise, the bakery settled into darkness. It would be a very silent night.

Chapter 30

Beau cranked up the portable generator. The little unit didn't produce a lot of power, certainly not enough to run the heating system in the house, but he'd managed to rig up a small heater, which he aimed toward the stalls at the far end of the barn.

He stared at his phone screen. Not a glimmer of light. He should have saved a little battery juice in case he needed to make an emergency call, rather than talking with Sam earlier. But it was important that he know she was safe indoors. It was the only way he'd ever fall asleep tonight.

Now, with the generator running, he could have plugged in his phone charger—except it was on the dresser upstairs in the log ranch house. It might as well have been ten miles away.

Danny came in the door at the other end of the big

barn, stomping his boots and unwinding the scarf he'd wrapped around his neck. Ranger and Nellie trailed along at his heels.

"We've got a little clearing near the door, boss," he said to Beau. "Wouldn't have that if you hadn't started shoveling it out when this mess began."

"We'll carve out pathways in the morning, and I'll see if my plow will make a dent in clearing the driveway. But all that can wait. It's dark and we're tired."

He showed Danny where he'd piled straw and horse blankets in the empty stall across from the two where the horses were now bedded down for the night.

"We each have a little spot here," he said. "Figured it was better than trying to keep the house warm enough for sleeping. We'd be up all night, stoking the fireplace. This way we can cover up and make it until morning."

Danny peeled out of his snowsuit and boots, and immediately rushed to the blankets, lying down on one and pulling two more over himself.

"You got a flashlight?" Beau asked. "I'm shutting down the generator now to conserve our fuel."

"Flashlight?"

"In case you gotta get up in the night to take a whiz?"

"Young guys like me, we don't need to do that," he said with a chuckle.

Beau shined his own small flashlight toward the ranch hand's face. "Well, just wait. Someday you'll be an *old* guy, like me."

Without the generator, the barn became quiet except for the gentle breathing of the horses. Beau shed his own boots and Levi's and crawled into his set of blankets. The two dogs settled near his legs. The white sky outside sent gentle gray light through the windows, comforting, once their eyes adjusted to it.

"My *abuela* would come up with a Christmas story for this," Danny said. "Us here, spending the night in the manger, you know."

Beau smiled into the darkness. But he would have rather had his warm bed in the house, with Sam snuggled in beside him. Maybe he really was turning into an old guy.

Chapter 31

Kelly poured the last of the wine into Emily's glass. They were on their third holiday rom-com movie and second bottle of wine when the power went out.

"Well, dead TV, and that's a good time for me to run to the little girls room," Emily said.

They'd lit scented candles for ambiance, and decided to watch their shows by the light of those and the tiny lights on the Christmas tree. Now, in near-darkness, Emily picked up a candle and headed down the hall, leaving Kelly with two others. She heard the tree branch scratching the window on the west side of the house again.

Maybe this was a good time to check in with home, see if the electricity was out all over town. Just as she was reaching for her phone, it rang.

"Hey, Mom. You guys sitting in the dark too?"

Sam chuckled and kept her voice low. "We are. We've settled into the kitchen where it's warm and cozy, and Miss Ana just drifted off to sleep. How are you girls doing at Emily's?"

"Good. Our movie just quit, but we'd both seen it anyway. I'm going to check in with Scott and then I guess we'll see how long it takes for the lights to come back on. If they don't, we'll go to bed."

"I'm glad you girls are having—" Sam's voice cut off, and Kelly saw that she'd lost the signal. She tried redialing but the call wouldn't go through.

She tapped Scott's number. Nothing. Something must have happened to one of the town's cell towers.

She wondered whether he finished his manuscript and got it emailed out to his editor. Not that anyone in New York would be working late on Christmas Eve, but she knew he'd really hoped to pass it along so it was off his desk. She smiled. Her husband was so cute. When he was writing he became totally immersed in the story and the words. And when he finished, he couldn't wait to get it out to the publisher and be done with it.

At his book signings, people would ask specific questions about what had happened in one of the novels, and he confessed to Kelly that he rarely remembered his reasons for writing a particular scene in a certain way. She read books to absorb them; Scott apparently wrote them to get on to the next story in the series. His mind was constantly in motion.

"Whew, better," Emily announced, coming back into the living room. "Hey, I was thinking again about the painting—the one my grandfather hid away. It looks so different at times, depending on the room and the lighting.

I wonder what it looks like by candlelight. Wanna take a look?"

"Sure." Kelly hopped up from the pillowy sectional and set her phone and wine glass on the table. "TV's down and phones have no signal. It's good we have something else to do."

Each holding a candle in its glass jar, Emily led the way to her grandfather's old study. She touched a place on the bookcase and it swung outward, revealing a space. The previous time she'd showed the picture to Kelly it was already out, lying on the desk.

"Wow, hidden spaces. I like it," Kelly said.

"Well, you live in a very old house, too. You must have come across a few such spots, along with all the creaks and groans in an old building," Emily said, pulling the painting out.

Actually, aside from the attic, Kelly hadn't gone poking around in the Victorian very much. She wondered if Scott had. She did know their old house had been the inspiration and served as the setting for his children's mystery series.

Emily set the painting on the small ledge of the bookcase, a space between the lower shelves and upper ones.

"Normally, if I want to look at it at night, I turn on this big floor lamp, but since that's not an option right now …" She held her candle closer.

Within the artwork, small golden lights appeared at the little cabin hidden in the snowy forest. Two deer were standing among the trees, their gold-brown coats showing up now. Their faces were turned toward the viewer and their dark eyes stared, questioning.

"I don't remember the animals at all, when I looked at this in daylight. It's as if the yellow candlelight is bringing out completely different aspects of the design."

Kelly stared. She had to agree, the differences were amazing. "How do you suppose the artist accomplished that?"

A voice came from behind her. "JC Freeman was extremely talented."

"Grandma Valerie!" Emily said. "You came on Christmas Eve!"

Kelly felt goosebumps raise on her arms. She whirled around, nearly upsetting one of the candles. The woman in the room with them was nearly as tall as Emily and appeared as any other person would, well, except for the wavy lines around the edges. She wore a long skirt and short-sleeved top, and Kelly's first thought was whether her arms would be cold. But that was silly—she knew she was seeing a spirit, not a real person.

"The hidden objects appear and recede in all his later paintings," Valerie said. "No one ever understood how he accomplished that, and as far as I'm aware no other artist has been able to successfully imitate the technique."

"It's … it's amazing," Kelly said, finding her voice.

Valerie's gaze shot toward the window, where snow had piled on the outside sill.

"Em, you need to close those drapes," she said, urgently.

Emily looked at the whitish sky and falling curtain of huge snowflakes.

"*Now*, my dear."

Emily stepped over and pulled each side of the drapes together in the middle. "Better?"

"Please be cautious, sweetheart, about showing the painting, about bringing it out of hiding."

"Kelly is Sam's daughter. They're the ones helping—"

"They are not the ones you should worry about,"

Valerie said with an indulgent smile toward Kelly. "There are others. Answers will be revealed, but you must be patient."

They all turned toward the painting once more, as if those answers might show themselves now. And when Kelly glanced over her shoulder a moment later, Valerie was gone.

"Whoa, Em. Do you suppose we just had a visit from the ghost of Christmas past?"

Chapter 32

Scott paced his small turret office, elated to have finished his manuscript. When the girls had first decided to stay away for the day, he was happy to have the extra hours to himself to work out his final edits. Now, he was bummed that Kelly and Ana weren't there to share his excitement. They had a little family ritual whenever he finished a book, one that involved champagne for Kelly and himself and a glass of sparkling ginger ale for Ana, followed by a big juicy steak that Scott himself cooked on the grill. None of that was happening tonight, obviously.

He thought, too, of the big unanswered question in their lives. Would Kelly be having a share of the champagne, or would she partake of ginger ale instead? As much as he loved Ana's idea of welcoming a little brother into the household, he also knew a new arrival would mean taking a hiatus from his writing career. And, he already had an idea brewing for the next book in his series, plus two more after that. Homeschooling one child was doable. Adding a second could be a challenge.

But he and Kelly had taken on the challenge of the old house and one child, just as he left his steady teaching career and she discovered many new things involving a strange book, an even stranger wooden box, and things she'd never known about her mother. They could surely slip another little inhabitant into the whole mix. He flopped onto his desk chair, deciding he would be good with it, no matter how the pregnancy test turned out.

For now, all he had to do was attach the manuscript document to the email he'd composed to his editor and hit the Send button. Then the lights went out.

His computer was on auxiliary power; nothing was lost. But with the loss of power, the internet died. He should have set the router up on a battery backup of some kind—he knew he should have. He pounded the desk with his fist. Ouch. *Funny how that never looks like a hand-breaking event when some guy does it in the movies.*

He could always flesh out the plot for the next book; nothing about being in the dark meant his mind wouldn't work. And ideas for new stories were always present. Maybe his protagonist, ten-year-old Maggie Plimpton, would need to solve a mystery on a dark night when the lights went out. He smiled to himself. People wonder where writers get their ideas—sometimes it's as simple as looking at the very thing that's going on in your own life at the moment.

But he didn't want to jump immediately into a new book right now. He'd just finished one. Taking a few days' break, being with his family, enjoying Christmas together—

that's how he wanted this night and tomorrow to unfold. He didn't like his little family being spread out in separate places.

"Okay, Scott Porter, get your act together," he said to the glow of his computer screen.

Eliza, the calico cat, jumped up onto the desk, sat down, and stared directly into his eyes.

"What? I know you have food in your bowl. I filled it right after lunch." But it was now after eight p.m. and maybe she needed water or something. "Okay, I get it."

He closed the lid on his laptop and the room went completely black. *Wow, guess I've been completely wrapped up in work.* He opened the computer again and used the screen's light to find his way across the room. There was a basket of little things on a shelf, alongside his research books. And there he found a small flashlight.

The batteries were dead. Okay. He knew there were batteries in one of the desk drawers. Once he'd located those and replaced the old ones he turned to the cat again.

"All right, let's see what you need."

She led the way downstairs, where Scott realized it was beginning to feel rather chilly. The propane-powered furnace would work without electricity, but the fan that distributed the warm air throughout the house needed it. He would need to figure out something, and he wished he had some idea of how long they would be without power. From experience, he knew all he could do would be to put in a call to the rural electric co-op, leave an automated message, and hope for the best. But his phone showed no bars whatsoever.

He trailed the cat into the kitchen, where both her food and water bowls were filled adequately for her needs. For good measure he picked up a small packet of cat treats and handed her a couple of them. The flashlight created long and jittery shadows on the walls.

"This is a little creepy," he told Eliza. "Let's get some candles going."

Kelly liked the scented ones in jars, so he went around and lit several in the kitchen, dining, and living rooms. He eyed the darkened Christmas tree in the front bay window, with the piles of gifts underneath. He should be tucking Ana in and promising that Santa would bring all kinds of cool stuff by morning. He could set the gifts out tonight and stick with the illusion, but it didn't feel the same at all. A frigid draft moved through the room and flickered the candle flames.

He'd never entirely bought into the idea that the spirit of Eliza Nalespar occupied the house, even though he had wondered if part of his writing inspiration came from the fact that another writer had lived here.

He rubbed his hands together, deciding he could do more good by rechecking all the windows and doors for the source of the draft, and perhaps making sure the pilot light on the old boiler hadn't gone out. Using his flashlight, he proceeded. The calico followed along with his every move.

The basement felt warm and cobwebby. He hadn't been down here since last fall when the weather first began to cool off and he'd lit up the heating system in preparation for winter. Spiders, he had to admit, were industrious and busy little critters. They'd already hung strands across the stairs in a few places and created elaborate webs in the corners of the high window that looked out into the back garden.

He looked at the furnace, shoving away an image from

that old Stephen King story, *The Shining*. He realized he'd rarely been alone in the house since they moved in more than five years ago, and certainly never in the basement in the dark. He could easily let his imagination run wild, but he would not go there.

Kel, I miss you.

And he realized that, after a lot of years as a bachelor living in a small apartment alone and teaching university classes, his life now completely revolved around his cute little wife and daughter. He couldn't imagine life without them.

His thoughts threatened to take a depressing turn, if he let himself imagine something happening to his girls, and he had to talk himself around, reminding himself that they were both in safe places and everyone would be back together tomorrow.

Mrroww!

Scott jumped at the sudden sound. Eliza sat at the top of the basement stairs, calling out, bringing him back to the moment.

"You're right. I probably just need to eat something."

He trudged back up the stairs and closed the basement door behind him. In the kitchen, he prowled through the fridge and came up with some sliced turkey and a block of cheese, which he stacked on a paper napkin and carried with him. At some point he would need to get some sleep, but where—build a fire in the living room fireplace and camp out there, or just crawl in bed with a big pile of blankets? Either place was likely to feel colder and colder as the big old house lost its remaining warmth, but he'd manage.

He stared out the front windows as he scarfed down his puny dinner. The sky was light, the ground covered in mounds of white that were impossible to judge. The snow had to be at least two feet deep.

Mrroww! said Eliza. She ran toward the main staircase and bounded up to the second floor where she called out to him again.

"Okay, I'll play your silly game." What the hell, there was no one else to talk to.

He touched the carved banister as he climbed the carpeted steps. By the time he reached the second floor hallway, the cat was on her way to the third. *Okay, why not?* He followed.

He found the cat sitting in front of the locked door to the attic.

"What do you want? Kelly's not there." He thought of the number of times he'd come up to find his wife reading or organizing shelves in here while the cat napped in the sunshine on the window seat. "You won't like your usual bed. It's not sunny in there right now."

Mrroww ...

"Okay, fine. I'll show you." He touched the top of the door frame and found the key for the attic.

When he opened the door, the room felt curiously warm, nearly comfortable. It had to be because this was the highest point in the house. Maybe there had been enough sunshine early in the day to warm the room and the heat just hadn't dissipated yet.

Eliza dashed in and leaped easily to the table top. A leather-bound book lay there, and the cat touched the cover with her paw.

"What? You're not pulling Ana's trick, asking me to read you a bedtime story, are you?"

Mrroww.

He lifted the cover and looked at the first page. The

title page was written in some kind of ancient-looking script, obviously in another language. And, oddly, all the other pages seemed to be in some strange combination of runes, cuneiform, or something. This must be the source document for the copies Kelly had once showed him and asked a university colleague of his to translate.

The cat watched as he flipped a few pages, seemingly interested.

"Makes no sense to me," Scott said, closing the book.

The cat had stuck a paw into one of the pages as he went by it. He reopened the book to that spot but couldn't see any reason for her interest. It was most likely the same as when he was working and she wanted his attention— she would lie down over an open book or try to drape herself over his keyboard.

"Okay, we're done. We can't disturb Kelly's stuff." He shooed the cat out of the attic and relocked the door.

Bored with navigating around the house by flashlight, he went back downstairs and gathered the candles he'd lit earlier. The jars were warm, and anything warm felt pretty good at this point. He would light them again in his small office in the turret, grab some comforters and quilts from the bed, and bunk on the small sofa in there. At least the small space wouldn't feel as lonely as the big bed without Kelly beside him.

His last picture, as he was drifting off to sleep, was of the Morton Library. It had been the site of much of Scott's research for his first book, and he had fond memories of Emily's grandparents and the wealth of information the family had collected over the generations. He hoped Kelly was sleeping well there.

Chapter 33

Christmas morning. Sam stirred and tried not to wake Ana with the groan that escaped her. Sleeping on a concrete floor in a sleeping bag wasn't nearly as much fun when you were nearing sixty. She inched her way out of the bag and tucked the warm fabric around the child.

In the bathroom she put on her warm pants and heavy coat. As she washed her face in icy cold water, she thought of the dream that had filled the night. She was at a party of some kind, in a big house, which she realized partway through the sequence was the Crawford house in its glory days. The crowd consisted of the people Sam had talked to about the fire and the missing painting—Phil Crawford, Camilla, Maurice Finstadt, Ben Martinez, Susan O'Malley and Bearcat Sowlow—plus some whose identities were vague. The fire chief, Arnold Brown, was there, and oddly,

Valerie and David Plankhurst.

In that surreal way dreams will do, Sam was in the crowd and yet seemingly invisible. She listened to people's conversations but they didn't interact directly with her. Camilla played the perfect hostess, moving among the guests and chatting with each, including those who would later interrogate the couple and the others. Sam could hear their words and their laughter, but none of it made a lot of sense to her. She tried to ask questions but, again, it seemed she was invisible to the others. She'd awakened with the frustrating feeling that she wanted to shout "look at me, listen to me" but even when she did in the dream, no one noticed.

Now, sitting on the toilet, she decided there was probably some psychology to that—the human desire to be heard—but for the moment she needed to figure out what to do next, in the real world.

She walked out into the kitchen and realized, for the first time, that Bobul's possessions were nowhere to be seen. Aware of the still-sleeping Ana, she whispered his name. Out in the salesroom, the same. No sign of him. Her heart began to pound.

Surely, he hadn't gone out into the storm. Her thoughts flew frantically around the possibilities. No one could wander about in this stuff, no one could travel any distance at all. She ran to the front windows.

The snow had stopped during the night, leaving nearly three feet of white fluff, as if all the confectioner's sugar in the world had sifted down upon them. Above, the sky was brilliant blue, and sunlight sparkled off every facet of every snowflake, leaving a zillion diamonds sparkling in the light. In front of the bakery, the snow seemed undisturbed, without a sign of a track. Bobul had not gone out this way.

She rushed through the kitchen and opened the back door. The silence outside was absolute. It covered Sam like a soft blanket, and she realized how few times in her life there'd been no residual background noise, no vehicles in the distance, no birdsong or human voices. At her feet, the snow sat in lesser depth than elsewhere, the result of what she had swept away and the places she and Bobul had walked last night. But there were no fresh tracks on top of the blunted edges.

He must have walked out in the middle of the storm, leaving the snow to cover his tracks. And if he'd been outside that many hours he was in grave danger.

I have to find him.

She found the snow shovel—where it had been all along, in the supply closet—and began scooping the powder away in a path toward her car. Ten minutes later, she realized what a hopeless task it was. She could walk to the car's door, but there was no way her vehicle, with snow more than halfway to its hood, would get out until the road department plows came. She stared down the alley. There was a slight indentation in the blank white slate, but no definitive sign that a person had pushed through there recently.

She went back inside and shed her Sorels at the door. Her cell phone still had no bars, and she remembered thinking the cell towers must have been damaged. She picked up the bakery's landline phone and got a dial tone.

The sheriff's department number answered with a recording. "If this is a medical emergency dial 911, but please be aware that emergency vehicles are unable to reach many areas. The highway department and town of Taos road department have dispatched all available snowplows and will be clearing streets as quickly as possible. Please bear with us during this difficult time, and please stay indoors."

Sam pressed the 0 on the phone, with little hope it would connect her to a human being. It didn't. But there was a 'leave a message' tone, so she did. She spoke as a deputy would, saying she wanted to file a BOLO on a missing person. She described Bobul and his clothing as accurately as she could, stated where he had been last seen, and that it was likely he was out in the open somewhere.

Next, she repeated the same message at the police department. She hung up the phone, feeling discouraged but knowing she had done what she could. Maybe as the plows got out, someone would spot him and get him to a warm place. She felt sad to think that the old man, who she thought of as a friend, might come to a bad end and last night might have been the final time she would see him. She turned on the radio, hoping for news.

Ana was stirring in the sleeping bag, waking with a smile on her freckled face. "It's Christmas, isn't it?"

Sam nodded. "And I'm going to figure out a great breakfast for us."

Ana sat up, holding the warm fabric around her shoulders. "Where's Bobul?"

Sam pasted her best smile on her face. "I guess he went on to the next place he needed to visit."

The child looked skeptical. "Out in the snow? How?"

"I think Bobul knows some magic," Sam said, realizing she believed it.

Chapter 34

The first outside sound came around noon, the sound of a large vehicle moving slowly. The plows were out, although they sounded several blocks away at this point. After making pancakes with blueberries for breakfast, Sam had gone out the front door of her shop and continued making what little headway she could with the shovel. She'd cleared the sidewalk in front of the door—at least melting snow wouldn't come in under it now—and part of the way across the shop front.

For the first time, she noticed a parked vehicle in front of the bookshop next door, a mounded lump she was fairly sure belonged to Ivan Petrenko, the owner. She trudged over the high snow to the front windows, peering in to see if he was all right. He was sitting in one of the wingback chairs, a blanket around his shoulders and a book on his lap. Well, if there was any better place to be stranded than a bakery, it had to be a bookshop, she supposed.

Ivan spotted her and came to the front door, which opened inward. His overhead awning had minimized the snow directly in front of the door. He stood there staring at it.

"Have you had anything to eat?" Sam asked. "I can bring you something."

"*Da*, Ivan is a survivor." He gestured toward the small display of cookies and chewing gum he sold near the front counter.

"You can't live on that stuff. Let me go back and cook you some eggs or something."

He smiled, his wrinkled face lighting up. "Is no problem. Had burrito—what you say, left over?—in small fridge. Cold, is not the best, but is filling." He patted his stomach.

"If you're sure …"

"Getting ready now to take walk," he said. He bent and picked up a pair of snowshoes that were leaning against the wall near his window display.

"You keep snowshoes at your shop?"

He gave a one-shoulder shrug. "Plan was to meet friends and hike in forest today. So, no way to get up mountain, but I can walk here, in neighborhood."

From deep in her coat pocket, Sam heard her phone's ringtone. She jumped. "Cell service!"

She pulled off her thick glove and reached down into the pocket for it.

"Kelly! You got through. Are you girls enjoying a leisurely morning?"

"Oh, Mom, something awful's happened."

"Oh my gosh, you're not hurt are you? Is it Emily?"

"We're both fine. We were shoveling a path between the house and the library, and there's … there's a woman out there. We're not sure if she's alive."

"Did you call 911?"

"They took the call but say they can't promise when they'll be able to get a vehicle in here. And the helicopter has to come all the way from Albuquerque and they have a lot of calls …"

Sam looked at Ivan and eyed the snowshoes. "Is it hard to walk with those things?"

"*Nyet*. Very simple."

"Kel, get the woman inside, as warm a place as you can find for her, then see if you girls can rig up a sled of some kind. I'm on my way."

She ran back to Sweet's Sweets, gathered Ana and a bakery box, and told her she was going to get a real Christmas treat—spending the afternoon in the bookshop, having cupcakes with Ivan.

"Why was Mommy scared?"

"What?"

"On the phone a minute ago at the bookshop. She was worried."

This kid. It wasn't the first time Ana had known when someone would call and intuited what they were about to say.

"It'll be fine. She just needs my help with something over at Emily's house."

Five minutes later, she was getting a quick lesson in how to strap on the snowshoes.

It took a half block or so to get the knack of walking with her feet wide apart. Once she could keep her balance reasonably well, she made good progress covering the few blocks to the Morton Library. She kept to the middle of the streets, where the snow was smooth and level, bypassing the large lumps that covered parked vehicles.

"I wasn't sure what you meant by a sled," Emily said, "so I put the word out to Grandma Valerie for help. She directed me to look in the storage shed behind the house. And look!"

It was an actual sled, one of the molded plastic ones kids could flop onto and slide down a hill.

"I used to play on this thing, and I'd forgotten all about it," Emily said.

"The tow rope doesn't look too great," Sam said, looking around and not finding anything better. "Where's the woman you found?"

"Kelly's with her in the kitchen." Emily seemed distressed. "I'm not even sure she's alive. We couldn't find a pulse and we can't tell if she's breathing."

"I once had an EMT tell me about hypothermia—'they're not dead until they're warm and dead.' She said she had seen some amazing recoveries."

They walked into the house where an inert form lay on the floor. Kelly had lit the oven and opened its door to spread warmth to the room, and she had wrapped several blankets around the victim. Sam dragged the sled through the doorway.

"Let's get her on here." Then she looked at the unconscious woman's face. It was Camilla Crawford.

Her face and hands had a pale blue-gray tinge. Instinctively, Sam pulled off her gloves and reached for the unconscious woman. Could her healing touch work now? But there was no reaction from Camilla. Sam hadn't handled the wooden box recently, so she wasn't surprised.

She sat back on her heels, her thoughts going in a hundred directions. What, how, *why* would Camilla be here?

"Kel, see if you can get through to 911 again. Find out what's the nearest intersection they've cleared enough for an ambulance to get to. Tell them the situation and that I'll meet them there. Em, let's get her on the sled and tied securely in place. I have no idea how steady a driver I'll be."

"I have cross-country skis. I'll come along to help," Emily said, bending to help Sam pull Camilla's inert body onto the bright orange sled.

By the time they'd found rope and figured out a way to secure the body to the sled, Kelly was at the back door. "They say Paseo del Pueblo Sur has a lane clear from the plaza to the hospital. They're working on Camino de la Placita now."

Sam draped the pull-rope around her middle, the sled behind her now, and took some tentative steps. The rig seemed to work all right. Emily had brought out her skis and poles and proceeded to step into the bindings.

"I'll ski along beside the sled and give it a little help if it starts to tip."

"We'll head for the intersection nearest the bakery," Sam told Kelly. She hoped the plows would have cleared la Placita to that point by the time they arrived. "Keep in touch with the 911 operator, if you can, and tell them we'll be watching for the ambulance."

It was much slower going, pulling the sled, and Sam had to adjust her grip on the tow rope several times. The flat street posed little problem, but everywhere the snow had drifted the sled tried to tip. Emily used her ski poles to give little nudges to the plastic conveyance to keep it as level as possible.

Two blocks from the library, Sam spotted a black BMW at what must have been the curb. It must have sat there since early the previous evening while vehicles could still move on the roads. The only thing that made sense was that Camilla, obsessed now with *The Ghost of Christmas*, had thought she could get into Emily's house and find it. Sam mentioned that to Emily.

"You think she was actually trying to break in? I mean, Kelly and I heard noises but there *is* that old elm tree with the branches that touch a couple of the windows. We just thought … Who is this woman, and why would she be after the painting?"

Sam had a hard enough time trudging along with the weight of the sled behind her, so she told Emily she would explain later. But her mind was racing. Last night's dream. There had to be clues in that silly party scene and the conversations she had overheard.

Chapter 35

Sam could tell by the EMT's expression that he didn't hold high hopes for Camilla's survival. He looked at her perfectly manicured nails, on fingers frozen white with frostbite.

"She's gonna lose some of those," he commented, almost under his breath. He peeled back the fuzzy purple coat and began cutting away the blouse and jeans, laying a heated blanket over Camilla.

"Did she actually think that fake fur would keep her warm in this weather? And those boots—fashionable, I suppose, but completely inadequate."

"I have no idea," Sam said. "I met the woman a couple of times, and all I can tell you is her name."

She watched while the driver wrote it down, along with Phil Crawford's and the names of the friends Camilla had claimed she was staying with. Sam and Emily watched the emergency vehicle pull away with lights flashing.

"Seriously? She was staying with these super celebrity types and no one called to report her missing?" Emily seemed shocked.

"Sad, huh. She and Phil never had children and she never remarried after their divorce. I have no idea if she has other family. I guess we can only leave it to the authorities to see if there are connections."

They turned back in the direction of the bakery.

Ana saw them coming and opened the bookshop door, shouting out, "Grammy, I want to play in the snow!"

"Maybe later, honey." Sam couldn't let go of the image of Camilla's near-frozen body. It might be a long time before she could think of snow in terms of fun again.

"You should come back to my place," Emily said. "We'll stoke up the fire and get plenty of warm clothes, and she can play in the snow there." She glanced up at Ivan, who was standing behind Ana in the open doorway, and included him in the invitation.

"So many women … no, *spasibo*, I will be to staying in my shop. Samantha, you keeping the snowshoes longer."

Sam laughed. He was right. Ivan would feel a little overwhelmed among all the females. She thanked him for the use of the snowshoes and said she would figure out how to get them back to him soon. She unstrapped them long enough to go into the bakery, check things, turn off the oven, and gather supplies they could use at Emily's. A few minutes later, they set off toward the library—Sam once again towing the sled, this time loaded with everything from her emergency kit, a box of food, and Ana. The four-year-old shrieked with delight every time they hit a bump.

Kelly was standing at the kitchen window when the others slid into the side yard and stopped near the back door.

"Did everything go okay?"

Sam relayed the fact that Camilla was now in the hands of medical personnel. "The bakery is closed up tight, and Em has been kind enough to invite us all to stay."

"As long as it takes to clear the roads," Emily said.

Ana shrieked with joy and Kelly gave her friend a look that said *I hope you don't regret that offer.*

While the girls chose bedrooms and Emily added extra logs to the fire, Sam checked her phone, thankful she'd remembered to include the charger she kept at the bakery. She received a weak signal, one bar. It was worth a shot, so she tapped Beau's number.

His voice came through, broken up by static. "Got … to house … charger." The signal cleared a little. "… and got both Danny's and my phones working again. You girls doing okay?"

She assured him they were fine and told him where they were. "We want to get home as soon as we can."

"Didn't catch … another day or two … county road … plows … They'll clear from the middle of town and move outward. The ranches will likely be last on the list. But I'm calling Joe." The static-then-clearing cycle of the conversation was frustrating.

Sam got enough to figure out that the big plows would handle the main roads, smaller county plows would get the country roads and, finally, the ranchers would use their own resources or call in those intrepid folks with snowplows attached to their pickup trucks to get their driveways open. Joe was the go-to guy for their area and he was familiar with their property. In reality, it would take several days to get around to everyone.

In the end, she could only tell him she loved him, and he told her to be careful. They would see each other when they could. Kelly and Ana came into the kitchen just as Sam was putting her phone down. She reported what Beau had said about the roads.

Ana was squirming at Kelly's side.

"Okay, okay. You can play outside, just here where I can watch you from the window." Kelly opened the back door and Ana dove for the deepest area where the snow had been shoveled away from the narrow path.

"She's going to be soaked in ten minutes, but we simply don't have any of her snow gear with us. I'll keep an eye, and when she comes in I'll strip her down and put this on her." She held up one of Emily's flannel nightgowns. "She can bundle up in front of the fire until her clothes dry."

"And by then she'll want to go out again," Sam said with a knowing look.

"You got it."

Emily walked into the kitchen and offered to heat soup for lunch. "I got on a real cooking binge last week, and I put a lot of it in the freezer."

She pulled out the frozen soup and a saucepan and lit a burner on the stove, while Sam stared out the window at Ana, whose snow angels were practically standing upright on the high snowbank. Then, all at once, the lights flickered a couple of times and stayed on.

"Yay!" Kelly shouted.

It was amazing how the silent house suddenly came to life with small sounds—the refrigerator, a beep from the microwave, even the light fixtures seemed to hum slightly.

A radio on the windowsill, pure 1960s vintage that must have belonged to Valerie and David, came on.

"Guess I'd better go around and see what else was left on when everything went dark last night," Emily said.

She reached for the radio dial but Sam stopped her. "Maybe they'll have updates on storm damage and road conditions." She was thinking of Bobul.

Emily turned the volume up slightly and headed for the living room.

The broadcast began with an update on the latest in road openings, then went on to say that all area churches had cancelled Christmas Eve and Christmas Day services, as if people hadn't already figured that out.

"In other news, police have now identified the body of the man who seemingly jumped from the Rio Grande Gorge Bridge last night. As reported earlier, it was only by luck that one of the county plows was on the bridge and the driver spotted the lone man at the moment he went over the railing. This morning, search and recovery teams helicoptered down into the gorge and discovered his body in the water. The victim was brought out and identified as Bearcat Sowlow of El Prado. Taos County Sheriff's Department deputies have notified the man's next of kin."

Chapter 36

Sam stared into the fire, a coffee mug in hand. She should be feeling relaxed and rested. The holiday rush at the bakery was over, her entire family and all her employees had survived the storm and were safe and warm. But the enforced confinement was beginning to wear her down. Aside from her concern about Bobul, she felt antsy to clear David Plankhurst's name in the theft of the painting. Camilla's condition was still unknown, the hospital personnel wouldn't tell her anything over the phone, and Bearcat Sowlow's suicide weighed heavily. Had Sam said something during their brief visit that had prompted the young man's drastic action?

A large vehicle roared by on the street outside. That was another thing—the awesome silence of two days ago had been replaced by the noise of snowplows and road crew vehicles, day and night. She couldn't complain about it—there were still many neighborhoods where people were stranded and, according to the radio, a few of the more remote places where electricity had not yet been restored.

All in all, Sam knew she was lucky to be where she was. She got up and carried her empty mug to the kitchen. Emily, bless her, had gone to great lengths to accommodate the unexpected guests in her home. She'd pulled out board games and even found some children's books from her own childhood visits here. But boredom was setting in, for all of them.

She put on her coat and walked out toward the front of the property, verifying what she thought she'd heard. The plow had, indeed, cleared the street in front of the library. A path to freedom! The only problem was, her car most likely was still under a mound of snow in the alley behind Sweet's Sweets. Still, she could check it out.

Back inside, she phoned Ivan at the bookshop. There was no answer on the landline, so she found his cell number and called.

"Yes, *da*—little road now clear. Bookshop no more—I am being at my home."

Sam took 'little road' to mean the alley, so she put on her boots and told Kelly her plan. She walked the few blocks to the bakery, where she cleared her car and prayed it would start. Considering the temperature had dropped below zero the past two nights, the hybrid vehicle answered her prayers. Letting the car warm up for a while, she stowed her shovel and broom, made sure the water lines at the bakery hadn't frozen, and got ready to leave.

Her strongest urge was to head for the ranch, to see where she might be of help to Beau and Danny, but she had already spoken with her husband by phone, and he confirmed her fear. She wouldn't be able to drive through. Stay in town, he advised.

There were a couple of things weighing on her mind, so she headed toward the hospital. Life was beginning to return to normal in the middle of town. Private plows had cleared about half of the Walmart parking lot, for instance. The snow they had removed sat in gigantic piles that covered the remainder of the property. Some intrepid souls were there—probably hoping the much-hyped post Christmas sales were still happening. Sam cruised on by.

The hospital entrance and parking lot were in better shape than most; emergency services had clearly received priority. Sam pulled into the visitor lot and parked, then made her way inside. At reception, she was informed that Camilla Crawford could receive no visitors. Her condition was listed as critical, but the person at the desk could not give details.

"I'm worried about a friend who was outdoors the night of the storm," Sam said. She gave Bobul's name and description. "He mostly likely wouldn't be carrying any identification. Can you tell me if he was brought in?"

The desk woman called to the ER and relayed Sam's question. When she hung up the phone, she shook her head. "No one."

Sam left, holding fast to the hope that Bobul had stayed safe. The man was a mystery—somewhat ungainly, yet an incredible artist with small details; awkward with English, perhaps uneducated, but by no means stupid. She remembered the tiny cabin in the canyon where Highway 64 headed eastward. Bobul had been living there the first winter he appeared at the bakery, and he'd somehow traveled there daily. After he disappeared that year, she'd stopped by the place and found it utterly abandoned, as if unoccupied for decades.

So Bobul *did* know how to adapt and survive. And that was the best she could hope for now.

She sighed and started the car again. She'd noticed a few items Emily's kitchen was running low on—bread, cereal, and milk. She could stop by the supermarket while she was out.

This was a crazy idea, Sam realized the moment she set foot in the store. People were lined up with carts wall-to-wall, many of them bulging with the strangest combinations of items. She spotted one customer with four 12-packs of toilet paper; another had an entire cart filled with peanut butter and at least fifteen loaves of bread. Hadn't these people just purchased enough Christmas dinner items to feed themselves for a week? And that was only three days ago?

She went to the bread aisle but felt guilty about taking the last loaf. She left it there, instead moving to the soups and picking up a Bear Creek mix for chicken and corn chowder. She thought of the ham and potatoes and everything Kelly had on hand for their own holiday dinner, all of it sitting in the Victorian and completely inaccessible. But that would hopefully be for only another day or two. She escaped the store and decided to get away from the main drag, if possible.

Civic Plaza Drive would take her to Camino de la Placita and then to Emily's street. She automatically slowed down as she approached the offices of the sheriff's department. How many times had she pulled in here, either to surprise Beau or to help him with a case? Her eyes automatically went to the walled employee parking lot. Evan Richards, the young former deputy who had taken over Beau's position, was standing near his cruiser, a newspaper tucked under his arm, looking down at the phone in his hand.

Sam wheeled over to the driveway and tap-tapped her horn. She had her passenger window powered down when he glanced up.

"Hey, Sam. I've been meaning to check up on you guys. Everything okay at the ranch?"

"Long story, in which I got stuck in town and Beau at the ranch, but yeah, we're fine. Although I know Beau will be relieved when the county plows get out that way. You know him—antsy."

Evan smiled. "He wants you home 'cause he prefers your cooking to his own."

"Maybe something like that."

He offered Sam the newspaper, dropping it onto her passenger seat, and turned his attention to his phone, swiping and tapping at something. "You're just off BA39, right?"

At her nod he tapped some more. "Okay, you're on the list. They'll put a priority on it."

"Evan, wow. You didn't have to do that. Really, I didn't come by to ask for special treatment."

"I know you didn't. But you and Beau have always been good to me and Riki. And this wasn't a huge favor. Your road would have been plowed by tomorrow anyway. I just moved it a touch up the list."

"Thank you. Sincerely, thank you." Sam stretched out a gloved hand and tapped knuckles with the sheriff. "Hey, there was something I did want to ask. The man who jumped from the bridge the other night."

Evan's smile dropped. "Yeah, sad. Had to be a scary way to go. We found some relatives, but no one around here. When things open up again, we need to get his body sent to a sister who lives in Texas, I guess."

"I met him. I went to his trailer out toward the airport and questioned him in connection with that old case I asked you about a couple weeks ago, the fire at Phillip Crawford's house. Turns out this Bearcat Sowlow is the one who started the fire."

"No kidding."

An official vehicle had pulled up behind Sam, a deputy wanting to enter the parking lot. Evan stepped back and waved her in, then came over and sat in her passenger seat after she parked.

"This fire, he admitted to you that he did it?"

"Actually, yes. He said someone paid him—an envelope of cash and a note with instructions left in the mailbox. He was a kid, barely fifteen. Obviously didn't think through the consequences."

Evan was staring out the windshield, focusing on nothing in particular. "Because this may just explain the suicide note we found at his trailer."

"What did the note say?" Sam held her breath. She'd had dreams and guilt pangs over Bearcat. Had she said something that prompted him to take his life?

"Just a few simple words. 'I lied. It was the owner.' We had no idea what it meant."

Sam's breath whooshed out. Was the arsonist saying the homeowner was the one who paid him? Because that would turn Phil Crawford's testimony upside down, along with everything she assumed about how a billionaire wouldn't be concerned about the few thousand the painting was worth.

Evan's phone vibrated and he glanced at it. "Gotta go.

Hey, thanks for that tip about the suicide victim."

Sam nodded distractedly. "I can add one other thing. The wife of the owner—well, according to her, she's the owner of that house now—she's been in town. In fact she got caught out in the storm and is in the hospital right now."

"Name?"

"Camilla Crawford. And, Evan? If you decide to go there and question her about that note, could I come along?"

"Of course. Not sure when I'll get out there. We're up to our necks, so to speak, in this whole winter storm thing." He held up his phone and got out of the car. "I'll give you a call."

Chapter 37

"Well, soup for dinner doesn't sound like much," Sam said when she unloaded her small grocery bag at Emily's. "I tell you, the store was crazy. But I feel badly that we've eaten up so much of your food, all the things you bought for your parents' visit."

"It's not looking like they'll make it up here this winter at all. My dad got in a fender-bender in Albuquerque because of the few inches of snow they got there ... Now he's saying he won't ever again drive in snow."

"Give him some time. Maybe he'll change his mind," Kelly said. "Meanwhile, you're coming to our place to join us for Christmas dinner, whenever we can actually get everyone there."

Emily stirred water into the soup mix Sam had brought and began to cut up some chicken to add to it. And Sam filled them in on the good news from Evan, that the road to the ranch should be cleared soon.

"Of course, I'm calling Beau before I head out there, to be sure we can get to the front door."

"Meanwhile, we'll have a good hot lunch, and there will be plenty left over for dinner or for tomorrow." Emily set the flame under the pot and wiped her hands on a towel.

"Do you mind if I take a look around outside?" Sam asked. "I've been thinking about what you girls were telling me on Christmas Eve."

"Thirty minutes for the soup to simmer … that's your only deadline."

If Sam was going to get a chance to talk to Camilla alongside the sheriff, she wanted to have a few more bits of evidence first. She put on Ivan's snowshoes again and started around toward the west side of the house. The sun had formed a crust on top of the snow, and her snowshoes broke through, giving her an awkward gait as they settled a couple of inches below the surface.

Rabbit tracks crisscrossed everywhere, the little critters lightweight enough to hop across the top of the snowbanks, and she saw what were probably either dog or coyote prints where the snow was thinner under the trees. And then she spotted something more—an indentation made by something larger.

She studied the pattern that trailed from the street, followed the western wall of the library, and came across the open space between the two structures. There was nothing as defined as a footprint; this was more like a channel made by someone pushing through snow that was above their knees. But there was more snow on top, and the pattern had become blurred and softened until she couldn't say for certain what had created it.

Out of curiosity she began to walk alongside the indented area. After meandering across the few yards of open space, the trail kept close to the house. It appeared wider near each window in Emily's home. If this was made by a person, they'd paused to look in the windows. At the third one, Sam peered in. It was the study where David Plankhurst had hidden *The Ghost of Christmas* inside the secret niche.

Now, of course, the painting was nowhere in sight, but Sam imagined what Kelly had told her, that she and Emily had brought the painting out two nights ago and stood in this room to admire it. Someone—and Sam knew deep inside that it was Camilla—had quite possibly watched them. Maybe she'd even tried to find a way inside the house during the storm?

Had Camilla seen Emily remove the artwork from its hidden niche? If so, she would know exactly where to look and how to get to it, once she was able. *If* she was able. Another good reason for Sam to know the woman's condition.

Down in her coat pocket, Sam's phone began to ring but with her heavy gloves on she couldn't reach for it. Oh well, it was time to get back inside anyway.

She parked the snowshoes outside the kitchen door and stomped the residual snow off her boots. Indoors, she removed her coat and retrieved the phone. The call had come from Beau. She listened to his voicemail message: "Good news. County opened 39 and I've got Joe on the way over to clear our drive. I'll call again when it's safe to come through. Can't wait to have you home."

She heard the longing in his voice, and her throat tightened. She couldn't wait to be home again too.

The newspaper Evan had given her was lying on the kitchen counter. Sam picked it up and scanned the front page, which mainly consisted of continuing news about the aftermath of the storm. Below the fold was a photo op type shot of the three candidates who had officially announced for the mayor's race. Ben Martinez stood next to the incumbent, and the opposing party candidate was on the opposite side. All three wore wide smiles. Sam started to read the story but her eye was drawn back to the photo.

In the background, behind the stars of the show, stood a large man dressed in drab colors, wearing a floppy knitted hat and a scarf around his neck. He looked directly toward the camera and had raised the fingers of his right hand to touch the edge of the hat. It was Bobul's way of letting Sam know he had survived the storm all right.

She felt emotion rise in her throat. Thank goodness!

Ana walked up beside her and spotted the photo immediately. Without a word she reached out and took Sam's hand in her own.

* * *

It was a little after three o'clock when Sam got the next call from Beau. She steered between the stone pillars at the entry to the ranch and made her way down the long driveway. In the back seat Ana stared out the windows, her mouth hanging open.

"It's higher than the car," she whispered.

Kelly seemed awestruck, as well. "I've never seen snow like this in my life."

It seemed the weather forecasters had got it right—this was the largest snowfall on record for the northern mountains. The snow thrown aside by the plows had created great hills, and it almost felt as though the car was driving through halls and rooms carved out of it.

Beau was standing on the covered porch. She could see that he'd shoveled the steps and carved out some pathways.

"You girls get settled in the guest room," Sam said as they unloaded their few belongings.

"I'm glad we were able to get out of Emily's hair," Kelly said, "but I really need to do some laundry. Both of us have been in the same clothes for four days now."

Sam echoed the sentiment. Borrowed pajamas had gotten them through, but it would feel so good to put on something different. Beau reached out and pulled Sam into a fierce hug the moment they were alone.

"Missed you," he murmured into her hair.

"Missed you more." She felt a hundred little details tugging for her attention, but right now she was content to stay in his arms.

Chapter 38

Scott called that evening. Ana was eyeing the wrapped presents under the grandparents' Christmas tree while Kelly and Sam folded laundry.

"We're on the list to get our driveway cleared in the morning," he told her.

"So excited. How have you and Eliza been getting along?"

"No problems, although as soon as I can get out, I'll need to make a cat food run to the store."

"I could do that—but no. My car is still sitting at the library. Guess I need to figure out how to get it back."

Scott was quiet for a few seconds. "I'll take care of it. It might not start right away."

"You're sure?"

"What else does a lady have a knight in shining armor for?"

"You're the best. And you shall receive an appropriate reward when I get home." Kelly blushed when she realized Sam, Beau and Ana were nearby. They talked about a couple of logistical items for the big family dinner before they ended the call.

To distract her daughter, Kelly agreed to let her open one gift, as long as she saved the rest for their belated Christmas celebration.

Sam's phone was buzzing too. She'd already checked in with Jen and Becky. Now she made sure Julio had a way to get to Sweet's Sweets in the morning, a ride that didn't involve bringing his Harley out on the slushy roads. It seemed the bakery would be set to reopen.

By morning, Sam was contentedly sipping her first cup of coffee as she stared out at the ranchland beyond the back windows. The sun had now been out for three days and, although the nights still got quite cold, the snow was visibly shrinking a bit each day. Kelly joined her, a steaming mug of her own in hand.

"Will it be weird to celebrate Christmas on New Year's Eve instead?" she asked. "I'm just thinking I need another couple days to get the house ready. I have no idea whether Scott kept things somewhat clean or not. All he's talked about is how much writing he got done."

"I think New Year's Eve is perfect. Two holidays for the work of one."

"Emily agreed to come, and I think we've got Riki and Evan lined up although Riki swears she's not going to eat a thing. Snowbound in the house, she says they've nearly gone through a pantry full of food. So, we're thinking just the family in the morning, and we'll open gifts and do a few brunchy foods, then the big meal in the early afternoon, then everyone slips into a big-meal coma in the evening."

"After they've gone home."

"Yes, I'm feeling the need to get Ana back into a normal routine."

"Kel ... what about the ..."

"Pregnancy test? Didn't have to do it—period came. I haven't told Scott yet. He won't be disappointed, but I figured it's news to deliver when we're together."

"Ana really is his whole world, isn't she?"

Kelly nodded. "We love the little family we have."

Small feet came charging into the living room. "Ana is what?"

"Ana is the princess of the Porter household," Kelly said, setting down her coffee and pulling her daughter into a hug. "And Princess Ana gets to see her daddy today. He'll call as soon as the driveway's done."

It was nearly noon when they heard the sound of a vehicle outside and looked out the front windows to see Kelly's car arriving, Scott at the wheel.

"Snowplow guy gave me a ride over to the library," he said. His grin spread across his face. "Got cat food, got groceries, and now I've got my girls."

Sam's phone rang as she was waving goodbye. It was Evan.

"I'm heading over to the hospital to talk to Camilla Crawford, and I'd promised you a call."

"I'll meet you there."

She found Evan standing outside the private room Camilla had been moved to, after her initial stint in the ICU.

"Nurse's doing something so she made me wait," he said.

"I wonder if Ben Martinez also plans to question her. The case was initially his department's."

"Doesn't look like it. I told him about the note we found, but he says the statute of limitations on the arson has run out. Six years."

"But the note is new evidence. Can't he reopen it?"

"Maybe, but the arsonist is dead. I suppose, technically, the insurance company could file a civil case and try to recoup what they paid on the house claim. But again, the statute of limitations and the fact that everyone has moved on … most likely it wouldn't go anywhere."

"What do you think?" Sam asked.

"A man died during the commission of the felony arson. No limitation on prosecuting that. I'd probably go for it—if it was in my jurisdiction." He unzipped his jacket in the warm corridor. "But the note is a little ambiguous. Saying 'the owner' isn't proof of much. If he'd stated a name … different story. It would be hard to prosecute."

"So you're going to see if Camilla will name Phil?"

He was interrupted when the door opened and a young nurse stepped out, giving them the go-ahead for the visit.

The room held three huge flower bouquets and a "Get Well Soon" mylar balloon. Camilla was sitting up in bed, wearing a peach-colored peignoir, her hair freshly styled and her makeup in place, including the thick false eyelashes she always wore. The only sign of her ordeal was her heavily bandaged hands, which she quickly tucked under the blanket. She smiled at Sam and eyed the handsome sheriff. Sam performed the introductions.

"Sheriff Richards wants to ask you a few questions, and then I have some of my own."

Sam could tell Evan wished she had told him about this out in the hallway, but he turned his attention to Camilla. When he told her about the death of Bearcat Sowlow, she attempted to furrow her brow, although her Botoxed muscles didn't move much.

"I don't believe I know that person," she said sweetly, "but I'm sorry to hear he died."

"Before he killed himself, Sowlow confessed to being the person who set fire to your house. Are you certain you never had contact with him?"

Camilla had been hanging around actors long enough that she managed a credible imitation of a person hearing shocking news for the first time.

"No, Sheriff. Never. Did this Mr. So—Sow, whoever, say that he knew me?"

Sam remained quiet, knowing Evan was trying to learn more about Sowlow's suicide note.

"So you don't believe your husband—sorry, ex-husband—could have done something like that?"

Camilla's eyes shifted. "What would happen to Phil if he did do it?"

"A death that happens in the commission of a felony is considered murder. Even all these years later, the perpetrator could be tried and convicted."

Her face took on a greedy glint. "And if Phil went to prison for something he did while we were married, would that overturn the divorce settlement and give me what was rightfully mine instead of the tiny portion I received?"

Sam could see where this was going. Camilla was desperate enough to sell out her ex in a nano-second if she thought it would set her up financially.

Evan kept a straight face. "I'm not familiar with divorce law, ma'am."

He took a couple of steps back, yielding the floor to Sam.

"Camilla, there was a painting, *The Ghost of Christmas*. You mentioned that to me before and said the owner of the Finstadt Gallery had an interest in it."

"Yes, I believe he does—I mean, he did back then. He sold it to us."

"Mr. Finstadt believes the painting somehow survived the fire, and if it should turn up after all these years it would be worth quite a lot more than it was at the time."

"Well, I suppose that would be the case. Everything costs more now, doesn't it?" Camilla fiddled with her blanket, quickly tucking her bandaged hands back under it.

Sam hoped Evan was paying attention to the subtext here.

"Camilla, you're in the hospital right now because you were found outside during the blizzard. You were next to the Morton Library. What were you doing there?"

"Library? I'm sorry, I'm not much of a reader. I don't remember any details about that day."

"The Morton Library is a smaller, private library that features books on the art and history of this area. A lot of researchers use it."

Camilla chuckled. "Do I look like a researcher to you?" She tried flashing a seductive smile toward Evan but didn't quite manage to pull it off.

"I know the owner of the library," Sam said. "In fact, the adjacent home is where I stayed after the blizzard passed, since I couldn't reach my own home. Yesterday, I explored around there a bit. You know, curious about how you got there and why. And I found tracks all around the house. Indications that you might have been spying on the house and peeping in the windows. If you were stranded outside in the cold, why didn't you knock for someone's attention? I'm sure Ms. Plankhurst would have taken you in."

Camilla flopped back against her pillows and half closed her eyes. "Everything's pretty fuzzy about that day. I don't remember."

"Maybe you were looking for something of value but you didn't want anyone in the house to know you were outside?"

Camilla squeezed her eyes shut and a tear trailed down through her blusher. "I can't believe you're accusing me of something like sneaking around someone's house, someone I don't even know. I'm in the hospital here—I nearly died. I lost three fingers, for god's sake!"

Evan's fingertips brushed against Sam's arm. "It seems Ms. Crawford is tired. We'll talk again later."

"I'm sorry," Sam said. "And really sorry about your fingers." *I wish you'd knocked on the door instead of creeping around the side of the house.*

They walked out of Camilla's room, leaving her in bed. Stopping at the nurse's station, Evan inquired when the patient would be released. One or two more days, according to her chart.

"I'd like a call before she leaves here," Evan said, waiting while the nurse made a note.

He and Sam took the elevator to the ground floor.

"She's not under arrest," he said. "I don't have enough evidence against her. But I don't want her leaving town. In her condition, she'll either have to be released to someone local or I suppose she could fly back to California."

"I get the impression she has no money. She's basically sponging off friends. I have a feeling she's poking around in search of that painting. Did you see the way her eyes lit up when she thought she might get more of Phil Crawford's money?"

"If I can spare someone, I'll send a deputy down here when she's released. It'll be interesting to know who picks her up and where they go."

"If your guys are tied up, I could do that. You know I have experience."

"Sam ... I don't know ..." He climbed into his cruiser without making any promises.

Sam felt a ripple of excitement, the kind she normally experienced when a case was winding down. But something still wasn't quite fitting together. Were the Crawfords in this together, and what would have been their motive?

Chapter 39

All the way home, her mind buzzed with various scenarios and suspects. When she got back to the ranch, Sam realized she simply needed some time alone, to process everything. Beau's truck was gone, presumably out to pick up supplies. She shed her coat and went upstairs to wash her face. The carved box sat on her vanity top and she laid her hands on it, allowing the wood's glow to warm her.

The overstuffed chair in the corner of the bedroom beckoned to her, and she settled there with a knitted blanket over her lap. With closed eyes, images from the dream she'd had a few nights ago began to come back to her. She focused her attention on Camilla, hoping to draw out more than what the woman was willing to admit.

Sam was back in the party scene at the Crawford house,

able to move around but seemingly invisible to others. There was a palpable tension in the room; it seemed to originate with Phil Crawford who was standing near a bank of windows with a wide view of Taos Mountain. She saw Camilla in conversation with Arnie Brown, the fire chief. Sam listened, but only caught bits about the party food and the chief complimenting her on their home. Ben Martinez came into the picture and conferred quietly with the hostess after Brown moved back to the food table. Camilla's eyes scanned the room, landing on another guest, Bearcat Sowlow.

Sam's eyes opened. She didn't remember the teenage boy being in her original dream.

She stretched and thought about the various players. She'd barely spoken to the fire chief, and something told her she might gain valuable information from another chat with him. She went downstairs and rummaged in her coat pocket for the little vial of the lie detector potion. It was empty. In the kitchen, the jar in which Kelly had poured the batch held almost none of the potion either. Sam dipped her finger in and swiped along the edges of the glass, licking off the small amount she collected.

The main fire station seemed to be hopping with activity when she drove up—lots of cars and people milling about in the big garage. Sam parked and walked in.

There was a festive mood among the crowd, and Sam noticed balloons, streamers, and a food table. Above it, strung across an entire wall, was a long banner that read: Good luck, Chief! Arnie Brown stood as the center of attention with a bunch of young firefighters around him. People held plates of food and at least some of the beverages appeared to be beer.

"Big occasion?" she asked a passing EMT.

"Chief's retiring. Everyone who's not on duty is allowed a drink or two," the young woman said, holding up a can of Coke. "Sadly, I'm one who is on duty, so it's soda for me."

The group surrounding Brown broke up and Sam edged her way toward him.

"I hear congratulations are in order," she said.

"Yep, the last day of this year, I'm outta here. There's a fishing pole with my name on it."

She saw that he meant it literally. Leaning against a nearby bank of lockers was a new rod and reel, and she could see his name embossed on the grip in gold letters.

"I'll make my way around all the lakes in the three-state area, and then I may just head to Alaska when the salmon are running. Maybe Beau would even love to come along." His perfect teeth showed when he grinned, an outdoorsy man with a lot of enthusiasm for his hobby.

"You'd have to ask him about that." She wasn't sure she'd ever heard Beau express any love for fishing. "Say, Arnie, before you leave your job, I wonder if I could ask one more semi-official thing? I've been looking into the fire at the Crawford house."

"Crawford?"

"Big concrete modern place, just a few blocks off the plaza. It was a very long time ago—twenty-five years—but I thought you might remember some details. I spoke recently with the man who started the fire."

Arnie stared toward the ceiling for a moment. "Yeah, yeah, I remember that house. Weird place. So modern, not much like most of the homes here."

"How well did you know the Crawfords—Phillip and Camilla?" Sam was watching for signs that Arnie could have been Camilla's lover, the one Phil had accused her of cheating with.

The fire chief's mouth did a little down-twist wrinkle movement. "Gosh, hardly at all. I seem to recall we had some questions for them, being that there was an accelerant used on the draperies in the main room."

From what she could tell, his words were truthful.

"Are you sure about the accelerant? The official case file the police kept doesn't mention one and they concluded the fire was an accident, caused by candles left burning too near the draperies."

"No, that's not right. I mean, it's possible for drapery fabric to combust with an open flame nearby. But for the fire to spread the way that one did … the entire ground floor was in flames when we got there. And the arson investigator would have checked carefully."

"Did you ever become friendly with the billionaire owner and his wife? It's always interesting to get to know people so far outside our own sphere, isn't it? Your name was connected with the governor's a few years back, and I got the impression you moved in those social circles."

He waved it off. "Not much. I guess I've met a few important people over the years. Can't say we ever became chummy."

Nothing he said had a false ring to it, and Sam had to admit she'd been on the wrong track in thinking he could have been Camilla's lover and conspired to hide the results of the fire investigation. She congratulated him again and moved on.

Near the food table she spotted Rico, one of Beau's deputies who still worked with Evan. He noticed her at the same moment and greeted her. As she looked around, she realized there were several familiar faces in the crowd. She picked up a small handful of tortilla chips and chatted with the deputies, gently quizzing those who might have been around at the time of the Crawford fire, to see whether any of them might drop some tidbit that would help her piece together how the arson had slid by as an accident, despite the fact that the arsonist had been brought in and questioned. No one knew a thing.

Sam worked the room for a short while before slipping out in time to avoid hanging around for speeches. She thought about everything as she drove home. She'd connected Camilla Crawford with the painting. Evan said there was a note connecting the arsonist with the home owners. The fire chief seemed to remember an accelerant being used in the fire, but that report had vanished from the official police file, presumably on some kind of order that possibly came from the governor's office. Mike Miera's family continued to grieve for the son who'd died. And no one had been held responsible.

What the heck was going on?

Chapter 40

S am, Evan here. I'm taking you up on your offer. Camilla Crawford is getting discharged from the hospital today and I don't have a spare deputy to send out to follow."

"Any idea what time?"

"Ha. You know hospitals. They just said it'll be after the doctor's rounds. They make it sound like a quick thing, but the final paperwork always seems to take forever."

Sam looked around the kitchen at Sweet's Sweets. They were still playing catch-up after the forced days closed. There were New Year's Eve party trays to make, and a couple of last-minute weddings seemed to have popped up, couples who wanted to tie the knot by December thirty-first most likely for tax reasons. Still, they wanted cakes.

"I'll get over there the minute I can," she told Evan. She had a strong feeling that she'd unleashed something when she told Camilla she had spotted tracks in the snow near Emily's house. It was important they find out what the woman's next moves would be.

"Can you manage things here?" Sam asked Becky.

"Sure. Go."

Bless her, Becky never asked for details. She had no idea where Sam was going or why. Just that it sounded important. Sam flipped through the order sheets one last time, just to be sure. She'd rather catch up on an investigation later than disappoint a customer. Becky was right—there was nothing that couldn't spare Sam from the bakery for a few hours. She'd work late tonight if she had to.

She backed into a parking space at the hospital, giving herself a clear view of the main entrance. After twenty minutes it occurred to her that she could sit here all day, never knowing whether Camilla had already been picked up. She phoned the main hospital number and asked to be connected to her room. When Camilla's voice answered, Sam hung up. It was all she needed to know.

Her mind raced ahead to how this whole thing might unfold. She couldn't imagine the woman would simply drop the idea of finding *The Ghost of Christmas*. She placed a quick call to Emily. She'd hardly posed her idea before a white SUV cruised up and parked under the portico at the hospital entrance.

A woman in a dark pantsuit with glossy brown hair done up in a bun got out of the vehicle and walked briskly to the front doors. Sam's first thought was of an administrative subordinate, a personal assistant, a gofer to someone in charge. She wasn't a boss type, but she radiated efficiency and competence, someone who was trained to arrive at precisely the right moment and take charge of the little details her boss couldn't be bothered with.

Sam had met enough of the rich and famous in the course of business to recognize the others—the entourage. The woman in black was one of those.

In less than five minutes, the woman appeared again, with a tote bag over one shoulder (the huge flower bouquets must have been donated to other patients). She clicked open the locks on the SUV and stood aside as an orderly steered a wheelchair out the door. Camilla Crawford rode in the chair, wearing a rust-colored sweat suit—probably the latest in designer comfort wear—and a new coat. Sam pictured her wealthy hosts having sent a personal shopper (maybe the woman in black) to outfit Camilla for her departure from the hospital. Certainly, it wouldn't do for their house guest to return in the now-ratty purple fake fur she'd been wearing the night she nearly froze to death.

The driver stowed the tote bag in the back of the SUV and walked around to take Camilla's elbow, ignoring the glaring white bandages on her hands. Camilla climbed into the back seat and the orderly disappeared with the wheelchair. None of them glanced in Sam's direction.

She started her car and followed as the SUV pulled away, keeping some distance between them until they got into traffic on Paseo Pueblo del Sur. She closed the distance as they approached the busy area near the plaza. She would need to keep the vehicle in sight if they headed toward the ski valley. Homes in that area could be tucked onto tiny side roads, and Sam needed to be able to report to Evan where they ended up.

But the white SUV detoured off the main drag, turning in the direction of the bakery. Okay, this could get awkward, Sam thought. But the vehicle bypassed her street and took the next. Ah-ha. It appeared Camilla was heading directly toward the library.

And into her trap.

Emily had turned on all the lights in the place and, there in the front window, she'd set up *The Ghost of Christmas* on an easel. An overhead light shone directly on the magnificent piece of art.

Sam watched the car ahead as it slowed to a crawl. In the back seat, Camilla appeared agitated, twisting to face the library and pointing toward the window. Sam pulled to the slush-filled curb, about twenty yards back, and picked up her phone.

"Em, it worked. She's here. If she gets out and comes toward you, set your phone to record whatever happens next."

"Got it."

It appeared to Sam that Camilla was reaching for the door handle inside the SUV, and the driver had turned, speaking over her shoulder to her passenger. She pulled into the library parking lot and quickly got out, saying something to Camilla before she closed her door.

Sam edged her car forward, remaining across the street, listening to the scraps of conversation she could pick up via the open phone connection. She heard Emily greet the woman in black. Some unintelligible words from the visitor, then Emily said, "It's not for sale. The painting is a family heirloom."

Good thinking, Em.

"My boss will pay rather a lot of money."

"Who's your boss?"

Sam held her breath, hoping the woman would reveal

Camilla's name. But she didn't. She turned toward the door, as if to return to her vehicle.

Despite her heavy bandages, Camilla had managed to grip the inner door handle somehow, and she jumped out of the SUV, practically crashing into the other woman, shouting something Sam couldn't hear. The assistant paused for the barest fraction of a second, then spun and ran back into the library.

Grabbing *The Ghost of Christmas* off its easel, she pushed it into Camilla's arms and threw herself into the driver's seat. Camilla barely had a grip on the frame, but she managed to tuck both herself and the unwieldy picture into the back seat. Emily had appeared in the doorway, screaming for help. She rushed out and made a grab for the passenger in the back seat, but the car door slammed and the vehicle whipped out of the parking lot.

Chapter 41

Sam felt as if a jolt of electricity had passed through her whole body. Camilla's audacious move was beyond belief. When she suggested setting up the painting as bait, Sam had assumed Camilla would just verify the painting's whereabouts and then figure out another time to break in and take it.

She wrenched her steering wheel to the left and hit the gas.

The SUV was two blocks ahead, slowing for an intersection as the driver apparently tried to decide which of the twisty roads to take. Sam slowed, hoping they hadn't noticed her yet. She picked up her phone and heard Emily's sobs.

"I can't believe I let them get away," she said.

"Don't worry about that now. I need to hang up and

call the sheriff."

She kept an eye on the SUV, which had turned right at the corner, and found Evan's cell number. In as few words as possible she told him about the blatant grab-and-run with the painting and gave her location.

"Crap, Sam. I don't have anyone in that area. Keep talking. Let me see who I can round up."

She put her phone on speaker and set it on the dashboard as she concentrated on following the route of the white vehicle. It became clear that the woman driving was not a local. She took the most direct route back to the main road and turned north.

"They could be headed toward the ski valley," Sam shouted toward Evan. "That's where Camilla told me she's staying. I'll have to move closer once they get on that road."

"Do it. Rico's up in Questa but I can have him head south and meet up with you. Just stay on the line."

Traffic increased as they went through El Prado, where it seemed all the after-Christmas shoppers were out in force at the small shops and the health food market. Sam allowed a couple of cars to get between her vehicle and the SUV. When they got to the intersection where SR150 branched off, she would need to move up. Being spotted would become an issue then.

But the white SUV didn't make the expected right-hand turn. The driver moved to the left and turned.

"Uh-oh, Evan. They're heading toward the airport."

"Oh, man. Okay. I'm on my way out to my cruiser, to hell with the mayoral candidates who wanted a personal tour of the department."

Sam could hear him breathing heavily as he must be pulling on his coat and dashing out the back door to the employee parking. Evan really could stand to lose a few pounds. So could she, Sam admitted to herself. She hoped he got there before she had to dash off on any big chase. The upside was, she handily outweighed Camilla and could take her down. But, with the help of that other woman, who knew how it would go.

Keeping the SUV in sight on the straight section of highway wasn't difficult. The downside was, it wouldn't be hard for the driver to spot her either. The other upside was that Sam knew exactly where they were going and she would be prepared for the turn. At least she hoped she knew. If the airport wasn't their destination, it could be a case of 'anything goes.'

She kept checking her rearview mirrors. With his lights and siren, Evan would make far better time. She kept a grip on the wheel and a hope that he would show up soon.

The Taos airport is small, with a half-mile two-lane entrance road, a small parking area, and one building where the fixed base operator kept things going. A few years ago, Sam knew the guys who worked here, but times and personnel changed and she didn't know if she could count on the current staff knowing who she was.

The driver of the white SUV spotted the turn, made it, and sped toward the facility. Apparently, she'd been in contact by phone because a private jet sat on the tarmac and one of the FBO guys was sliding open the chain link gate that allowed access. The vehicle dashed through and the attendant started to close the gate again.

As Sam got closer, she could hear the plane's turbine engines at idle, waiting for its passengers to board. Behind her, there was still no sign of Evan.

Sam's heart sank.

She recognized the gate attendant as one of the guys who had worked here for years. She pulled up beside him and shouted for him to leave the gate standing open. "The sheriff is on the way!"

His expression faltered, puzzled. Was the sheriff one of the passengers on the charter? Was someone in trouble? Was Sam speaking officially?

She let him work it out on his own. Mainly, she was thrilled to see flashing lights behind her in the distance. Evan's vehicle made the turn from the highway to the access road. Sam moved her car out of the way, her head swiveling as she kept watch on the approaching cruiser and the two women at the SUV.

Unfortunately, they spotted the cruiser too and started moving double-time. The woman in black ran around to the back of the SUV and pulled out a large suitcase and the tote bag she had carried out of the hospital. Camilla awkwardly scrambled out of the back seat and tucked the painting under her left arm, balancing it with her bandaged right hand. They were shouting back and forth, but Sam couldn't make out their words over the loud whine of the jet engine.

Camilla started up the steps to board the jet. A uniformed flight attendant started to offer help but Camilla brushed her away. She turned to the assistant, who shoved the large suitcase toward her.

"Hey, you can't leave that here," the gate guy shouted, pointing to the SUV. The women ignored him.

Sam abandoned her car and ran over to the airport employee, who was staring wide-eyed at the whole scene. Camilla was inside the plane, the flight attendant was wrestling the large suitcase through the doorway, and the woman in black stood on the steps, keeping an eye on the oncoming flashing lights.

"Open the gate, wide enough for Sheriff Richards to get through!" Sam yelled at the young guy. The cruiser was into the parking lot now.

Sam grabbed at the chain link and helped the young guy push the gate fully open, just as Evan's cruiser roared past them.

In a movie-worthy maneuver, the cruiser skidded to a stop in front of the plane, blocking it. The jet's engine slowly whined to a stop.

Evan jumped out and drew his weapon, keeping his vehicle between himself and the suspects.

Camilla's assistant had lost every bit of her cool-and-calm; her expression crumpled and her neat chignon was coming unraveled. She froze, there on the steps, and slowly raised her hands. The startled flight attendant dropped the suitcase to the ground, where it split open and spilled bright clothing on the ground. Evan motioned the two of them to walk slowly down to the tarmac.

"Camilla Crawford," Evan called out, "exit the plane with your hands up."

Easier said than done, since Camilla wasn't about to give up the *Ghost*. She stood defiantly in the doorway of the plane, gripping the valuable painting under her arm.

"Evan ... don't shoot the painting," Sam cautioned in a low voice.

Evan repeated his warning to Camilla, and she finally came slowly down the steps.

"Camilla Crawford, you are under arrest for grand theft, attempting to flee, and possession of stolen property." He holstered his weapon and pulled handcuffs off his belt as he approached his suspect.

"This is my property, Sheriff," Camilla said, batting her eyes and putting on a smile. "It was taken from me and I was just getting it back."

Evan reached out and took the painting from her, handing it to Sam.

"No! That's mine! It's really mine!" Camilla's polite veneer vanished.

A second cruiser drove up just then and Rico got out. He took charge of Camilla, cuffing her and escorting her to his vehicle. Evan apprehended the other woman. Once she was tucked securely into his car, he gathered the broken suitcase and its contents, stowing that and *The Ghost of Christmas* in the trunk of his cruiser.

The pilot of the plane had come out, presented his credentials and swore the plane and crew were only there because they'd received a call the previous evening to charter the aircraft for the relatively short flight to L.A. Evan took names and let them go.

He turned to Sam. "Now, it'll get interesting. Come in for the interrogation if you'd like."

Oh yeah, she would definitely like.

Chapter 42

It had been a while, Sam thought as she walked into the observation room located between the department's two interrogation rooms. Camilla and Shanaya Blackburn—the PA—were separated and kept that way.

In interrogation room A, Ms. Blackburn opened up right away. She worked for the California couple in whose home Camilla was a guest for the holidays. Her employer had sent her to pick up Camilla from the hospital and deliver her to the local airport, and she would fly home.

Surprisingly frank, Blackburn gave the opinion that the house guest had worn out her welcome and it was worth the price of the charter jet to get her out of their mountain home. Camilla was the type who came to visit and didn't leave, Blackburn said. Apparently, she and others in her position—personal assistants, pilots, household staff to the rich and famous—talked among themselves and had a good feel for what was what.

When asked what she knew about the painting, Blackburn said, "I'd never heard of it. After I picked up Ms. Crawford from the hospital, she asked me to make a slight detour on the way to the airport, and it was that little library where she asked me to stop. I was told to go inside and inform them the painting had merely been on loan to the library and the owner wanted it back. If that didn't work, I could offer to buy it. The girl inside basically laughed in my face. No way, she said. When I started back to the car, empty-handed, Camilla told me to just grab it and run."

Shanaya hung her head. "I knew it was wrong, doing that. I guess I'm just so used to these rich people making crazy demands, and we're expected to go along with whatever it is, with a 'yes ma'am' and no questions. Before I could think it through, I had the picture in my hands and Camilla was shouting at me to drive, drive! I can't believe I actually did it."

Evan left the suspect alone while he walked into the observation room. Sam agreed that what the young woman said matched what she had witnessed.

Blackburn was crying now, shaken by the morning's events. Evan instructed a deputy to offer her coffee or a soda and let her sit there a little longer.

"I don't believe she had a role in this, but it won't hurt to let her think there will be consequences for simply following orders."

Sam turned and watched the mirrored window facing the other room, the one where Camilla sat on a hard metal chair in front of the hard metal table. Her designer sweatsuit was looking rumpled, but she had taken the time to observe herself in the mirror and fix her messed-up hair. She kept looking toward the door, as if expecting her rich friends to show up and pull her out of this jam.

Evan walked in and ignored the flirtatious look she sent his way.

"Do you understand the charges against you?" he asked.

"Actually, no. The painting is mine. It hung in my home here in Taos and I believed it was destroyed in a fire there, twenty-five years ago. Imagine my surprise when I saw it on display in the window of that little place—what is it? A library?"

Sam sputtered. Camilla wasn't even going to address the fact that she'd been spying on Emily's home, and getting caught out in the blizzard was what led to her hospitalization.

"I merely sent my assistant inside to inform them of the fact that the painting belonged to me and I wanted it back."

Evan played along. "How do you suppose the painting got there, since it was supposedly destroyed in the fire?"

Camilla worked up some genuine fire in her voice. "I think David Plankhurst stole the painting from my home and replaced it with a fake. Knowing I would spot the fake rather quickly, he probably even set the fire."

"And you knew this David Plankhurst? How would you guess he was behind all this?"

"Um, well, slightly. My husband used to enjoy history as a hobby—he's a powerful hedge fund manager, you know. He spent some time with Mr. Plankhurst, doing research on Taos history."

"So, Plankhurst had been invited to your home?"

"Oh no, I don't believe so. He was definitely not of our social cl— I mean, he wouldn't have fit in with our set of friends."

"So he never went to your home?"

Camilla nodded agreement.

"Then how did he know about the painting? He couldn't have seen it there."

That one had Camilla stumped. Sam fist-pumped a big *yes* for Evan.

Evan didn't give the suspect a chance to come up with an argument. He changed tactics. "In the hospital I asked if you knew a man named Bearcat Sowlow. Do you remember him now?"

Camilla put on a puzzled expression and shook her head.

"He knew you. He also killed himself very recently, apparently in remorse for knowing you."

"What? I don't see how that's poss—"

"He left a note, written before he jumped from the gorge bridge." Evan pulled out a half sheet of paper that looked like it had been torn from a spiral notebook.

"Sowlow was questioned at the time of the fire at your home. The police had good reason to suspect he had set it, but because of some missing evidence and because of Sowlow's age—he was only fifteen at the time—he was not charged."

Camilla studied the unbandaged fingers of her right hand, probably thinking she was due for a manicure. Sam wondered how that would go, considering she was now missing the little finger on her right hand and two from her left. But Evan's next move brought her attention right back to the interrogation.

"So, the note. It's a confession," Evan said, unfolding the sheet.

He was watching Camilla's face as he did so. She visibly tensed but didn't say anything.

"It says, 'I lied, it was the owner. She paid me to set the fire.' Those were Bearcat Sowlow's last words."

She paid me. Sam realized Evan had not shared that information with her, and she'd been under the impression that 'the owner' was Phil Crawford. More pieces fell into place.

"The owner. She. That's you, Camilla. Isn't it?"

A little war was going on inside Camilla's head, Sam could tell. Years of keeping the secret, the stress of losing her beloved painting, her divorce, and the fact that she'd blown through her money and was now living off the goodwill of a very flaky set of friends … It was all catching up. Camilla should have said, "I want a lawyer" but what she really said was, "Oh, shit. It's over."

Chapter 43

Sam couldn't contain herself any longer. She left the observation room and tapped on the door to the room where Evan and Camilla sat. He stood up and let her inside.

"The bakery lady?" Camilla said, clearly confused.

"Sam was once a deputy here in the department. She still helps out now and then."

That wasn't strictly true. It was more accurate to say Evan and his deputies came to her aid when she suspected something amiss, such as had happened this month. But she put her shoulders back and assumed the role he was handing her.

Taking a seat at the table, she leaned toward Camilla. "You said it's over. Just now. Do you want to explain, or shall I fill in the blanks? You knew the painting that was lost in the fire was a fake because you had already taken the real *Ghost of Christmas* down, and my feeling is that you had asked David Plankhurst to hide it for you. Am I close?"

The last of Camilla's bluster was gone. "I did know David, yes. He was such a nice man, always willing to do little favors for Phil and me."

"Go on," Evan said. Sam imagined the recording equipment in the other room picking up every bit of this.

"I knew I couldn't retrieve the painting for a few years because of how famous JC Freeman was. Too many people knew we had purchased it, and there were questions from the police and, mainly, the insurance company. I knew I would have to make them think I believed that it burned up, probably for a long time. Realistically, in the scheme of what my life was then—married to a billionaire and having unlimited money to spend on anything I wanted—the Freeman painting was just a whim. Twenty-five thousand simply wasn't that much money to us. I just loved the picture."

"It really is an amazing work of art," Sam said.

"Then Phil and I divorced and he totally screwed me over. Although we lived in California, our permanent legal residence was in New York, and that's where he filed. He and his team of lawyers managed to hide assets and screw me out of everything."

All but two million dollars, Sam recalled.

"I did the best I could with the money I did get, but it's an expensive lifestyle. I'm stretched pretty thin now. You don't know how embarrassing it is to admit that." Indeed, a lot of the spunk had gone out of the sad woman's demeanor.

"So, last summer I started thinking about the Freeman painting again, and I wondered if David still had it. It had to be worth a whole lot more now, since Freeman died a few years ago. Work by famous artists always goes up in value when they're dead, right?"

Sam wasn't so sure about that, but she let it ride.

"I came to Taos and stopped by the library to see David. But he was gone and his wife wasn't very friendly. She said David was now in a care facility."

Sam nodded. "You met his wife then?"

Camilla nodded.

"She suspected you and David of having an affair. Did you realize that? Or I suppose I should ask, did you have an affair with him?"

Camilla sat back in her chair. "David? Seriously? Completely not my type."

"But there was an affair, and that was part of the reason Phil filed for divorce."

Camilla tilted her head in acknowledgement. Sam got the feeling there had been more than one lover, and somewhere along the line Phil became fed up.

"So, back to the painting," Evan brought up. "You asked David Plankhurst to hide it for you—why?"

"Phil found out about my affair and threatened to sell the house and all its contents. I took the real painting because I loved it, and because it could always be my little nest egg, just in case he really followed through. I commissioned a replica, one close enough that no one but an art afficionado and someone familiar with Freeman's work would recognize."

"Maurice Finstadt—was he the one you were involved with?" Sam should have figured that out.

"Maurice? Oh no. He knew where the money was. He would have ratted me out to Phil right away."

"Then …?"

"Doesn't matter. Ben and I were over fairly quickly. I came back here last summer and, after being turned away by David's wife, I started poking around whenever I got the chance. But, no luck. Then, a few months ago, I happened to see a mention someplace that a Valerie Plankhurst had passed away. It's an unusual enough name that I figured she must be the wife. I was excited to think I might have the library all to myself, to really search it thoroughly, but then this young woman moved in."

"She's their granddaughter," Evan said.

"Anyway, I couldn't get back up here until the holidays, and having a place to stay with friends … it seemed like the perfect time to look around again." Camilla held up her bandaged hands. "And look what that got me."

Tears welled in her eyes and she suddenly seemed defeated. Something had stuck in Sam's mind, but she let Camilla talk first.

"I feel like the painting is about the only thing I have left. It's the only way I know to come up with the money to keep up with my lifestyle."

"You never considered a different lifestyle? Cutting back, getting an actual job, living in an ordinary home instead of a showplace?" Evan clearly couldn't comprehend Camilla's choices. Neither could Sam.

"I have nothing else. Where will I go? Phil and I never had children, and my family is pretty scattered. My sister in North Carolina is about the only one I ever hear from."

"She could be a good place to start," Sam suggested.

Evan held up a hand. "Not to burst your bubble about some happily ever after life here, but there are still serious charges against you. Grand theft of the painting, for one thing."

"But it's mine. I only asked David to keep it for me, but

by all rights, it's *mine*."

"Except that an insurance company paid the claim when you said it was destroyed. Technically, it now belongs to them," Sam said, although she really hoped it didn't come down to turning over the stunning *Ghost of Christmas* to someone in a big underwriter's corporate office.

Evan continued. "The more serious charge, the one with no statute of limitations, comes from the fact that Mike Miera's death happened during the commission of a felony. It's murder."

"But—but—I didn't start the fire," Camilla wailed.

"You hired the person who did. And that makes you equally guilty."

And that's when Camilla uttered the words: "I want a lawyer."

Before Evan could shut her down, Sam interrupted. "This is a personal question, if I may? You named the man you were having the affair with as Ben. Would that be Ben Martinez?"

Chapter 44

The final pieces clicked into place. Evan ordered Camilla taken to a cell and Shanaya Blackburn released. Sam was practically squirming with excitement as the two of them walked through the squad room and into his private office, formerly Beau's.

"I don't have the actual evidence for this," she told him once they were both seated. "That's up to you and your guys to find, conduct interviews, whatever. But here's what I'm pretty sure happened."

Evan sat back in his chair and took a long pull on the straw in his McDonald's cup. He made a face; apparently the soda was now flat.

"Ben Martinez had to be the one who took the incriminating page out of the police report. Arnie Brown told me that the arson investigator's report included the fact that they had spotted traces of an accelerant in the Crawford home. It's how they knew to go looking for an arsonist. But without the written report, that aspect of the police case fell apart, and that's why they eventually closed the case and called it an accidental fire. I have a feeling Ben is the one who planted the idea that word had come from up high—the governor's office—that he wanted the arson squashed."

"I read some of this," Evan said. "There was a call from a female admin person in the governor's office."

"Who could easily have been Camilla, pretending. She arranged for the fire to be set. The original plan was probably to have the house torched while she and Phil were away in Mexico, with witnesses to back up their alibi. She'd talked David Plankhurst into hiding the real painting, so her most valued possession wouldn't go up in flames. Neither she nor Phil loved the house, so they could quickly walk away with a decent insurance payout. But everything changed once Mike Miera died there. Camilla was probably terrified of being caught.

"Officially, if the fire was set purposely it was a murder, and eventually Bearcat would have cracked and admitted that he'd been paid to set it. Camilla would have been found out and convicted. She and Ben probably worked together to conceal the facts. To protect her, Ben could have planted the idea in his chief's mind that the governor was a friend of Phillip Crawford and—whether it was true or not—that's the story they stuck with and eventually it became a fact, in everyone's mind."

Evan had been rapidly scratching notes on a tablet. "Wow, Sam, it's amazing you put all this together. I'll be taking it to the prosecutor's office as soon as we put the details together. Looks like it'll be the end of Ben Martinez's political aspirations. An affair could be overlooked, but a cover-up of arson and murder ... nah, he's toast."

She gave a little diffident smile, not admitting that some of the connections had come to her in a dream.

"Can I ask one favor in return?" she asked.

"Name it."

"Let me return *The Ghost of Christmas* to Emily Plankhurst."

He sputtered a little.

"Your case revolves around the fire, the death of Mike Miera, and both Camilla and Ben's involvement in that. The painting was—still is—incidental to all that. Since the painting was removed from the house before the fire, I'll make the argument that it's a case of the owner of an item making a gift of that item to someone. Camilla admits she gave it to David, and the fact that she didn't return for it until more than twenty-five years later ... Well, doesn't that kind of seal it that she meant for the Plankhursts to keep it?"

"What about the insurance company that paid for its loss?"

"I have an idea on that, too. Emily comes forward and says it has recently come to her attention that a mistake was made. Someone else—the Crawfords—claimed this as an insurance loss but it has since been recovered. If she offers to reimburse the amount paid out, the twenty-five thousand dollars which was its insured value at the time, I feel sure they would let her keep it, free and clear."

He seemed skeptical for a moment, then relented. "Well, it would ease my mind not to have responsibility for it. I've never had a million-plus dollar item in our evidence locker before. And I suppose Emily's family has managed to keep it safe all these years. She's obviously got some way to do that."

"I wouldn't reveal the news publicly," Sam cautioned. "About a newly discovered JC Freeman piece here in town. Emily's got some decisions to make, whether she'll sell it, keep it, how to go about getting it insured ..."

"Right. Got it." He stood up and led the way out to his cruiser, where the valuable artwork still lay, locked in the trunk.

Sam handled the framed piece carefully. Suddenly, this felt like a huge responsibility, and she couldn't wait to get it back in Emily's hands and safely locked away in its hiding spot again. She placed it in the back of her car and said goodbye to Evan, with a quick reminder that he and Riki were invited to Christmas dinner at Kelly's.

She drove away from Civic Plaza, thinking of Camilla sitting in a cell right now. Such a sad case, this woman who once had it all and risked everything over a fling with a man and a piece of art she couldn't hold onto.

At the library, Emily greeted Sam and accepted the painting with tears in her eyes. "I felt as if Grandpa's soul was snatched away when Camilla drove off with this," she said.

Sam told her most of what had gone down at the airport and sheriff's office. Following Em into the house, she watched as her young friend opened the secret niche and placed the valuable artwork inside.

"It's sad to keep it locked away, out of sight where no one can enjoy it," Emily said, giving the piece a final look before she closed the bookcase. "I'll have to decide what to do about that."

Sam gave her a hug and walked back to her car. Feeling as though she'd been through the wringer, Sam knew she had one more stop, and she might as well get it done today.

Once again, she noticed woodsmoke trailing upward from the chimney at the Miera home. This family had endured so much, pain that never went away. She realized she didn't need to be the one to deliver this news, but imagining herself in their place she wouldn't want to see it on the front page of the newspaper.

Nina saw her through the front window and met her at the door. Her smile brightened and she invited Sam inside. Jorge stood before the fireplace insert, adding a log.

"I wanted to let you know that your son's case has been solved and an arrest has been made."

Nina dropped to the nearest armchair. "*Dios mio.*"

Jorge rushed to her side. Somehow sensing that something was going on, Roberta came out of the kitchen, wiping her hands on a towel.

"What's up?" she asked.

Sam told the whole story, including Camilla's switching the paintings and hiring the arsonist. "It seems that her instructions to the boy who started the fire were not very clear. She swears she didn't think anyone would be in the house at the time."

"But why?" Nina asked. "A crazy rich woman wanting to burn down her own house? It makes no sense to me."

"It was a spiteful act, meant to hurt her husband who had caught her having an affair—with a rookie cop, of all things. For Camilla, it was a quick, unimportant fling but it ended up threatening her way of life. I suppose she thought if she couldn't have the big beautiful house, she wasn't going to leave it for the husband. I don't know. It was crazy thinking. And she's going to prison for it. The man who set the fire is dead. I know that doesn't change anything for your family, but I thought you should know."

Nina continued to stare at the floor, absorbing it all, with her husband at her side. Roberta walked Sam to the front door and stepped outside with her.

"The rookie cop," she said, "was it Ben Martinez?"

Sam looked up, surprised. "Yes, actually."

Roberta's eyes grew moist, and all at once Sam knew.

"Were you involved with him too?"

Roberta's face twisted. "Involved. But not in the way you're thinking. I had a job as a dispatcher at the police department, my senior year in high school. Ben came on to me relentlessly. These days it would be sexual harassment, a clear case. But back then we girls just learned to brush off guys who were pushy."

"I know. Been there."

"Ben was … so charismatic. I don't suppose he ever had a girl turn him down, so he really didn't take no for an answer. I told him I had a boyfriend. It didn't matter. One night after work, he caught up with me at my car and pulled me into the back seat."

"Oh, no."

"A few weeks later I knew I was pregnant. I'd never had sex with my boyfriend. We had this old-fashioned idea of saving ourselves for marriage. I didn't tell anyone but my mother, and it shamed her so badly. My boyfriend knew—he could tell I was different. When I was four months along, I was sent to stay with an aunt and uncle in Colorado and the baby was given up for adoption. A year later, there was the fire, and Michael was dead. My parents couldn't cope with anything more."

Sam remained quiet. This was the big Miera family secret, something that would make no difference in many families, but quite a big deal to them.

"If he forced you, you could still come forward," Sam said.

Roberta shook her head. "No, it's old history. What would be the point?"

"Your case may not be the only one. If Ben behaved that way with other young women, maybe he's still acting that way now …"

"I don't know. It wouldn't surprise me, but I've purposely stayed away from him. Maybe I should have spoken up, taken on that battle, but I have already felt guilty every day of my life since I was seventeen. Sam, I just can't put my parents through anything more."

Sam nodded. "I understand." Plus, she had a feeling Ben's public image would soon be ruined anyway, once Evan and the prosecutor brought out the facts of the old arson case.

"Don't say anything—to anyone," Roberta begged. "Please. Somewhere out there is a young woman who was raised by a loving, adoptive family. I doubt she will ever come looking for me, but if she does, I don't want this awful story to become hers. I'm content to drop the subject and move forward with my life."

Sam pulled her into a hug and they stood that way for a long time. She'd had her own pregnancy journey. She could understand how personal the decision was. She wished Roberta a peaceful new year, and then she left.

Chapter 45

December thirty-first dawned clear and cold. When Sam rose that morning, knowing it would be an activity-filled day, she bundled into her heavy jacket and Sorel boots and carried an insulated mug out to the front porch. Both dogs ran out into the snow, which had melted to half its previous depth, cavorting and romping and doing their doggie business before racing back to the house.

Sam stood at the top of the porch steps, staring up at the dark sky. Orion was still visible in the southwest, with the bright star Sirius nearby. She sipped her coffee and absorbed the silence. When the tip of her nose began to tingle, she went back inside and scooped food into bowls for Ranger and Nellie.

She had thought a lot about the past since yesterday, wondering what it would have been like for her if she'd given Kelly up for adoption, as Roberta had, instead of taking on the challenge of raising her daughter on her own. She couldn't imagine never knowing the closeness they now had.

She'd also thought about Ben Martinez. There should be consequences for him. Evan felt there was a good case but, in reality, could it be proven that Ben was the one, the rookie cop, who tampered with the police file? Would Camilla name him when her case went to court? And if so, would it matter? In recent weeks, Ben had made no secret of the fact that he intended to use his mayoral run as a stepping stone. Once he gained experience in public office, aiming for the governor's office or perhaps a congressional seat wasn't out of the question. A decade or so building his credentials and meeting all the right people within his political party … he could even aim for the White House. It had been done before, and by men with every bit as shady a past.

Sam shoved those thoughts aside as she hung up her coat. Today was reserved for her family, for the Christmas celebration they'd missed last week. She went to the storage closet and pulled out a large cardboard carton, then packed up the presents under the tree for the trip to Kelly's house. Beau would be finished with his barnyard duties soon, and they would get an early start, just as if it really were Christmas day.

* * *

Beau's truck had barely come to a stop when Ana came running out the front door of the Victorian. She threw her arms around Sam's legs, and then insisted on helping to carry the huge box of presents. When it became obvious that wasn't going to work, Beau handed her a reasonable-sized package and he carried the rest.

The table gleamed with crystal and silver, and Kelly had outdone herself on decorations.

"Well, I figured we're celebrating both Christmas and New Year's Eve—had to bling it up a bit."

They had already discussed whether the party would continue into the night, with midnight champagne. Kelly had just laughed. "I don't know what planet you live on, but no one in this house has been up until midnight in years."

"We'll toast the new year at twelve noon," Sam said, "and if Beau isn't too exhausted, he and I might stay up late enough to watch the east coast celebrations on TV."

Scott joined in with that sentiment. He seemed in an ebullient mood and when Sam asked, he said it was because his editor had already given the new book a quick read and she'd loved it. There would be a little bit of back-and-forth editing, and they would give it a huge publicity push and release the book at the beginning of summer, just when kids were getting out of school.

That news called for a toast, and since it was barely nine a.m., the celebration was performed with hot cocoa.

"Presents, presents!" Ana demanded, running about to round up the adults.

As on Christmas, the family gathered near the tree in the living room for the ritual of ripped wrapping paper and exclamations over the gifts. And the frenzy was over before Sam could take a deep breath.

By late morning, the other guests began to arrive. Emily brought cinnamon rolls in a Sweet's Sweets bakery box, for which Sam chided her. She didn't need to pay for those.

"I bought them a week ago, and when it turned out my parents couldn't drive up from Albuquerque, I put them in the freezer. Your baked goods keep really well that way, did you know?"

Riki and Evan walked in, and the moment their coats were off, he sought out the rolls. "Riki doesn't let me do this often," he said, patting the belly that was beginning to reach out over his belt buckle.

"And with good reason," she scolded. The petite British expat hugged Emily and Sam and admired Kelly's dining table. "Who else is coming?"

"I invited Zoë and Darryl, but their place is filled with guests and they couldn't break away. Rupert would be here, but the poor thing is still enduring that Caribbean beach. So it's a little smaller group than usual," Kelly said. "Just us."

Out in her Jeep, Emily had another surprise. She unpacked the easel first and set it up near the dining room window. Then she set *The Ghost of Christmas* in place. With the full light of the northern exposure, every detail revealed itself. Sam felt her breath catch.

"I wanted to give it a proper audience among friends before it goes on, to its first ever art show. The museum in Albuquerque is doing a special exhibit on the life and art of JC Freeman, and they were thrilled to include our lovely *Ghost* as the star. They're selling special tickets to view it, and the proceeds are going to Alzheimer's research."

"You got this all arranged on short notice," Sam said.

"Ever since I discovered the painting, I've been thinking about what to do with it. Grandma Valerie sort of suggested the idea of generating some money for charity, and this one is close to our family."

"It's incredible," Riki said, unable to take her eyes off it.

The men seemed similarly impressed. "It's too bad Camilla Crawford was so obsessed with this," Evan remarked, "although now that I'm seeing it I can understand somewhat better."

"So true," Sam said. "She could have gone about her life, enjoying the perks of being wealthy, but she messed up."

"Messed up badly enough to be responsible for two deaths," Evan said. "Of course she's got lawyers now, but they'll have a tough job trying to spin her actions in any positive way."

Sam stared at the painting, her heart heavy. So sad that the allure of the beautiful work of art had led to death and destruction.

She turned to look at the faces around her, everyone in the room admiring the incredible and lovely snowy holiday scene. Their gazes and the awe in their expressions really showed the painting's enchantment, what *The Ghost of Christmas* was all about.

It was time for the piece to come out of hiding, she realized, to be enjoyed by large audiences, to share its magic with the world.

Thank you for taking the time to read *The Ghost of Christmas Sweet*. If you enjoyed it, please consider telling your friends or posting a short review. Word of mouth is an author's best friend and is much appreciated.

Thank you,
Connie Shelton

Get another Connie Shelton book—FREE! Sign up for Connie Shelton's free mystery newsletter at con-nieshelton.com

and receive advance information about new books, along with a chance at prizes, discounts and other mystery news!

Contact by email: connie@connieshelton.com
Follow Connie Shelton on Twitter, Pinterest and Facebook

Made in the USA
Monee, IL
11 October 2021

79812194R00173